NO
STRINGS
ATTACHED

Previously published Worldwide Mystery titles by
JULIE MOFFETT

NO ONE LIVES TWICE
NO TEST FOR THE WICKED
NO WOMAN LEFT BEHIND
NO ROOM FOR ERROR

NO STRINGS ATTACHED

JULIE MOFFETT

WORLDWIDE®

TORONTO • NEW YORK • LONDON
AMSTERDAM • PARIS • SYDNEY • HAMBURG
STOCKHOLM • ATHENS • TOKYO • MILAN
MADRID • WARSAW • BUDAPEST • AUCKLAND

For my two boys, Alexander and Lucas.
Love you to the moon and beyond. oxo

Recycling programs
for this product may
not exist in your area.

No Strings Attached

A Worldwide Mystery/June 2017

First published by Carina Press

ISBN-13: 978-0-373-28413-9

Copyright © 2016 by Julie Moffett

Printed in U.S.A.

Acknowledgments

A novel is rarely a solitary effort and this book is no exception. Thanks to all of my true-blue tech head family: my nephew, Kyle, who works at Google; his wife, Julia, who works at Yahoo; my brother, Brad, who is brilliant at all things tech and storytelling; my sister, Sandy, who is a great writer and always knows everything about everything (really!); my mom and dad, fantastic editors and Lexi's first fans; my niece, Katy, who also beta reads for me; my sister-in-law, Beth, who watched Lucas more times than I can count so I could do the writer thing; and Carina Press editor extraordinaire Alissa Davis, for knowing Lexi and the gang inside and out and always making the BEST freaking suggestions. Love you all! oxoxo

ONE

"To the general public, the word *hacker* often conjures a vision of someone who breaks into your computer and steals your bank account information or locks your computer, holding it for ransom. Most of us are in agreement that this type of hacking is considered cracking, or black hatting. But what if we do these same things to someone on behalf of our client? Does that make us black hatters or white hatters?"

I paused, looking at the participants of my workshop *Black Versus White Hatting: Ethics for the Security Professional.* I was wrapping things up—thank God. I hated speaking in front of people. I'd agreed to do this presentation because I felt the topic was important. So, I—along with four hundred other geeks—had gathered for HACK CON, a popular hacker convention at the Capitol Heights Hotel near Washington, DC. We convened annually in one giant nerd herd to learn about the latest in security design, network penetration and hacking shortcuts, mostly from each other.

My interactive workshop had gone well except for the jerk who sat front and center, apparently feeling like it was his duty to prove I was some kind of fake geek girl. I'd done my best to ignore him, but I could see he was far from finished with me.

"Miss Carmichael," he said with a heavy emphasis

on the *Miss*. He paused for dramatic effect. "I have an answer for you."

Lexi Carmichael, that's me. My job as Director of Information Security at X-Corp—a cutting-edge cyberintelligence business in Washington, DC—had gotten me a first-class ticket and an invitation to present at HACK CON. I'm a twenty-five-year-old reformed hacker, a fangirl and a dedicated gamer who also happened to work in a heavily male-dominated industry where—for some reason—I had to constantly prove I belonged because I didn't have a Y chromosome.

I crossed my arms against my chest, leaning back against the table and hoping my tone sounded neutral instead of annoyed. "Okay, Mr. Corbin. What's your answer?"

"My answer is if it's in the best interest of our client, it's ethical. We're getting paid for it, right? May the best man win."

"I see." I pretended to think it over. "So, you're saying it's okay to break into another company's system and screw it up or bring it down if it's in the best interest of your client?"

Corbin smirked. "If they don't have the balls or skills to keep us out—then they deserve what they get."

"Really?" I said, trying not to sound exasperated, "Although I'll be the first to admit there is no clear-cut answer to ethical behavior in our rapidly evolving field, I'm confident the 'May the Best Man Win' strategy would not be considered ethically sound."

I'd pissed him off. His eyes narrowed and his face flushed red. He leaned forward in his chair, resting his arms on his knees. "What do you know anyway?

Everyone in this room knows there is only one reason you are here."

The room fell deadly silent. I kept my voice even. "And what would that be?"

"Quota." He sat back in his chair, smug. "That's why you're here. I'm just keeping it real."

My gaze locked on to his. "Okay, let's keep it real. In the past year, I've had four different articles published in the *Journal of Adversarial Infosec, Cryptologia* and *Red Teaming Today*. Since the conference has strict guidelines that in order to be invited to speak all presenters must be extensively published in peer-reviewed journals on the topic, I guess I do meet a certain, rather exclusive, quota. But now that you've mentioned it, I don't recall seeing your name on any articles on this topic. When were you last published?"

There were several snickers as Corbin fell silent, seething. I lifted my hands. "Anyway, in conclusion, I think the most important takeaway from this presentation is that as white hatters, we should consider the defensive route as the most ethical one. Protect and defend. Yet, having said that, I do acknowledge there may be situations where black hatting methods may be required, especially if in defense of critical infrastructure or lives. Regardless, be aware that the line between black and white in our profession is constantly shifting. Ethical standards need to be regularly revisited. Thank you for attending."

The room erupted into clapping before people rose to leave. Corbin stalked out of the room without a backward glance. I chatted with a few of the participants before the last person left. Gathering my materials, I straightened up the room before tucking my laptop under my arm and heading for the elevator. I switched off the light as I left the conference room. The area in front of the elevators was empty, which probably meant I'd just missed one. I hoped I didn't have to wait too long. In the past twenty-four hours the power to the hotel had gone off six times. Unsurprising, with several hundred hackers gathered in one hotel. While the little show of power was impressive, the consequence was a nasty backup of the elevators. *That* was a royal pain for all involved, myself included.

The button illuminated, so at least the elevators were working. However, seeing as how I was on the thirty-seventh floor, there'd be a wait for it to arrive.

I checked my watch. Two thirty. Maybe the hotel bar would be empty. I needed to sit somewhere quiet and plan the bachelorette party I was supposed to be throwing next week. I'd booked a place and sent out invitations, but there was no menu yet and Basia had been dropping hints that these parties usually included inappropriate games and alcoholic beverages named after body parts. I wasn't fond of either, but she was my best friend and I was her maid of honor. This was the most important party of her life. If that meant researching cocktails and learning how to set up a dirty version of bingo, I was going to have to stop procrastinating and get to it.

When the elevator door opened, I stepped in and nodded at the young couple inside—a guy with a shock of blond hair and a young woman in shorts and braids. The lobby button had already been pushed, so I smiled at them.

The woman smiled back shyly. She wore a T-shirt

that read We're Not in Kansas Anymore. Both of them had shiny gold bands on their ring fingers.

The guy glanced at my laptop. "So, what's going on at the hotel this weekend? There's, like, a ton of people."

As the doors closed, I leaned back against the elevator. "HACK CON." The blank expression meant he clearly had no idea what I was talking about. "Computer stuff. Cybersecurity. Hacking."

"Oh!" Understanding dawned. "Gosh, that's pretty impressive. I know almost nothing about computers except how to type on one. I'm a vet. Well, a vet-in-training. I work with my dad. Sarah and I are here on our honeymoon from Kansas."

I glanced at the woman's T-shirt. "Oh, Kansas. Right. I get it. Congratulations."

His grin widened. "We thought it would be cool to visit Washington, DC and check out all the monuments and stuff. Our parents chipped in to help us stay here."

Jeez. Two clueless kids on their honeymoon from Kansas in the *same* hotel at the *same* time as four hundred hackers. Who the heck in Kansas had thought *that* would be a good idea?

I braced a hand against the elevator wall. "Look, guys, listen to me very carefully, okay? You have cell phones?"

The guy's smile faded and the girl shifted anxiously, pressing into her new husband's side and clutching her small purse. Like maybe she thought I'd reach out and snatch it or something. But I didn't need to touch her phone or her money in order to take either.

"Why do you want to know?" the guy said. Our moment of friendly interaction vanished and he looked at me suspiciously. "Sure, we have cell phones. Doesn't everyone?"

"Possibly." I tried to keep my tone light. "Take them out right now and turn off the Wi-Fi. It is critical you do *not* have them on for the entire duration of your stay in this hotel. When you get downtown, at least six blocks from this hotel, you can turn it back on. But while you are here, do *not* have the Wi-Fi on. And please do not, under any circumstances, use the free hotel Wi-Fi or access anything on your phone or computer that requires a password, even if you're on your own network or hot spot. Also, don't send any text messages from here that you wouldn't mind other people reading or that contain passwords. Finally, do not—and I repeat—do *not* use the ATM in the hotel. Do it at a bank or elsewhere, okay?"

Their eyes were wide as the elevator dinged. I stepped off and gave them my friendliest smile. "Uh, have a great honeymoon."

I crossed the ornate lobby, passed the fountain and headed toward the bar. I hadn't meant to scare them… much. Probably 60 percent of the attendees were white hats—no malicious intent, but they might still invade people's privacy with the hopes of scaring them into taking better security precautions. Regardless, it was still a 97 percent certainty those kids would be hacked *before* they left the hotel if they didn't take precautions, and a 60 percent chance even if they did.

I strolled into the bar, then stopped. The place was freaking packed. Every table, every seat at the bar and every square foot of floor near an outlet had been taken. I wandered to the back of the bar near the bathrooms and, to my delight, spotted an empty table with two chairs. I made a beeline for it and then stopped when I saw the white Reserved sign on it.

"Crap."

There was absolutely nowhere else to sit. I debated going back to my room, but I was hungry and thirsty. Hoping the people who had reserved it never showed up, I slid into the chair, looking around for a server. My plan was to sit and work while I got a bite to eat. If the people who reserved the table did show, I'd just get up and hope by then another table would have opened up.

I wound my brown hair into a ponytail, securing it with a scrunchie before opening up my laptop. Actually, it wasn't *my* laptop. It was a company laptop with absolutely nothing of any interest or value on it. Even though I'd protected it six ways to Sunday, I had no illusions that it was safe—hence, no important data had been stored on it. To protect myself further, I wasn't even carrying my actual phone, but a burner one. I knew better. Everything and everyone was game at this convention.

I'd just put on my computer glasses and started to type when a guy about my age slid onto the other chair. He wore a pair of dark sunglasses, jeans and a long-sleeved black T-shirt with white lettering that said Hack the Planet. He held a thick manila envelope in his hand.

"You're early." He set the envelope on the table and folded his hands on top of it.

I lowered my glasses to look at him, realizing he must be the person who'd reserved the table. "Oh, look, I'm sorry about—"

"No, no. It's all good," he said, cutting me off. He started to jiggle his foot wildly, shaking the table and my laptop. He had a wet sheen across his upper lip, which he wiped with the back of his hand. "Let's just get this over with. I'm not good at this kind of thing."

"What thing?" I said, starting to stand. Was this some kind of blind date setup? "Look, I think you've got this all wrong. I'm not—"

He grabbed my arm, yanking me back into the chair. "Sit down and zip it," he hissed. "Don't draw attention to us."

His frown grew as he rested his arms on the table, staring at me. "I know this is totally nerve-racking. They didn't give me much information either, which is the way it should be. I don't *want* to know more." He kept looking over his shoulder. His leg jiggled against the table so many times I had to put a hand on my laptop to keep it from getting bounced off.

"Do I know you?" It was hard to see his face clearly with the oversize sunglasses on. Had he been in my workshop?

He gave me a sharp glance and lowered his voice, leaning over the table. "Of course you don't know me. Don't be stupid. I don't want to know your name either. I will never speak to you again after this."

"You won't?"

"No. In fact, this concludes our little interaction." He pushed the manila envelope across the table at me. "Look, it's all in there—half now and the other half deposited when you're done. Good luck and have a nice life. Forget you ever saw me."

Before I could say another word, he got up from the table and disappeared into the crowd.

I lurched to my feet. "Hey, wait." I held up the envelope, but he was gone.

What in the world? I sat down and examined the envelope. There were no words on the outside and it wasn't sealed shut. I pulled it open, shaking out the contents onto the table.

Stacks of neatly bound hundred-dollar bills spilled out, followed by a single, folded sheet of paper.

TWO

HOLY BANK ROBBERY!

For a moment I stared slack-jawed at all the money. I stuffed the stacks of cash back in the envelope, then glanced around the bar, but no one seemed to be paying any attention. I unfolded the sheet of paper. It contained a username and private SSH login key, followed by a string of code. My eye caught the IP address 30.42.120.4. The NSA's network block. I recognized it from my time at the agency.

OMG! Alarm bells started clanging in my head. As I scanned the code, I began to see where this was headed…and it wasn't good. Still, I had to know for sure.

Code was my forte, so I opened my laptop and started following along. A knot formed in my stomach. Two keystrokes later, I backtracked, then slammed my laptop shut, my pulse jumping. I hadn't followed the trail far, but far enough to know that seriously bad things were afoot, especially when accompanied by what looked to be about fifty thousand dollars in cash.

"You're early."

I looked up as a young woman slid into the chair recently vacated by the other guy. She was Asian, pretty and probably in her early thirties. Her thick black hair fell to her waist and her eyes narrowed in anger as her gaze fell on the envelope and the code lying open just to the left of my laptop.

"What the hell do you think you're you doing?"

"What am I doing?" I glanced at the code like a kid getting caught sneaking a cookie. "Ah…ah…" Nope. Nothing even remotely plausible leaped to mind.

To my dismay, she reached across the table and snatched the envelope with the money and the paper from the table. I would have grabbed them back, but she slid them inside her black purse and snapped the clasp shut.

"It's all here, right?" she asked.

"It?"

"The money."

My mind raced. "Ah, yes, it's all there."

"It better be." She leaned forward, her expression irate. "You weren't supposed to open the envelope. For a well-paid courier, that was a stupid and dangerous thing to do."

I didn't miss the threat her words and tone carried. This was serious stuff.

I decided to play along. "I was curious. No harm, no foul."

"Why were you looking at the code?"

I feigned surprise. "That was the code—that jumble of numbers? Didn't mean a thing to me."

"That better be true." Her words carried an unmistakable warning. "So, what about the rest of the money I'm due? How will I receive it? What's the plan for that?"

I paused, considering the significance and risk of what I was about to do. But things had escalated to a point of no return. I didn't see another choice.

I crossed my arms against my chest and rested my elbows atop the laptop. "The plan is—the hack is off. You can keep the money for your trouble, but your services are no longer required. So, give me back the code. You won't be needing it."

Surprise and then anger crossed her face, but to my relief, she didn't bolt. "That's impossible. This directive came from the very top."

"Well, the very top is calling it off. A last-minute thing, I guess."

"Why?" Her eyes narrowed as she looked at me, most likely wondering if she could trust me. After all, I was nothing more than a courier. I held my gaze steady, afraid that the slightest waver would tip her off.

"I don't ask why." I lifted my shoulders. "Not my place."

"What about the other half of the money I was promised?"

"I have no idea. You'll have to take that up with them."

She pressed her lips together, presumably deciding whether she believed me or not. After a moment she spoke. "Fine, but I risked a lot to do this. This doesn't make any sense."

"Agreed, but this is what they instructed, so this is what you do. If your services are further required, you'll be contacted. The code, please." I held out my hand, but she didn't make a move to hand it over.

Instead, she rose, wrapping her fingers tightly around the straps of her purse. "No." She studied my face. "Not yet. You can tell them I was curious, too."

Before I could protest, she turned and strode away from the table, her dark hair swishing behind her.

I stood up, sliding the laptop beneath my arm. I would have followed her, but she had already disappeared, melting into the crowd.

I took a deep breath, thinking. I needed to stop the hack. But first, I needed expert advice and quick.

THREE

MY HEART POUNDED as I jogged toward X-Corp, bypass-
ing my office and heading straight for the parking garage. No way could I start an exploration of that hack
from official X-Corp equipment.

As I was pulling my red Miata out of the garage, I
punched in a number on my cell. It rang twice before
a computer answered, informing me the person I was
trying to reach was unavailable and to leave a message.

Crap. He wasn't answering, probably because he
didn't recognize the number. I spoke fast. "Slash, it's
me. Call me quickly at this number. I'm on a burner
phone and I've got a problem. A big one."

Luckily for the world, my boyfriend is one of the
good guys behind the keyboard. He works for the NSA
in a capacity that is unknown to me because I don't have
the proper clearance, and hadn't, even when I'd worked
there myself. Slash is a brilliant hacker. His skill at the
keyboard and deep knowledge of cyberspace make him
vital to national security. As a result, he has a special
FBI detail on him 24/7, kind of like the President.

My phone rang and I answered. "Slash?"

"What's up, *cara*?"

"I intercepted a serious hack. We need to talk. Now."

"Where are you?"

"I-95, headed toward your place."

"I'll meet you there in thirty minutes."

"Great."

He paused. "Are you okay?"

"Not really." My hands were shaking. I gripped the steering wheel tighter, concentrating on calm, even breaths.

"Can you tell me what happened?"

His voice carried a hint of warning, reminding me not to share anything classified over the phone.

"It was a total case of mistaken identity." I tapped the steering wheel nervously. "There was nowhere to sit at the hotel bar at HACK CON, so I figured I'd just have a quick bite to eat and work on the details for Basia's party at a reserved table. I'm sitting there when a courier passes me written instructions for a hack, along with an envelope stuffed with bills. Then, *bam*, he splits. Apparently he thought I was the person who was *supposed* to be sitting there."

I switched lanes, looking over my shoulder and into my rearview mirror.

"Did you recognize him?"

"It wasn't just one person. There were two. After the courier, I met the actual hacker—the one who was *supposed* to be sitting there. The courier was about my age and wore big sunglasses, which means I didn't get a good look at his face. The hacker was female, Asian. The guy passed off the code and the money to me. Then the real hacker showed up and snatched everything off the table before I could stop her. She thought I was the courier. So, I pretended the hack had been called off. I'm not sure she believed me."

"You called off the hack?" His voice was incredulous.

"Well, it seemed like the right thing to do at the

time." Now that I actually thought about it, it had been kind of ballsy. "What else should I have done?

"Nothing. You did the right thing. Did you actually see the code?"

"Yep. Saw it and actually followed it a little way, before it got too hot for my blood. First of all, I'm on a sterilized computer without the right software. Second of all, I'm sitting in a crowded bar with a dozen hackers sitting around me. Didn't want to advertise where I was headed. Good news is, I've got the whole code here in my head." I tapped my temple. "Photographic memory for the win."

"What about the written code?" he asked.

"The hacker took it, along with the money, even though I told her the hack was off."

"That's not good."

"You think? It's why I'm in a hurry to get to your place."

I glanced in my rearview mirror. A small black car weaved through traffic behind me. My concern grew as the car pulled up beside me. I looked over at the driver and recognized the hacker from the bar.

"Slash, she just pulled up beside me. The hacker. She's got a gun!"

"A gun?"

"I'm in trouble," I shouted as she raised the gun and pointed it at me.

FOUR

I LIFTED MY foot off the gas just as the driver's side window exploded. Somehow I hadn't been hit. Her car screeched ahead of me as I swerved into the far right lane and nearly sideswiped a blue minivan. Traffic was too heavy for any fancy maneuvering, not that I even *knew* how to do that.

Slash shouted something, but I couldn't make it out.

The shooter cut to the shoulder, slowed down, then fell in behind me again, boxing me between a truck and a silver Honda. She fired, this time from behind me. I heard the ping of the bullet hitting the metal frame of the car. I was a sitting duck.

"She's shooting at me," I yelled.

At this point, I had only one real option. If I stayed where I was, it was only a matter of time before she hit one of my tires and I'd be forced to pull over. I swerved to the shoulder and hit the gas, roaring off at the next exit.

"The hacker is shooting at you?"

I ran a red light and shot past two cars on the wrong side of the road before yanking the car back to my lane. She stayed with me. To my great dismay, no police car turned on its lights and started following us.

"Yes! The Asian woman from the hotel," I screeched. "Guess she didn't buy my 'the hack is off' story. She's in a black two-door sports car. I can't see the license plate clearly. I'm too busy driving for my freaking life."

He swore. "Don't get off the freeway."

"It's too late. I didn't have a choice. Traffic was too heavy and she was shooting at my tires. But I'm not sure which exit I got off on." I ran another red light and so did she. She almost hit a red Toyota. Car horns were blaring and I imagined several middle fingers were being shot my way. Panic gripped my throat. "Seriously, I can't shake her, Slash."

"Hold on, *cara*. Whatever you do, don't stop the car. I'm already on the way to your location." I could hear the wail of a siren and assumed he had placed the light on top of his SUV. "I'm tracking you via your earrings. My ETA is about seventeen minutes."

"What about your FBI tail?"

"They're trying to keep up."

Slash's recent Christmas present to me, in addition to a gun, had been a pair of earrings that came with a tracking device he'd designed. They were our secret. Seeing as how a little black cloud seemed to follow me around, we'd agreed that for the time being, both the gun and the earrings were a good idea. Still, seventeen minutes seemed like an eternity.

"I don't know if I can last seventeen minutes." I swerved and nearly took out a guy on a motorcycle.

"*Si*, you can. You've got this. Stay calm." Slash's voice remained steady, while my heart galloped. "Are you on a two-lane stretch of road?"

"Still four-lane."

"Good. Keep her behind you if you can. I've already alerted the police to your position. Help is on the way, I promise. Hold the course. Stay calm."

I glanced in my rearview mirror just before she slammed into the back of the Miata. I swerved to the left, clipped a green pickup truck coming the other direction. Pulling up on the right side of my rear bumper, she fired another shot through the back windshield. I hunched over the steering wheel as the bullet shattered the rear window and lodged somewhere in my car.

"What happened?" Slash asked.

"I'm okay, but my rear window is toast."

We pulled into a forested stretch and the four-lane road turned into two lanes. "Bad news, Slash. We're now on two lanes and I think I'm screwed. Not much traffic along this stretch and she's a better driver than me."

"But you're smarter. You've got this."

Easy for him to say—he wasn't being chased by a lunatic with a gun. Plus, I'd never told him I hadn't gotten my driver's license until I turned twenty-one, and I'd failed the driving test twice.

Sure enough once the cars coming from the other direction had passed, she gunned forward, pulling up to the driver's side again. I tried to sideswipe her, but she managed get out of the way. She raised her gun again.

I hit the brakes just as she fired. She hurled past me, and the bullet pinged off the hood of my car. Unfortunately, the abrupt stop cost me. I was traveling at such a high rate of speed that the Miata skidded sideways, screeching across the asphalt. It slid into a spin.

"Noooo," I shrieked, wrestling with the steering wheel. The car veered off the road, Slash shouted something and I held my breath. For a moment I was airborne, then the car crashed and I blacked out.

FIVE

I BLINKED INTO CONSCIOUSNESS. Everything was blurry and an acrid smell filled the car. My air bag had deployed. Swallowing the panic, I pushed aside the bag and yanked on the handle of the door. It opened and I fell out of the car, rolling to my knees and crouching, coughing and squinting at my surroundings in the sunlight.

Luckily the car had fallen over a short embankment and not off a freaking cliff. I hadn't hit a tree, a pole or anything solid either. I'd just come to a jarring, bouncing stop in a cleared, grassy area.

A quick shake of all my limbs indicated I was in one piece, although my car was totaled. There was something wet on my forehead. When I swiped at it, my fingers came away bloody.

A car squealed to a stop at the ledge above me.

I limped to the tree line and hid. A door slammed shut. The woman from the bar appeared on the ledge, shading her eyes and peering down at my car. Glancing over her shoulder at the road, she pulled her gun, then started down the incline sideways.

I wasn't in any condition to outrun her, but it looked like I wasn't going to have a choice. I started moving quietly through the trees. My heart pounded so loudly I was afraid it would lead her right to me. It would take her just a moment to see I'd left the car and then she'd be after me.

I kept walking as quickly as I could, focusing on putting as much distance between us as possible. After a couple of minutes, I paused, leaning back against a tree and panting. It was quiet. A squirrel climbing a tree, some crackles of the leaves here and there. How was I supposed to know what was her and what were normal sounds of nature?

I didn't want to stay in one place too long. I pushed off the tree, stepping carefully through the foliage. My foot landed on some branches covered by leaves. It made a loud cracking noise.

Jeez, I was probably as easy to track as an elephant.

I took a few more steps and ducked behind a large boulder. My knee hit the rock and I hissed through my teeth at the stab of pain. A rustle sounded to my right and I froze. If she was coming, how would I protect myself?

I scoured along the ground for something and came upon a rock the size of a baseball. Misdirection always seemed to work in the movies, so I figured it was worth a shot. I didn't have any illusions about completely shaking her, but I was out of ideas.

I heard another noise, a rustle. It sounded too equally paced to be an animal, so I counted to three and threw the rock as far as I could.

It made a crash. The rustle became louder, thankfully moving away from me. I headed in the opposite direction, trying to hop onto areas that were clear of rocks or leaves to limit the noise. A life-and-death game of forest hopscotch.

After a few minutes of that I began to feel winded. A

new resolution was to add cardio to my daily workout, which at this time was monthly, possibly bimonthly… oh, who was I kidding? It was nonexistent.

I was breathing so hard it was difficult to listen. I hadn't heard anyone overtly following me, but that didn't mean she wasn't right behind me at this very moment. She was probably just a heck of a lot better and faster than me at this. In my defense, I'd started up an embankment and moving at an upward angle on crumbly soil was killing my knee, as well as my stamina.

My back foot snagged on a log. I threw out my hands to catch myself, but landed partially on my knee.

Ouch!

I rolled over, clutching my knee. As it was, I'd probably already made enough noise to alert anyone a mile away to my location.

I rolled to all fours, took a second to wipe the dirt and leaves from my nose and cheeks, then stood.

The cold barrel that pressed against my temple made me rethink my decision to move.

I'd been found.

SIX

"CARA?"

"Slash?"

I opened my eyes in astonishment. Sure enough, it was him.

Yanking his gun away from my head, he pulled me into his arms. *"Mio Dio*, you're okay. I wasn't sure it was you, with all the leaves in your hair and the funny way you were walking."

"I'm limping. Thank God you're here. Did you catch her?"

"Not yet." He released me and looked around, keeping a hand on my arm. He took a radio from his belt and spoke quietly. "I've got her. The target is still at large."

A quiet voice replied. "Roger that."

Slash attached the radio to a slot on his belt. "Let's go."

"Wait. How many people are out here looking for her? Maybe she'll head back to her car."

"There are three officers out here, one waiting by her car. We're running the plates now. It's time to get you out of here."

"What about her?"

"You're my priority. When I saw your car… Let's just say it took me ten years closer to the grave. I'm running out of decades."

"I was lucky I didn't hit anything like a tree."

He cupped my cheek, turning it so he could inspect my forehead. "How do you feel? Looks like you might need a stitch or two."

"It probably looks worse than it is. Head wounds bleed a lot. Luckily I didn't hit my nose again." I'd recently broken my nose in a plane crash and it had just finished healing. I touched it. There was a small bump on the ridge, but thankfully right now it didn't hurt.

"I hope this doesn't become a habit—banging up your face."

"Believe me, it's not intentional." I winced as I shifted my weight on my feet. "My knee is bruised, I think. I can walk."

Not taking my word for it, he knelt down and inspected it, making me bend it a couple of times. "You sure you can walk out of here?"

"Of course."

He reached beneath his shirt and pulled out a gold cross, pressing a kiss to it. Then he slid an arm around my waist, shouldering much of my weight. "Let's move."

Keeping his gun out, he led me back to my ruined car.

WE STOPPED AT the emergency room, where I got away with one small liquid stitch on my forehead and a three-day prescription for painkillers. The doctor patted my hand and told me although I had a mean bruise on my knee, nothing was broken. I hoped the injuries would heal before my parents returned from their European vacation. They'd lock me up for good if they knew I'd been hurt yet again.

"Any news on the woman?" I asked Slash as the nurse put a salve on my elbow where I'd scraped it.

"Unfortunately none." Slash walked over to the tray where the nurse was picking up some cotton balls. "She vanished. The plates on her car were traced to a rental company. She paid in cash. Her driver's license, phone number and address are bogus."

"No surprise there, I guess." I wondered what the final verdict on my Miata was. I really didn't want to know, but better to ask. "What happened to my car?"

"I'm sorry, *cara*. It's totaled. It's been towed to the police station. It's part of the crime investigation for now."

"Great." I tried not to be too broken up about it, but it was hard. I really liked that car.

Thankfully the NSA had been able to expedite my police interrogation at the hospital after Slash convinced them it was more important to get me in front of a computer than to have me answer questions. I had to agree to talk with them later after we'd had a chance to examine the hack and provide additional details on the woman and the chain of events leading up to the car chase.

"Are you sure you're up to this, *cara*?" Slash shifted in the hard plastic chair. "Maybe I should take you to your parents."

"My parents are in Venice right now on an anniversary trip. I'm shaken up a bit, but fine. Really. Besides, I think we're all in agreement that time is of the essence. We've got to follow that hack right now."

He nodded, but he didn't look happy about it. "Okay, but we do it from my place."

One of the FBI agents leaned down. "I'm sorry, sir. We've instructions to take you to the NSA."

Slash didn't even look up. "Not even a chance. We're going to my place and use my equipment. I don't know what's been compromised at the NSA. I need a clean look."

The agents exchanged a glance, but didn't argue. One of them slipped out of the room, apparently to break the news to someone at the NSA that Slash wasn't coming in.

Slash put a hand under my elbow and helped me up. He kissed me on the cheek and murmured, "It's a good thing you've got excellent medical benefits at X-Corp."

"Ha-ha," I replied, but it made me smile. He always seemed to know how to do that.

We were quiet in the car with the FBI trailing behind us. Slash's phone vibrated twice but he didn't answer or even look at who was calling.

He put a hand on my knee and kept it there. "Are you sure you're well enough to do this?"

"I'm sure, Slash. They really, *really* don't want me to follow that thread, which makes me eager to do just that."

"Regardless, you were just in a car accident. It can wait."

"It *can't* wait. We both know that. If I can think, I can hack. Seriously, I'm fine."

He opened his mouth as if to say something, and then shut it. Instead, he reached over and turned on the music. Soothing sounds of a piano riff filled the car. It was Hai Tsang, our favorite pianist.

I closed my eyes and leaned back against the head-rest. Being near Slash, listening to the soft music and the effects of the painkillers relaxed me. I had spoken the truth when I said I was good to go. I knew he'd do the hack for me if he could, but seeing as how the information was locked in my head, I had to be the one at the keyboard.

When we got to his apartment, he pressed his wallet to the pad on his door and it clicked open. He ushered me in and then tapped out a code on his alarm before closing the door behind me.

"I know you're ready to go, but how about a bite to eat and a quick rest first?"

"I'm not hungry yet and the painkillers are working their magic. I'm in a good place for the time being. Let's just get started, okay?"

I could see he wanted to argue, so I held up a hand. "I'm serious, Slash."

He got the picture, so after a moment of hesitation, he nodded. "Okay."

He led me to the safe room in his apartment where he had all his specialized and unregistered computer equipment and secure networks. He endured a biometric scan and spoke in Italian to confirm a voice imprint before the steel-enforced door opened.

We entered and made our way past a couple of closets and a piano until we came to a workstation with several laptops and a couple of thirty-two-inch monitors.

"Sit," he said pointing to a swivel chair in front of a laptop that was connected to one of the large monitors.

"There's only one chair in here," I protested.

He dragged the piano bench over and straddled it. "I'll get another chair in a minute. Let's work while you still can."

He leaned over me, signing in and readying one of

the laptops. His fingers flew over the keyboard. I observed him jumping from place to place, making our own point of origin hidden from anyone who might want to trace us.

After a few minutes, he glanced up at me. "Ready?"

"Ready."

He scooted aside and I pulled the chair closer to the laptop. Taking a deep breath, I started the hack. I took my time, careful to follow the code I'd memorized. After less than two minutes, I heard Slash draw a sharp breath.

"This is as far as I got at the hotel," I said. He sat so close to me that his breath warmed my cheek. One of his hands rested on my back and I could feel the heat through my blouse.

My fingers steadily tapped the keyboard. "You can see where I'm headed." I pointed to the IP address on a data stream on the monitor.

Slash hissed, his brown eyes narrowing as he shoved off the bench and stood. "The NSA."

"Bingo."

I paused, leaning back, rolling my neck. "I have a feeling it's going to get real exciting from here. My guess is that there's a back door at the end of the rainbow."

"Undoubtedly."

"Do you think she's already been there?"

"Doesn't matter." His expression darkened with anger. "Someone created that door, so regardless, we have to assume the information has been compromised.

The question is where does it lead and what did they want?"

"The only way to know is to follow the yellow brick road."

SEVEN

HE PUT A HAND on my shoulder. "Not yet. I've got to make a call." He pulled out his cell from his jeans' pocket and punched a button. After a moment, he began issuing instructions to his team at the NSA. Then he snapped the phone closed and sat back down. "I need everyone on alert and looking for anomalies. Are you sure you're up for continuing?"

"I'm sure. We're getting close. Let's do it."

"Okay. Let me get a decent chair first."

He returned a few moments later, carrying a chair. He set it down and left the room again, this time bringing back a couple of bottles of water, a box of crackers and two apples. He handed me a water bottle and an apple, then sat down, facing me.

"Drink and have a bite first."

I unscrewed the top of the bottle and took a long slug before biting into the apple. "Thanks."

He hooked a finger under my chin until I was looking into his eyes. "We stop when you are in pain, tired or hungry. No negotiation."

"Understood." I nodded. "Let's get going."

His finger lingered a moment longer on my chin before he released it and sat back in his chair.

I steadied myself and took a minute to review our path and determine where we were headed. Despite my pain and exhaustion, I felt the surge of adrenaline that

I always got when starting a hack. My fingers tingled and my pulse kicked it up a notch. Even though I had permission to follow this path, hacking the NSA was *not* for the faint of heart.

I went slower than usual, partly because I was nervous and partly because the painkillers were starting to wear off and a dull ache was interfering with my concentration. I didn't want Slash to know, so I forged ahead. As we maneuvered deeper into NSA territory, I realized that whoever had written this code had inside information. I knew Slash had figured that, too. I could feel his tension rise at each juncture, although he didn't say a word.

Finally I lifted my fingers from the keyboard and turned to him. He was staring at the screen, his focus intense and singular. When I spoke, he actually blinked.

"You know what this means? Slash?"

I glanced sideways at him as his jaw tightened. "Insider threat." His voice was grim and cold. "I'm going to find the bastard and nail him. Or her. No mercy."

I not only believed he would do it, I sincerely hoped he would succeed. All tech heads know there is a special place in hell for the insider threat. There was no doubt in my mind that Slash would get him. But first we had a door to find so we could open it and see where it led.

"Okay, who's orchestrating this and what do they want?" I grabbed my water bottle and took a drink. The hack was getting harder and deeper, but a clear and careful path had been laid. "The insider needs cash or has a political ax to grind, which means there must be a path leading somewhere for some specific purpose."

"Let's postulate a theory once we see exactly where the door opens."

"Fine." I leaned forward, inspecting a data stream. "Seriously, though, whoever created this path is good, Slash. Really good. If I hadn't intercepted the hack…"

He raised a hand. "I don't want to go there. Do you mind if I take over now? You can guide me. I want to check out some peripheral items as we go along."

"Sure." I scooted to the side and he pulled his chair into my place. He angled two more laptops toward him and started typing while occasionally referring back to what we'd already done. After a few minutes, he dipped his head at me.

"I'm ready."

"Then let's finish it." I snatched a cracker as I gave him initial instructions.

The deeper we got, the quieter Slash became. The penalties for hacks on intelligence agencies were severe, involving lengthy jail time, not to mention the security was state of the art, so the chance of getting caught was extremely high. No question this was an extremely dangerous hack, but someone had cleared a path right past several of the NSA's top security levels and traps. Slash paused every now and then to jot down a string of code on a pad of paper or type into one or both of the adjoining laptops. The fact that we'd already gone so far undetected was scary and to Slash, completely unacceptable.

"There," he finally said pointing to his screen. "The back door."

I peered at the monitor. At some point, our room had become dark, lit only by our monitor. I had no idea how many hours had passed since we started. Our bottles of water were long empty and my forehead was throbbing. I rested my chin on his shoulder.

"I must be tired. I don't see it. Where exactly?"

His elegant hacker fingers tapped the screen. "Here. Damn it. Right here."

I finally saw it. Cleverly hidden, but there nonetheless. I could almost feel the anger vibrating off Slash. At least we'd found it, which meant we could close it. Safe…at least until the next hack.

Slash yanked his cell phone out of his pocket, punched a button and began barking out a number of commands to someone on the other end. After he hung up, he sat back down at the monitor. He looked furious.

"What's wrong?"

"We had another intrusion. Thirty-nine minutes ago. They are trying to isolate it, but we're already here, so we'll find it first."

"She got in."

"I'm afraid so. Let's see where this trail goes."

I hesitated. "Am I cleared to see what's in there?"

"As of right now you are. I don't have to explain confidentiality to you."

"No, you don't."

He tapped on the keyboard and waltzed in through the door. His fingers paused, hovering over the keys.

"So, where are we?" The weariness, pain and hunger all disappeared in the excitement of the discovery.

He leaned forward, hit a few more keys. "A personnel database."

My brow furrowed. "Well, I sure didn't see that one coming."

"Me neither. It doesn't make sense. There are a lot more sensitive spots they could have hacked given this level of inside support." He opened several windows on his screen and began jumping around. "Definitely odd."

"I know, right? All this time I was thinking more along the lines of a hack into a sensitive countersurveillance operation or an attempt to steal nuclear passwords. You know, something exciting."

He made a few more keystrokes. "This is interesting, though. This hack is specific to one department."

"Which department?"

"IAD."

"IAD?" I whistled. "Seriously? Someone provided instructions for a hack into the personnel database for the NSA's Information Assurance Directorate?"

The Directorate was responsible for protecting and defending the nation's computers from the incessant stream of hacks on government and private sector networks in accordance with National Security Directive 42. Directive 42 provided strict guidelines for how American national policy and operational procedures must be conducted in regards to information technology and computer systems. The NSA executed the duties of the Directorate, while the Department of Defense oversaw the entire program. This was super top secret stuff—way above any clearance I'd ever had.

So, the fact that someone went to the significant trouble of hacking into IAD for the purpose of penetrating a personnel database was…weird. No top secret info there. Just a list of employees.

"That's what it looks like." Slash's jaw tightened. "No question that whoever built this door is an insider. Stand by."

"Are you going to close it?"

"No. I'm going to set a trap."

EIGHT

As Slash set his trap, I stood, stretching my arms above my head. My forehead and knee were throbbing, which meant it was way past time for a painkiller. My stomach growled and I tried to remember the last time I'd eaten something other than the apple. Breakfast had been about seven thirty. No wonder I was starving.

"I'm stopping now," Slash said, looking up from the monitor.

"You're not. You just got in. You've got to finish. We both know the dangers of leaving in midtrap. I'm good for a bit more. I'll go get some water to take my pills."

He hesitated. "Are you sure?"

"I'm sure. Finish it up. I mean it, Slash. Either you do it or I will."

He stared at me for a moment longer, then turned back to the monitor. I went out of the room, wedging a book in the doorway so I wouldn't have to bother him to come back in.

I grabbed a water bottle from the fridge and washed down one of my pain pills. A few glugs later and I had finished off the entire bottle. My purse was on the counter, so I took out my cell phone. I'd turned it off while at the conference, and I had one call from my mother and three from Basia. My stomach flipped when I saw Basia's number. She'd left three messages, but I was afraid to listen to them. She probably wanted to set up a time to do something horrific, like try on bridesmaid dresses or shoes. Or maybe she wanted an update from me on the plans for the bachelorette party. I had nothing. Paralyzed by party planning—that was me.

Why in the world Basia wanted to have the bachelorette party a full month before the wedding remained a mystery to me, but since I knew absolutely nothing about weddings and parties, it wasn't my place to second-guess her. Still it had shrunk my timeline for planning, which wasn't very helpful, especially when I had no idea what I was doing in the first place.

I started to panic, more scared of a freaking party than I was of being chased through the woods by some crazed hacker with a gun.

"Calm down, Carmichael," I said aloud. "It's just a party."

Since Slash was still preoccupied with setting the trap, I decided to do a bit of browsing on my phone for party stores in the area. There were about one gazillion party stores, so I refined the search to bachelorette parties. I wasn't sure exactly what I was looking for, so I started scrolling through the list. I hovered over one store name because it said Faylene's Bachelorette Parties and Supplies. I had yet to see a store so specialized, so I figured if that was all they did, they must be doing pretty good business. The hours said the store was open until eleven o'clock at night, which seemed kind of late, but maybe people only planned bachelorette parties at night. It wasn't like I had any frame of reference.

After two rings someone picked up.

"Faylene's Bachelorette Parties and Supplies." The woman sounded like a heavy smoker. "We do it all for you. How can I help you?"

They'd do it all for me? That sounded promising. *Really* promising.

"Uh, hi. I'm supposed to plan a bachelorette party for my best friend. I wondered if, well, you really do it all. Decorations, games, food, supplies and planning."

"Sure, we can do that. You provide the parameters and we do the rest."

Parameters. *Now* we were talking my language. "What kind of parameters do you need?"

"Well, how many guests are coming, what kind of theme you want, what type of food people want to eat, will it be alcohol or dry and what do you want to do for the entertainment? That kind of thing."

"Oh." It sounded a lot like I was going to have to do something. In no way did I want to give her that impression. "Look, I'll be honest with you, I've never planned a party before, let alone a big one like this. There are going to be about ten women and the bride-to-be is, well, a free spirit. That's as much as I've got in terms of parameters. Well, and it's this weekend. I've got a place rented and invitations mailed, but that's it."

There was silence. "That's a fast turnaround and not much to go on. I guess I could come up with some ideas and run them past you."

"Great." Relief flooded through me. "Really great. Thanks so much."

"You're welcome. By the way, I'm Faylene."

"Oh, hey, Faylene. I'm Lexi. I guess this must be your shop."

"It sure is. I'll take good care of you. Don't worry."

"I won't. I can't wait to hear what you come up with."

We exchanged contact information and she promised

to call me soon. I'd just put my cell back in my purse when Slash came out to the kitchen.

"Who were you talking to?" he asked, tugging on my arm and pulling me into his arms. He kissed me before letting me rest my head against his shoulder.

"Oh, I was just party planning."

He raised an eyebrow. "At this hour? It's nearly ten o'clock."

"Lucky for me, the store is open late."

"So, how's it going?"

He didn't have to ask me which party. It wasn't like I even *went* to parties, let alone planned them.

"According to the timeline of *How to Plan the Perfect Bachelorette Party*—which, by the way, was the only thing I understood in the entire book—I'm in serious trouble," I said. "However, I think I've finally got a thread I can pull in terms of assistance."

"It's *this* Saturday, right?"

"Right." I gulped. "No worries. I will not panic. It's all under control."

Wisely he questioned no further. He was invited to Xavier's bachelor party, which was also this Saturday. The details of that party were apparently top secret because no one had told me anything, including Elvis.

"So, is the trap set?" I asked, changing the subject.

"It is." Slash tucked a strand of hair behind my ear. "Let's put it away for a while. I want to take care of you. What do you want to do for dinner? Unfortunately, my pantry is a bit understocked."

"I know. I checked."

"Want to go out?"

"I don't feel up to that. We could order a pizza, though."

"Excellent idea. I'll order from Amicci's on South High Street. It's only about fifteen minutes away. They have good pizza."

"Perfect. I completely trust your judgment on pizza."

He smiled as he picked up his cell. He must have ordered from them before, because he asked for the regular and gave nothing more than his telephone number before hanging up.

He went to the fridge and grabbed a water bottle, tossing it to me. "I'd open some wine, but you're on painkillers. This will be better for you."

I caught the bottle. "I know. Thanks."

He pulled another water bottle for himself, unscrewed the top and took a long swig. As he put the cap back on, he considered me. "I'm afraid it's going to be a long day for you tomorrow. They want to question you at the NSA about the players in this little drama."

I twisted my hair around my finger. "I don't have a lot to tell them. Still, I'm willing to talk as long as we don't have to go to the police station."

"Not a concern. This is way out of the hands of the police at this point. The FBI and NSA will run interference for you on this."

"Thank goodness. The fact that I'm on a first-name basis with the police at the station these days is not a good thing."

"I'm with you on that." He suddenly snapped his fingers. "That reminds me. I almost forgot. I have a present for you."

"A present for me? It's not my birthday. But more importantly, why does talking about the police station remind you that you have a present for me?"

He smiled. "It's a replacement for something you lost the *last* time we were at the police station."

"Slash, you know you don't have to—"

"I know." He held up a hand, stopping me. "I *know.* Just close your eyes, okay?"

Swallowing my objection, I closed my eyes. He took my hand and led me to a spot, ordering me to stand still and not peek.

I heard a rustle. "Okay. Open your eyes."

We were in the bedroom. He motioned to the bed, where a gorgeous blue coat lay.

I looked at the coat and then at Slash. "Wow. You bought me a new coat?"

"To replace the one that got ruined in New York." He held it up and helped me slide my arms in it. "This time instead of white, I opted for sapphire blue. What do you think?"

I ran my hand across the soft material. It fit perfectly and fell just below the top of my thighs.

I turned around to face him and he rested his hands on my hips. "I love this coat for multiple reasons, Slash. First, I adore this shade of blue. And second—"

He pressed a finger against my lips, interrupting me. "Let me guess. You *love* that you didn't have to go shopping for it."

I laughed. "Wow. You *do* know me well."

"I'm working on it."

"Thanks." I touched the stubble on his cheek with my fingertips. "I mean it. It was a thoughtful thing to do."

"You're welcome." He took my hand and lifted it to his lips, kissing the inside of my wrist.

I slid my arms around his neck and he pulled me closer so I could rest my head on his shoulder. "I have a little present for you, in return," I said. "You can take the coat *off* me now…if you know what I mean."

He tilted his head back, lifting my chin with his finger, a smile touching his lips. "I think I do." He gently touched the wound on my face with a fingertip. "But what about your injuries and the pizza?"

"I believe I will feel exponentially better and more relaxed after your, um, ministrations. In regards to the pizza, based on my calculations—including the time it will take them to make the pizza and drive to your apartment—I figure we have about fifteen minutes left. Can you work within those parameters?"

"I'll certainly do my best," Slash said as he carefully slid the coat off my shoulders. "But after that and the pizza, you're going straight to bed. No arguments."

"Deal." I sighed in pleasure as he lowered his mouth to mine.

NINE

THE NEXT MORNING we headed to NSA headquarters at Fort Meade. I'd wanted to call Finn Shaughnessy, my boss, to let him know what was going on, but Slash stopped me.

"Can you wait a bit more? I'd prefer to keep this confidential for the time being. You weren't supposed to go into the office today anyway, right?"

"No. I'm supposed to be at the HACK CON."

"Are you presenting?"

"No. I did that yesterday. I'm just a participant now."

"Good. No one will miss you then. We need to get clearance for how much of this you can tell Finn, okay?"

"Hey, you called him Finn. Are you guys becoming friends?" I hoped so. People admired Slash, but he generally kept them at a distance. Aside from his family and me, he didn't have many close relationships. Definitely nothing like what I had with Basia, Elvis, Xavier and Finn.

Slash gave me a sideways glance. "We're acquaintances with a person of mutual importance between us. Friendship is a possibility."

"Yay. That's progress!"

He smiled and I looked out the window at the passing spring scenery. Flowers were blooming and there was an occasional warm current in the spring air of Washington, DC. Soon it would be time for the annual

Cherry Blossom Festival, which was one of my favorite times in the city. This year, Slash and I would go see them together.

As we approached Fort Meade, Slash stopped at the guard gate and showed his identification. I had to show mine, too. The guard cross-referenced me with the tablet he held and then waved us through. Slash pulled into the parking lot in front of two large glass-front high-rise buildings. We walked to the entrance of the building on the right. Because I was a visitor this time around and no longer an employee, I went through a different line than Slash. I sent my purse through the X-ray machine and endured a full body scan. Finally, I pressed my palm to a biometric pad and signed my name on a tablet before I was admitted. Slash bypassed most of the initial entrance drama and waited for me on the other side. He'd hung his security badge around his neck. It was the first time I'd ever seen it. His lanyard was red, which meant he could access any part of the building he wanted. No surprise there, but it was cool for me to see the red lanyard close up.

We walked together to the elevators. To my surprise, instead of going up the stairs to where I used to have my office, Slash pressed his palm against a panel above the elevator's up and down buttons. When they lit up, he pressed the down button. Although I'd heard about the "Hole"—as NSA employees often referred to it—I'd never actually been there. Rumor had it there were extensive tunnels and offices, ten acres' worth, below-ground.

"Whoa. Are we going to the Hole?" I asked, trying not to look too excited.

"We are. It's where IAD has its offices."

I hadn't known that, but then again, we were heavily compartmentalized at the NSA to keep things as secret as possible.

The elevator door dinged open. No one was inside. Slash ushered me in and followed, pressing his badge against another keypad and pressing the button that said G2.

"So, exactly whom in IAD will I be talking to?" I kept my focus on Slash, trying not to look at my bruised reflection in the mirrored walls of the elevator.

"Several people, including the Director of IAD, Grant Durham, and our Lead Facility Security Officer, Shawn Moore. There will likely be several others, possibly reps from the CIA and FBI. I already briefed Grant."

"You filled him in personally?"

"Of course. He's my boss."

I stared at Slash in astonishment. I'd been dating him for several months and, although I knew he worked at the NSA, he'd never been permitted to tell me exactly in what capacity or department. That kind of information was top secret, as in I-can't-tell-you-or-else-I-have-to-kill-you secret.

"You work in IAD? Really?"

"Really. But not exclusively. I am occasionally…well, often…tagged for duties elsewhere as needed."

He didn't offer more information and I didn't ask. I knew he couldn't tell me even if he wanted to.

The elevator dinged and we stepped off. I'm not sure why I hadn't considered IAD, except I'd figured him as better suited for a spot in cyber research and development. IAD handled pretty dark stuff like network worms, Trojan counterattacks and semantic analysis.

Plus, IAD agents were often used by other agencies, such as the CIA, FBI and the military for intelligence operations. Now that I thought about it, IAD did make a lot of sense for a guy with Slash's talents. I slid a glance at him, wondering what other secrets he had hidden from me.

He took my elbow, steering me down a hallway. Florescent lighting illuminated the dim corridor as we walked past rows of identical sea green doors with no identifying information other than gold-plated numbers. We passed two men with green lanyards around their necks. They greeted Slash, who nodded back at them.

"Are we going to your office?" I wasn't sure why I was whispering except somehow I felt like I was on hallowed ground.

"No. It's too small. We'll convene in the IAD war room. They'll be waiting."

He abruptly stopped at a door with a gold plate that read G266 and pressed his wallet against an electronic pad anchored to the wall next to the door. The keypad whirred and then opened. Slash pressed his forehead to a biometric pad for a retinal scan. The door clicked and Slash pushed it open.

I took a breath and steeled myself for my first step into the legendary IAD.

TEN

SLASH MOVED TO the side and insisted I enter first. I strode into the room, looking around curiously.

Six men sat around a large, polished mahogany table. A large smart board was lit up, but nothing was displayed. No women in the room other than myself. Not that I was surprised.

All of the men had laptops open in front of them. One man was typing while two others huddled at the same laptop looking at something on the screen. Everyone glanced up at me. An older man with a shock of gray hair rose from the head of the table and came to greet us. He looked to be in his mid-fifties and wore his white shirt rolled up his forearms. A sports jacket was draped on the back of his chair. When he shook my hand, his grip was firm and swift.

"Hello. I'm Grant Durham, Director of IAD. I'm glad to have the opportunity to finally meet you, Ms. Carmichael. I've heard quite a bit about you."

"Well, you can't believe *everything* you hear," I joked. To my relief, he smiled.

Grant shook Slash's hand, too. While neither man said anything, Grant patted Slash on the back in a gesture of familiarity. "Have a seat both of you, please, and let's get started." He motioned toward two empty seats adjacent to him.

Slash pulled out my chair and I sat while Grant returned to his seat at the head of the table.

Grant closed his laptop and slid it aside. "Welcome to our war room, Ms. Carmichael. Everyone here is aware of who you are and what happened to you yesterday. Let's do quick introductions around the table so you will know us. Gentlemen, please introduce yourself to the young lady."

The man next to him nodded at me. "Good morning. I'm Trevor McMasters, Deputy Director of Operations, IAD. Nice to finally meet you. Your reputation precedes you."

He didn't smile when he said it, so I had no idea if that were good or bad. A young Asian man seated next to me went next. "I'm Charlie Hsu, Head of ISS."

ISS stood for Information Systems Security. It would be Charlie's job to oversee the installation and implementation of security software to prevent cyberattacks, as well as respond to successful attacks with appropriate countermeasures.

"Hey, Charlie," I said, and he nodded.

A middle-aged man with black hair sitting next to me held out a hand. "I'm Sam Nelson, Vulnerability Analyst."

"Hey, Sam. I'll be interested to hear your analysis of the hack."

He grinned. "Happy to provide it."

The introductions continued around the table. Marek Krupka from the Office of Security Investigations was next. A handsome African-American man named Shawn Moore, the Lead Facility Security Officer, or FSO, rounded out our group.

Slash didn't introduce himself.

When the introductions were finished, Grant leaned forward on the table, folding his hands on top of his laptop. "So, Ms. Carmichael, can you walk us through exactly what happened?"

I figured they'd already heard the short version from Slash, so I reviewed the entire chain of events, providing as much level of detail as I could. Several of the men jotted notes as I spoke.

"So, you had no prior knowledge that this exchange was going to happen?" Sam, the vulnerabilities guy, asked me.

"Nope. I was just in the wrong place, right time."

"You never saw either of these individuals before?" Shawn asked.

"Never. They might have been conference-goers or they could have used the busy spot as cover to pass off the hack. But we'd never met and I don't recall either one being in my seminar either."

"We've already pulled the attendance records for HACK CON," Grant said. "We're running them now."

Marek, the guy from the OSI, tapped his pencil on the table, studied me intently. "So, how did you know it was a hack?"

"I didn't at first. I examined the code and even followed it a little way on my laptop. It didn't take me long to figure out where it was headed. Taken in context, I had a dangerous virtual trail toward the NSA and a lot of money in cash. It all pointed in one direction."

"So you just decided to stop it?" Sam asked. He looked surprised.

"Well, I tried. Obviously, she didn't buy it. She knew I'd gotten a look at the code, so she tried to kill me."

Slash tensed beside me and I resisted the urge to reassure him with a pat on the arm.

"Why didn't you keep the code?" Grant asked.

"By the time I'd realized what it was, it was too late. She was already there and had snatched it from me."

Shawn tapped something on his keyboard and a picture appeared on the overhead screen. "We've retrieved security footage from the hotel. There is no hotel surveillance footage in the bar, but the hotel does have security cameras on several of the hotel entrances. Our team has reviewed the past twelve hours of footage so far. At this point, we've only found the time of arrival and departure of the young man who gave you the money."

A grainy picture appeared on the screen. Shawn tapped a few more keys and the footage magnified. Sure enough it was the guy with the T-shirt who had handed off the money and code. The oversize sunglasses and cap obscured his face, but the T-shirt was unmistakable.

"That's him," I said.

"Are you sure?" Grant asked.

"I'm sure. He seemed young, nervous, inexperienced. I think he really was just a courier. And a bad one, at that."

"It's not enough for the facial recognition software," Slash mused.

I glanced down the table at Shawn. "Did you get any footage of the woman?"

He adjusted something on his screen. "We're not sure. We need you to look at the possibilities. Can you go through the footage with us?"

"Sure."

We spent the next fifty minutes reviewing the video

from the hotel entrance stopping on females who generally fit her profile. None were a match.

I leaned back in my chair. "She's not there."

Trevor rolled a pen back and forth between his palms. "So, how did she get in and out of the hotel?"

Shawn shook a head. "Either she wore a disguise or she must have known about the cameras. My guess is that since she was able to follow Ms. Carmichael so quickly after they met, she deliberately chose an entrance without a camera. Which meant she was paying attention to security. That smacks of a professional."

"A hacker who does wet work?" Charlie asked. "Really?"

Trevor's gaze swiveled to Slash before Grant cleared his throat. "We can't assume her dual abilities are coincidental. It's unusual, but a thread to pull."

Shawn glanced at me. "Did you get a look at her when you were in your car, Ms. Carmichael?"

"I did, which is why I can say with one hundred percent certainty that the woman in the car who was trying to kill me is the same one I met in the bar."

"Then we have to assume she's a pro and trained in methods other than hacking," Grant said. "She did her homework in advance and didn't leave anything to chance."

"Did you lift her fingerprints from the car?" Charlie asked.

"We got nothing," Shawn answered.

"She was wearing gloves," I said. "I saw them when she pulled up alongside of me and shot at me."

Marek made notes on his paper and then rubbed his forehead, his pen still between his fingers. "Ms. Carmichael, would you be willing to work with an FBI forensic artist to try to recreate this woman's face?"

"Of course."

The room fell silent and all eyes went to Grant. He exhaled a deep breath, running a hand through his hair. "Okay, no point in delaying it any further. I've got more bad news. We've been doing some hard digging these past twelve hours. I wanted to be sure that the IAD hack was an isolated incident. I'm sorry to report it wasn't. We found another intrusion of similar style."

Slash tensed. "Where?"

I winced inwardly on his behalf. I hated that all of this, *any* of this, was happening on his watch.

"SIGINT."

SIGINT is the NSA's Signals Intelligence, which involves collecting foreign intelligence from countries' communications and information systems. There was absolutely no freaking way the system could have been penetrated, along with IAD, without high-ranking insider help. This mole was way more serious than I had envisioned, and I had envisioned something pretty serious.

I inhaled sharply. "So, I only intercepted one hack."

"Yes." Grant pushed his pad of paper away. At the moment he looked a lot older than the fifty-plus years I'd pegged him for. "There may be even more. We can't remain complacent thinking we've found them all. We've mobilized a few additional teams and are searching for more."

Charlie tapped some keys on the laptop. I couldn't tell what he was doing. "The good news is that the hacks are similar in style. Our insider either wasn't comfortable with mixing it up or it was too dangerous and time-consuming to make them all different."

"He, or she, only needed one of the hackers to get through," Slash murmured. "If one hacker failed, there would be another trail to the door."

We all digested that along with the sickening thought that there could be a lot more hacks occurring undetected at this very moment.

Grant inclined his head. "So, does anyone care to speculate on any theories as to who ordered the hack and who responded, in terms of the insider?"

"The woman in the bar who met and subsequently chased Ms. Carmichael was Asian with a slight accent." Trevor crossed his arms, rested them on the table. "I think we have to put the Chinese on the table."

Whether it was intentional or not, several people glanced at Charlie.

He whistled and held up his hands in a time-out motion. "Whoa. Let's not start racial profiling here. My grandparents were from Taiwan. None of us harbor any love for the communists. I've passed every single security clearance with flying colors. If you don't believe that, you can put me first for another round of lie detector tests. I've got nothing to hide."

It seemed totally unfair that Charlie was being singled out because of his heritage. Apparently Slash didn't like the direction this conversation was taking either.

"We have no proof the woman in the bar and chasing Lexi was Chinese," he said. "If we do put the Chinese on the table, it has to be because of our capture of Jiang Quon and…" He let his sentence trail off without finishing.

"And what?" Marek asked.

Slash exchanged a glance with Grant and Trevor, but no one answered Marek's question.

I narrowed my eyes. "Look, if you want our help, you're going to have to fill us in. Otherwise, we're hamstrung."

Trevor looked up and he, Grant and Slash seemed to come to an unspoken agreement.

"IAD has been working on a counteroffensive against the Chinese, led by Slash." Grant dipped his head in Slash's direction. "We've been assisted by Jiang Quon, who has been, ah, cooperating with us."

"Quon's alive?" I asked in surprise. I'd had a personal run-in with Quon just a few weeks earlier when he'd tried to kidnap me in an attempt to lure Slash to him. Some torture involving me had occurred, but that was another story. In the end, we'd nabbed him. The last time I'd seen Quon, Slash had been dragging him off a plane for a "professional discussion," which I didn't think involved tea and crumpets.

"Yes. He's in CIA custody and providing us with valuable intelligence," Grant replied.

I didn't know how or *why* Quon was cooperating and figured they wouldn't tell me if I asked. Not that I really wanted to know.

"Okay, then I'll ask the painful question." Grant took a moment to assess each of us. Perhaps he thought he could elicit a guilty confession or determine guilt by evasion using the sheer power of his eye contact. As he went around the table, the room remained silent. After a moment he asked, "Any theories as to who among us is helping the hackers?"

The silence was deafening. Several of the men shifted uneasily in their chairs, but no one offered a theory. Slash sat motionless. His jaw was tight, his eyes angry. Someone had penetrated his domain and he didn't like it one bit. Not that I liked it much either.

As the silence stretched on, I tried to take the tension down a notch. "It might be easier to determine who the insider is and why, if we figure out the reason IAD and SIGINT personnel databases were two of the targets."

"Maybe the hacker was looking for someone in the department to blackmail," Sam offered.

"Like they need *more* names after the Office of Personnel Management hack," Charlie grumbled.

Millions of Americans who applied for a security clearance or had been interviewed in the process of a security investigation had their security information stolen in a massive hack that had been traced back to the Chinese.

"They could be fishing," I offered. "Even if they can't trace your counteroffensive back to this department, they've got to know it's being run by IAD. It's just a simple leap of logic. But what they intend to do with the personnel data is potentially alarming."

"This isn't making any sense." Trevor referred to his notes and then shook his head in defeat. "If they know who or what they want, why the complicated hacks? I'm just playing devil's advocate here. If you've got someone on the inside at this level, why not memorize simple data like that and pass it on without lifting a finger. These are hacks with a purpose."

"A landing point?" Sam suggested. "A jumping spot to something else?"

"No." Slash's voice was hard and clipped. "We haven't been able to find any evidence the hack served as a jumping point. The personnel databases were the intended targets. We need to figure out why."

"I believe that the most pressing matter at the moment is *who* we are looking for within our own ranks." Grant's gray eyebrows met together in a frown. Someone in the company had betrayed him and everyone else working here, and it was sure to be someone he'd trusted. I knew firsthand how much that kind of betrayal could hurt.

"The first-pass analysis of the code indicates it could only have been written from someone among our ranks here in IAD," he continued. "That means we have a mole among us. Therefore, unless I personally authorize it, there will be no vacations or absences for you, or anyone in your departments, without clearance from me first. We start drilling now."

Having worked at the NSA, I knew what he meant by drilling. Everyone in IAD would now be undergoing a lie detector test and extensive interviews in the next couple of weeks. There would also be a thorough investigation of finances, health, marriage and sexual history. That was part of the reason I'd left the agency. I'm a private person, and they left no stone unturned, no matter how embarrassing.

At this moment, my history would be thoroughly analyzed, even though I was no longer an official part of the NSA. Luckily a good look at my bank account and personal assets wouldn't raise any unusual flags. But my personal relationship with Slash would certainly raise an eyebrow or two, and that would be thoroughly investigated. Even though I had nothing to hide, I felt my cheeks heat.

The hunt for the mole was on.

ELEVEN

As Slash and I left the NSA, I slipped my hand into his. His eyes were hidden behind dark sunglasses. I could already see the start of a five o'clock shadow on his cheeks and chin. "So, do you think I'm still in danger?"

He nodded and I appreciated that he wasn't going to sugarcoat it for me. "We have to assume so. Right now you are the only one who can positively identify her."

"Only *if* I see her again."

"You will," Slash corrected. "We're going to find her."

"I believe that, Slash. But we can't assume she's operating alone. What if someone else comes at me? What about the mole?"

Slash abruptly stopped, lowered his sunglasses and put both hands on my shoulders. "If someone comes at you, they have to go through me. Which means no one is going to hurt you. Not on my watch. Not ever. Okay?"

I nodded, so he took a deep breath and adjusted his sunglasses before taking my hand and heading for his car. "Just so you know, we've each been assigned an FBI detail in case we have to split up," he said. "But I don't foresee that happening, because I'm staying with you as much as possible until this situation is resolved."

I had no idea how long that would take, but the thought of being with him in perpetuity didn't bother me. Apparently our relationship was progressing.

"So, what's the next move?" I asked as I climbed into the car. I fastened my seat belt and rolled my neck a couple of times to release the tension and stiffness. My forehead and knee hurt, which meant I needed another pain pill. "I suppose everyone in that room is removed from investigating the hack. They're all suspects. Us, too, I guess.

Slash hopped in and pushed the key in the ignition. "It's standard protocol. OSI will assign an outside team to investigate the insider threat. Officially our job is tracing that hack back to its master. Just so we're clear, it won't stop Grant, Trevor, Charlie, Sam or me from investigating each other."

"I figured."

"So, where are we going to start?"

He kept his eyes on the road as we passed by the guard gate. "With a consult."

"The Zimmermans?"

He nodded. There was no one in the US who would know as much as Slash did about the NSA's networks other than the Zimmerman twins. Elvis and Xavier were two of my best friends in the world and also former NSA employees.

"Do you know if the twins are available?"

Slash slid his cell phone from his jacket pocket and punched a button. "I'm about to find out." Pressing the phone to his ear he listened and then said, "It's me. Are you and Xavier busy? I need a consult."

He paused, listening. "*Si*. Twenty minutes." He hung up and slid the phone into his jacket pocket. "They're available."

"Wow." I lifted my hands. "No hello? How are you? What's up?"

He lifted an eyebrow. "I'm a guy. The rest is extraneous. Since when did you care about social niceties anyway?"

I thought about it. "Good question. I don't know. It just seemed to matter for some reason. Oh, jeez. Does this mean I'm becoming socially proficient? My mother won't believe it."

Slash smiled and turned on the stereo. Piano music soared through the car. I rummaged in my purse, pulled out my bottle of pain pills, then tapped one onto the palm of my hand and took it, stealing Slash's bottle of water in the cup holder to wash it down.

It took us twenty minutes to get to the Zimmermans' ranch-style house, which was about ten minutes from my apartment.

Elvis opened the door before we knocked. He was dressed in a light blue flannel shirt and jeans. Despite the cool air, he was barefoot.

"Hey, Slash. Lexi." He looked at my forehead. "Wow. What happened to you?"

"A small accident."

"Again? You okay?"

"I'm fine."

The way he looked at me meant he knew better, but he didn't press. "Come in." He stepped to the side, holding open the door. "Xavier is already getting things set up."

Elvis glanced over my shoulder as two dark sedans pulled over to the curb and parked. His eyes met mine. "Two tails? Do I want to know what that is about?"

"You will soon enough," I murmured as I passed him.

Elvis closed the door behind us and led us into the

living room, which had been converted into the twins' command center. Computers, laptops and monitors stood on nearly every inch of flat surface with cords, wires and cables running across the floor and along the baseboards. Because of the sensitive electronic equipment, the room was kept at an especially cold temperature. I picked up a blanket that had been tossed over the back of a chair and wrapped it around my shoulders. The twins kept it there primarily for me. I wondered if anyone else ever used it.

Xavier, in a short-sleeved black T-shirt with a picture of Darth Vader on it, swung around in his swivel chair and waved. His shirt said Let's Get Sith Faced. I chuckled and gave him a thumbs-up. He winked at me and stood. "Hey, dudes. Good to see the both of you."

"Always a pleasure," I said, walking over and giving him a hug. "Nice shirt."

He grinned and looped an arm around my shoulders. "I'll give you one for Christmas."

"Promises, promises."

Elvis shook his head at us with a smile and then turned to Slash. "So, what's this consult about? If you need our help, I know it's going to be interesting. What are you looking for?"

Slash took off his sunglasses and hooked them on the front of his shirt. "I'm not looking for anything quite yet. I need an official consult before I start looking, which means whatever I'm about to say stays between us."

Elvis blinked, clearly startled by the statement. "Wait. You want an official consult? Here?" He held out his hands to encompass the living room.

Slash glanced around. "Are you clean?"

The clean Slash referred to was not the vacuuming or dusting kind. He was asking if it was safe to talk about classified matters. Because of the high incidence of industrial spying and the sheer amount of work the twins did out of their home office, they had a lot of special monitoring and security equipment that probably made their house as safe as Fort Knox, and most likely safer than any government facility. I presumed Slash already knew that, but regardless it was very unusual for Slash to read the twins in on something this classified in a setting that wasn't officially protected. I guess after the penetration by one of the NSA's own, he didn't have a lot of confidence it would be any safer discussing this matter in an NSA conference room.

Elvis exchanged a glance with Xavier who shrugged. "As of 0600 this morning. If you can wait three more minutes, we'll do another pass to make sure."

"Do it," Slash said.

Xavier got to work on his keyboard. After a few minutes he looked up. "Confirmed. We're clean. So what's going on that requires a special consult with us?"

Slash motioned to me. I sat beside him on the couch our knees touching as he gave them an abbreviated rundown of my interception of the hack and the subsequent activities, including the attempt on my life and our discovery of the insider threat at the NSA.

Elvis's eyes got wide when Slash told them about the attempt on my life. "What the hell, Lexi? Someone tried to kill you? Again?"

"Little black cloud." I pointed up. "Best friends, apparently."

Xavier rubbed his temples. "What's this world coming to? Another insider threat at the NSA? Lexi under attack again? This is just ugly, people. What do you guys know so far about the hack?"

Slash rested his hands on his knees. "Not much, unfortunately. I've done a first-pass analysis. It was definitely engineered from someone on the inside."

"And this hack led where?" Elvis asked. "If you are permitted to tell us?"

"I'm permitted. IAD. There was another hack into SIGINT, as well. There could be others. We're investigating now."

Elvis whistled. "Damn, that's bold. What parts of IAD and SIGINT?"

"This is where things get interesting," Slash said. "The personnel databases."

"Huh? The personnel databases?" Elvis took a minute to digest that.

Xavier rested his feet on top of his desk and hooked his hands behind his head. A thoughtful expression crossed his face. "Well, that's totally random except it's not. Why go to all the trouble of such a deep hack to get into a personnel database?"

"Trust me, that's the thousand-dollar question," I answered.

Elvis jotted something on a pad of paper. He looked over at Slash. "So, how many employees were compromised?"

"IAD has forty-two employees listed in this particular database. SIGINT has one hundred and four."

"You included?"

Slash hesitated and then nodded. "Including me."

TWELVE

XAVIER HOPPED UP from his chair and disappeared into the kitchen. He returned carrying several beers. He popped the tops and handed them to us. I took one even though I was on the painkillers. I figured a little extra assistance in the relaxation department was warranted after the events of the past twenty-four hours.

"Any idea why IAD and SIGINT in particular were targeted?" Elvis asked Slash.

"My first-pass analysis has been inconclusive so far." Slash ran his fingers through his hair. He looked tired. Neither of us had slept well last night. "My best guess at this point is the Red Guest."

"Those Chinese bastards who kidnapped Lexi in Papua, New Guinea?" Elvis asked.

"One and the same."

Anger crossed Elvis's face. "Damn it. Then you can count me in on any counteroffensive. If Jiang Shi or his group is trying to harm Lexi and hacking into the NSA, it's a priority for me."

"Me, too," Xavier added. "As of this moment. Let the hunt begin."

"We're not hunting," Slash said. "If it's the Red Guest, I already know how to get at them."

I saw Elvis's eyes spark with interest. Despite my apprehension at such an approach, I felt my own little thrill of excitement. What could I say? I loved a challenge and the Red Guest would certainly be one. I wouldn't be the first one to back down from a battle of wits with them. In fact, after what they'd put me through, I'd actually kind of welcome the battle. Not sure what kind of person that made me, but it is what it is.

"So, what's the deal with the Chinese?" Xavier asked.

"After getting nabbed for a bunch of high-profile and ugly hacks on us and other countries, they are backpedaling, at least publicly," Slash said. "The government is facing serious international backlash and dealing with a lot of internal upheaval in their upper echelons at the moment. Apparently, they've decided to publicly clean house to try to save face. Numerous high officials are being tried for bribery, fraud, stealing funds from the government and so on. It's a bit of a chaotic situation. All of this high-profile activity means I'm not convinced the hack on the NSA database was sanctioned by their government. Certainly not at such a sensitive time for them."

"Whoa," Elvis said. "You think the Red Guest went rogue?"

Slash shrugged. "Honestly? I think Jiang Shi is on the hunt for his brother."

Elvis whistled. "Okay, then what's the end game?"

"End game is I want to reverse engineer the hack."

Xavier and Elvis exchanged a glance. Elvis leaned back against the chair and crossed his arms against his chest. "I'm pretty sure you don't need us to do that."

"I do if I want to replicate and morph a code for self-destruction."

I choked on the mouthful of beer I'd just put into my mouth. Elvis and Xavier seemed equally as shocked.

Slash patted me on the back until I managed to swallow.

"Self-destruction?" I spluttered.

Slash met my gaze and nodded.

We were silent as we studied Slash to make sure he wasn't kidding. What he was talking about—replicating a code designed for self-destruction was dangerous. Beyond dangerous. There were a million things that could go wrong. The code could go awry, or be diverted, copied, or used for a multitude of destructive purposes, none of which might have been the intended target.

"Wait. You're not talking full-on self-destruction, right?" I asked Slash. "The so-called nuclear option?"

"That's exactly what I'm talking about." There was no indecision in his voice, no wavering. He was deadly serious. "Look, to protect ourselves, our country, this can't just be an attack on the Red Guest, it has to go all the way to the top. But we get at them through the Red Guest to make a point."

I couldn't speak. I just looked at him in total shock.

Either Slash didn't notice my disbelief or chose to ignore it. "We'd start with an attack through the routers, targeting the systems and control infrastructure of the country. We'll not only take it down—we'll keep it down. We'd then disable central communications by encrypting the software that talks to each other, preventing them from a restart even if they wipe things clean. That's it. If we take down the electrical grid and communications, they are dead in the water. They can't retaliate, counterattack or launch their own offense. They will be helpless."

I swallowed hard. So many thoughts were racing through my head I was having a hard time sorting through it all. What Slash was talking about—creating and releasing a dark code—was something seldom ever discussed in cybersecurity. In addition to the initial destruction it would cause, a domino effect could take down or cripple additional critical infrastructure. People, primarily those most vulnerable, would be at serious risk. There would certainly be deaths if hospitals, transportation systems and electrical grids were affected, even if the attack was used purely as a show of power and could be reversed at some point. That also meant once the code had done its initial work, the consequences would be out of the hands of its creator—Slash. It would then be up to the politicians to decide what to do about a helpless China. Given the state of things in Washington at the moment, that alone scared the bejesus out of me.

All of this in addition to the singularly perilous fact that once the dark code was out there, it could be used by other coders and black hatters savvy enough to find and replicate it. Those people could be agents of other nations or cyber mercenaries out for themselves. It was beyond scary to think Slash would be providing tools for other nations or organizations—benign or not—to become nuclear players in the cyberwar. In my opinion, spreading nuclear cyber power around was *not* a good idea.

My breathing quickened. So many things could go wrong with a self-destructive code that such code was rarely ever used, even by the most sophisticated of black hatters. I'd never even *seen* such a code, not even in an academic presentation. Yet here was Slash, my boyfriend, calmly proposing to go all Darth Vader and do exactly that.

Elvis leaned forward, his hands hanging between his knees. His blue eyes were intense and interested, but wary. "Okay, Slash. You have my full attention."

"Mine, too, dude," Xavier added. He'd swung his feet down from the desk and was staring at Slash in anticipation.

Slash turned to me, lifting an eyebrow. I swallowed hard. I wanted to warn him against even thinking such a thing, except he already knew the dangers. He was well aware this kind of hacking crossed the line from white to black. I was more than a little taken aback he was considering it, even if a valid argument could be made that it would be done in the name of national security.

"Slash, I don't know about this." I hated to be the only one voicing opposition because I was his girlfriend and I should support him. But I couldn't in good conscience go along with this until I heard more of his reasoning. My hopes he would be easily talked out of this course of action were dwindling. I knew him well enough to see he was already committed, given the grim look in his eyes and the hard set of his jaw.

He put a light hand on my knee. "Hear me out, *cara*. Okay?"

After a moment, I nodded. I owed him that.

"Despite vocal and official protestations by the Chinese government, the Red Guest is supported by the state," he said. "Maybe they know about the latest attack on the NSA, maybe they don't. Regardless, their goal is to bring down the political and economic infrastructure of the United States and her allies though concentrated cyberattacks. Now they are murdering our people. I don't need to tell any of you in this room that this isn't a game. The Red Guest are housed in the communist-supported Chinese People's Liberation Front, which is run by the Chinese military. This past year we've been engaged in some serious warfare, none of which has been made public. It's getting ugly. As you all know, there are international rules in hacking—legal rules the US and the West have been playing by. But the Chinese have not. They are getting bolder, believing us to be hamstringed by our obedience to a moral and legal code they don't follow. They think we won't do, *can't do*, what we need to do to stop them. They are wrong. It will take only one concentrated and successful attack to make them rethink their position."

"Maybe." I set my beer bottle down on the side table and scooted forward on the couch. "But one attack of this nature, even if it worked precisely as it was supposed to, wouldn't shut them down forever."

"Not forever. That's not the goal. But it would indicate we mean business, and we're able to play the game by their rules, or lack thereof, if we have to. It would also put a serious crimp in Chinese cybersecurity operations, especially if we take out the Red Guest in the first sweep."

"Whoa, dude, when you say 'take out' what exactly are we talking about?" Xavier tossed his empty beer bottle into a recycling tub on the floor near his desk. It was half-full of Mountain Dew cans and beer bottles.

"Total destruction." Slash's expression didn't change an iota. "The Red Guest must be compromised, humiliated and rendered completely inoperable."

I pressed a hand to my right temple, where a headache was brewing despite the pain pill I'd just taken. "This sounds like a strategy to spring a kind of cyber Pearl Harbor."

"That's not a bad analogy," Slash replied. "The Chinese must be forced to move on to someone other than the Red Guest to front their effort. Perhaps next time they will choose with more circumspection."

"And if they don't?" I asked.

"I believe our show of power will cause them to think twice about their escalating efforts. Or at least the threat could stimulate a new approach to cyber détente."

"Cyber détente," Elvis said thoughtfully. "An electronic standoff between two superpowers. Historically sound, but I don't see this gaining official approval from Congress anytime soon."

"He doesn't intend to go through Congress or the NSA." I suddenly understood what was happening here. "Which I presume is why we're having this *official* conversation in a *nonofficial* setting."

Slash didn't correct me, so Xavier laughed. It wasn't a sound of humor, but of nervousness.

"Look, guys, we've all worked at the NSA," Xavier said. "We know they're fully aware we're having this little conversation, so there is no need to pretend. Let's just put it on the table. They're tagging us to be some kind of black ops cyber team, right? It's all got to be hush-hush, off the record, off the books. Official deniability to the last keystroke."

Slash still didn't say anything, but he didn't have to. We all understood what was at stake.

I felt like I was still missing a critical piece of the puzzle.

"What else aren't you telling us, Slash? If you're asking us to be a part of this, we have the right to know. No detail is too small. Spill."

He hesitated for a moment and then said, "Quodan."

THIRTEEN

XAVIER JUMPED UP from his seat. His swivel chair spun around wildly. "Quodan? The extremist terrorist group from Iran responsible for blowing up the train station in Italy and three major hotels in Prague? You've *got* to be kidding me."

"I wish I was."

"Wait. You're saying the Chinese are interacting with extremists?" Elvis said, his expression incredulous. "That's low. Really low."

"It's purely business." Slash's voice held a hard, cold edge. "I told you this had progressed to an ugly stage. The Chinese and Quodan share a mutual goal—they just go about accomplishing it in different ways. It shouldn't be that much of a surprise that the two groups have decided they can profit from each other, at least for now."

Quodan as a player was a surprise to me—and definitely not a pleasant one. Ugly, indeed. My stomach churned. "How can you be so sure they are working together, Slash?"

"The NSA has intercepted multiple correspondence threads linking the Chinese to Quodan. They are willing to sell intelligence information to Quodan even if the price isn't right. It's all in the name of the end game."

"Man, you've got to give me a minute to wrap my

head around this." Elvis pressed both hands to his temples. "Unfathomable. Unreal."

"Unfortunately it's our reality right now."

My head was spinning, too. I needed to think, sort things out. The implications of such a partnership were staggering. "Okay, even if the Red Guest is behind this hack, supported by Quodan, you know better than most that reverse engineering and morphing a code for self-destruction…it's rogue. So much could go wrong. If something *does* go wrong, that's on us. We're talking about thousands, no, *millions*, of innocent people who could get hurt."

Slash's expression didn't change. At all. "I know. That's why I've got to get this code just right. That's the purpose for this request for consult. Each of you has unique strengths and talents. I can build the code myself, but I would appreciate a peer review. But I'm not asking any of you to go any further than that. This code, the rest, it's on me. Alone."

I couldn't believe what he was saying, what he was taking upon himself—the responsibility, the darkness. I felt sick. "Look, Slash, we don't even know for sure these latest hacks came from the Red Guest."

"No. Not yet." He stood, unhooked his sunglasses from the front of his shirt and put them back on. "But we will. Who's in?"

Elvis exchanged a long glance with Xavier and then me. Finally Elvis nodded, keeping his eyes on me. "I'm in."

Xavier seemed to wrestle with the thought for a moment, then swore. "Damn it, guys, my bachelor party is Saturday. *This* Saturday. That's six lousy days. This better not interfere with that."

It seemed both ridiculous and thankfully normal that he would be concerned with that.

A smile touched Slash's lips. "Trust me, Xavier. Even I wouldn't let world events interfere with your bachelor party. I can write the code before that. I've been working on it for some time already."

My mouth gaped open. Slash had been working on a black code…for some time? And he'd never mentioned it to me?

"Okay," Xavier said, leaning back in the chair and linking his fingers behind his head. "We all know full well the best people to do this are right here in the room. So, yeah, I'm in, too."

Suddenly every eye in the room was on me. I knew Slash, Elvis and Xavier were doing this partially for my sake, but somehow it felt like it was up to me to validate this crazy idea.

I swallowed hard. "Look, I'll be honest, guys. I'm on the fence about the dark code. Can we first determine for sure whether or not it was the Red Guest? I'll decide at that point whether I support moving forward. Can you live with that for now?"

Slash nodded. "I can." He turned to the door. "Let's go."

WE HEADED DOWNTOWN to FBI headquarters, where forensic artist and FBI agent, Kip Montgomery waited for me. Kip was an affable guy with a shock of brown hair, glasses and ruddy cheeks. He wore a white shirt, red suspenders and a red bow tie.

Kip greeted us cheerfully as we entered his office, making small talk and offering us coffee or water. We both declined. After speaking for a moment to Kip, Slash left to meet with someone else.

Kip insisted I sit at the small round table, where he carefully explained the process I was about to undergo.

"I want you to think back to these individuals and describe them the best you can. We'll start with the woman and then take a stab at the guy. Don't try to stress out about remembering every little detail, let's just start with an overall concept and refine from there. Be sure to mention any distinguishing characteristics you might recall. No worries."

"I'm not worried. I have a photographic memory. I'll give you every detail down to the last mole if you want."

He looked a bit taken aback. "Oh. Well, that's great. That sure will make my work easier. Are you ready?"

"Yes."

He stood and brought a laptop back to the table and started typing. Unable to help myself, I tried to peer around the screen.

"What program are you working on?"

He looked at me in surprise. "You know forensic art?"

"Not really. But I know computers."

He angled the laptop my way. "It's a program called FACES. It will allow me to draw and adjust the photo right on the screen."

"Can it do 3-D?"

"Sure."

"Great. I've got a good spatial memory, too. We are going to rock these composites."

"I wish all my interviewees were as optimistic."

"Well, I didn't get a good look at the young guy because of his sunglasses, but we can make logical assumptions based on skin and hair color as well as facial structure. We can totally nail every detail of the woman, though."

"You're making me a happy man, Lexi. Let's get started."

Before he even drew a line, Kip asked me several general questions about the woman and her facial structure, jotting notes to himself. When he felt he had a good grasp on her, he got started on the computer. I wanted to peek at what he was doing, but he kept the picture to himself until he had a basic composite drawn.

Eventually he turned the computer screen my way.

I studied it. "Wow, Kip. That's good. Really good. You have a unique talent."

We worked together to further refine the drawing according to my memory. Since I was able to provide enough detail, he was able to create a 3-D version of her face.

I stared at the composite. "Her forehead is slightly too high here." I tapped the monitor.

Kip fixed it and we sat back to contemplate. We were so engrossed neither of us heard Slash come in.

"That's her?" he asked, putting his hands on my shoulder and studying the screen with us.

"Yes. That's her. I can't think of any more ways to refine the composite. It's near perfect."

Kip leaned back and stretched his arms over his head. "Damn, you've got an incredible memory, Lexi."

"I'm glad I could help. A photographic memory does provide the necessary level of detail."

"We're fortunate you were sitting at the table when you were," he said.

"We certainly are," Slash said. "Can you send that

image to Agent Martinez right away? We'd like to run it through the facial recognition database while you two work on the young man."

"Consider it done." Kip tapped a few keys on his keyboard and stood. "I'm going to get a cup of coffee and then we'll get started on the kid. You up for another round, Lexi?"

"Absolutely. But this time can I just take a little peek at your program before we get started?"

FOURTEEN

"REMIND ME WHY there are FBI agents accompanying us to my wedding dress fitting?"

Basia slid me a glance as she pulled into the parking lot of the expensive and exclusive Thompson's Bridal Boutique. It had been a long morning between the FBI and a visit with Slash to X-Corp, where we finally were able to provide my boss with a sterilized version of what was going on. Not surprisingly, Finn hadn't been happy about it, mostly because I was in danger again. But at this point, there was little he could do about it. There was a fine line between what he could and could not argue about with the FBI and NSA, his excellent lawyer background notwithstanding.

As for Basia, there was no way in hell I was going to tell her about the events of the past twenty-four hours. She was living on the edge as it was. Ever since announcing her engagement to Xavier a few weeks ago, she'd morphed into Bridezilla, obsessed with getting every detail right for the forthcoming nuptials. I didn't want to add to that anxiety in *any* way, especially since I was part of the reason her fiancé was currently involved in a top secret, dangerous cyber operation.

"Because Slash is in the middle of an important operation and they are keeping an eye on me as a courtesy to him so he can concentrate and not worry about what trouble I'll get into next. Little black cloud and me, remember." I pointed to my forehead. "I'm a walking accident."

I'd told her I'd walked into a door. She'd actually seen me do it before, so it wasn't that big a stretch. Right now, however, she didn't seem to be buying it. Still, she didn't press. I think she just didn't want to know. I didn't blame her one bit.

She nervously pushed her short dark bob off her shoulder, her lovely engagement ring glinting in the sun. Xavier had bought her a big, round-cut diamond surrounded by small red rubies in a platinum setting. It was delicate and pretty without being pretentious. He'd chosen really well. In fact, she loved it so much she got all teary whenever she looked at it, which was a lot lately. I was beginning to think being a bride required riding on some invisible, emotional roller coaster and forcing the maid of honor, and all in her orbit, to go along for the ride.

"They aren't going to, you know, come into the dressing room, right?" she said.

"No, of course not." I tried to sound as sure of myself as possible, although I knew no such thing. "Hey, look, the parking lot is almost empty, well, except for the FBI guys pulling in behind us. I bet that means we'll have the whole store to ourselves. Yay!"

I jumped out of the car and tried to look as enthusiastic as I could, considering I was about to spend an hour in this store with nothing more to do than look at expensive, fancy dresses. Why I had to tag along was a mystery, except it was apparently an important responsibility of a maid of honor, in addition to throwing the bachelorette party. I also had to try on my bridesmaid gown, which I was dreading. Not because the dress wasn't pretty—it was. It was a soft red dress that fell just below my knees with short sleeves and a high, cinched waist. The reason I was dreading it was because mine had to be taken in around the boobs. That meant someone would be prodding and arranging me there, which I hated. But I sucked it up and smiled like there was no place I'd rather be.

"Come on, let's go in," I said.

As I held open the door for her, I saw the FBI agents getting out of the car. OMG! Were they really going to come in?

The bell on the door jangled and a perky young blonde with too much makeup on rushed out to greet us. "Hi, I'm Amanda, your bridal consultant for the day. Which one of you is Basia?"

Basia stepped forward. "I'm Basia Kowalski. This is Lexi Carmichael, my maid of honor."

Amanda turned to me and then stopped. "Oh, Lexi, what happened to your face?"

"I walked into a door." I grimaced. "I'm a major klutz. It will all be cleared up by the wedding, I'm sure."

I was a rotten liar and Amanda looked suspicious, but she didn't say anything. "Well, I'm so thrilled to meet you both. We're going to have so much fun today. Basia, I'll make sure you are an absolutely stunning bride. Now remind me, when is the wedding?"

"In thirty-two days…not like I'm counting." Basia threw up her hands. "Who am I kidding? I'm a nervous wreck. But I can't wait to see the dress."

Basia had special ordered a custom-made wedding dress online through a subcontractor of the boutique's. Now that it had finally arrived, she'd be able to try it on and have any necessary alterations made in plenty of time for the wedding.

"Your dress arrived last night," Amanda said. "I haven't even had time to unwrap it yet."

I glanced around. The store was completely empty.

Amanda glanced over my shoulder as the FBI agents in suits and dark glasses entered the store, the bell on the door jangling. One agent remained by the door with his arms crossed while the other starting walking through the racks of dresses, apparently looking for lurking perpetrators.

Jeez.

"Are they with you?" Amanda asked.

"Ah, them?" I jerked my thumb toward the one by the door.

The FBI agent by the door stared at me without expression. Not that you could actually see an expression behind the large sunglasses.

"Yes, them," Amanda said. Her tone indicated she thought I was slow.

"Well, yes, they are with us, but they aren't *with* us, if you know what I mean. They're just watching. Ignore them. I'm the only official one in the party today."

Amanda seemed puzzled, but this was Washington, DC, where people follow people around all the time, so she didn't protest. "Okay. Well, ladies, please follow me to dressing room number one. Let me gather your dresses and I'll meet you in there."

We followed her to the dressing room. It was a decent-sized room with a small stage in front of three full-length mirrors, presumably so you could see yourself and the dress from every angle. There was a long white couch, two comfortable armchairs and a coffee table covered by a white paper tablecloth upon which sat a silver bucket with two bottles of pink champagne on ice. One bottle was already open and six crystal flutes were artfully arranged around the bucket. Guess Amanda had been expecting a larger party. I almost felt sorry that Basia had brought only me, especially since I wasn't at all certain how much I could contribute to this excursion.

"Oh, it's all lovely," Basia said, clapping her hands together happily. "Look at those lovely tea lights and scattered red rose petals. Every detail is perfect."

It didn't strike me as overly perfect, but I had exactly zero expectations for a bridal dressing room, so what did I know? I guess the tea lights, which were actually just small oil lamps, the champagne and the rose petals did kind of look pretty.

Amanda came bustling into the room with two dresses wrapped in plastic over her arms. She hung them both on a hook near the door. I wanted to try on my bridesmaid dress as much as I wanted a pap smear. But it would have to be done, so I had to endure.

Amanda pulled my dress out from beneath the plastic cover. It was pretty on the hanger, but I was sure that, without any discernible curves, I'd look like a red Popsicle in it. Regardless, I smiled and pretended it was the most gorgeous dress I'd ever seen.

Basia inspected the dress and held it up against me. "Perfect. You're going to look lovely, Lexi."

"If you say so." I could barely look at myself in the mirror. God, I needed a drink.

As if she'd read my mind, Amanda walked over to the table. "Before we get started and see your dress, Basia, let's celebrate with champagne." She pulled out the chilled bottle and poured two flutes. She handed one to Basia and the other one to me.

I happily lifted the glass to my lips when Amanda started shrieking at me.

"No, no, no! Stop! You have to toast first."

I reluctantly lowered my glass. "Sorry."

Amanda collected herself, smoothed down her blond bob. "You, Lexi, as the maid of honor, must provide the toast. Please, toast to the dress."

"Excuse me?" I looked at her as if she'd lost her mind. "You want me to toast…the dress?"

"Of course." Amanda and picked up an empty champagne flute. She clinked it against mine. "You know… to the *dress*."

I didn't know why she was looking at me like I was a total idiot. Did people really toast dresses? I guess it was possible, but it had never crossed my mind. Then again, I'd never been to a wedding dress fitting before, so what the heck did I know? Maybe people across the world lifted their glasses to wedding dresses all the freaking time.

Fine. I could toast a stupid dress if it was protocol. Playing my part of the dutiful maid of honor, I held up my champagne and clinked my glass against Basia's.

"Um, here's to the dress. May it fit and be acceptable to you."

There. That hadn't been too hard.

Amanda rolled her eyes at me over Basia's shoulder. I guess my tone had been wrong. Or the emotional introduction had been missing. Or it was painfully clear I thought this whole toast-to-the-dress thing was colossally ludicrous. Narrowing my eyes at Amanda, I lifted the flute to my lips just before Basia burst into tears.

I lowered my glass. "Basia, don't cry. I can do a new toast. A better one. I promise. Just give me a minute to think one up."

Tears slid down her cheeks and she wiped at them with the back of her hand. "Oh, no, Lexi. It wasn't the toast. It's just I can't believe I'm getting married in just over a month. I mean, I've dreamed of this day since I was a little girl. Now it's happening. It means so much that you are here with me, sharing in this special moment. You're my best friend in the world."

She set down her glass and threw her arms around me, sobbing. I awkwardly patted her back and tried desperately to come up with an appropriate response. It was hard when I still wasn't sure exactly why she was crying. Were they tears of sorrow, tears of relief or tears of joy? How the heck was I supposed to know? The urge to bolt was overwhelming.

When I didn't say anything—because I couldn't think of a freaking thing to say—Basia started to sob harder. Panic gripped me, but a single intelligent comment that was both safe and reassuring refused to present itself. I was lacking significant parameters and was deathly afraid a wrong comment would make things worse. Amanda disappeared and came back with a box of tissues.

"Oh, honey, you are going to be a beautiful bride," she said, handing Basia a tissue. She shot me an exasperated look. Maid of honor epic failure. Again.

"Seeing yourself in the dress for the first time really brings it all home, doesn't it?" Amanda added, patting her on the back. "Don't worry. You're going to look beautiful."

Basia pulled away from me and dabbed her eyes with

the tissue. "Oh, thanks, Amanda. I'm sorry I'm being so emotional."

A cranky little monster arose within me. It wasn't fair that Amanda had so effortlessly been able to find the right thing to say. The playing field wasn't close to even because she probably had a lot of practice at this, while it was my first time soothing a bride-to-be.

"Nonsense, you're being a normal bride." Amanda took Basia's champagne flute and set it on the table. "Your wedding is the most important day of your life. Who wouldn't be emotional about that?"

Amanda glanced over at me and I saw the answer in her eyes. I gulped the rest of my champagne and filled it up again. We hadn't even tried on the dress yet and one bottle of champagne was almost gone. I wasn't much for alcohol, but I was already fighting an overwhelming urge to flee. If we had to be here much longer, I was going to need something a lot stronger than champagne.

"Let's try on your dress," Amanda said to Basia. "Strip down now."

Thank God we weren't trying on my dress first. I needed to have more alcohol before I could do that.

Basia started taking off her clothes while I polished off my second glass of champagne and filled a third. I then began pacing until Amanda pointed at one of the armchairs and instructed me in a stern voice to sit down.

I sat, hoping I would have no greater responsibility than to offer an appropriate nod and encouraging smile every once in a while before it was my turn to try on the dress. Amanda slipped her hand under the white plastic cover of Basia's dress, taking hold of the hanger. Before she pulled the dress all the way out from beneath the cover, she told Basia to cover her eyes.

"Let's make this a surprise. I'll tell you when to open them."

Standing there in just her underwear and covering her boobs with her hands, Basia smiled and closed her eyes. Amanda carefully pulled the dress out from the wrap and held it up.

"Voilà!"

My champagne flute nearly slipped from my fingers. "Holy crap. What is *that*?"

"What is what?" Basia asked, opening her eyes.

Amanda stood still as a statue. The expression on her face was one of frozen horror.

Basia saw the dress and gasped. "Oh, my God. That's supposed to be a rose on the waistband. The seamstress said she could embellish the dress with a tiny, delicate rose." Her voice broke. "But that looks like a…a…"

She couldn't say it.

I couldn't say it either.

Instead of a rose, that *thing* on her dress looked more like a large, exact scientific replica of a pink, female private part. Blossoming open.

On her freaking wedding dress.

FIFTEEN

I DARED A WORRIED glance at Basia. Her face had drained of all color except now there was a faint green tinge. I thought she might faint or vomit. I had to say something to break the awfulness of the moment, but what?

"Ah…uh…" I stuttered.

Basia looked at me, clutching her hands to her naked chest. "Oh, my God. Oh, my God."

I had to do something. I was her best friend. The maid of honor. The responsibility was on me to save this situation. But what the heck did I know about wedding dresses?

"Hey, no worries, Basia." I cleared my throat, tried to sound confident. "We'll just cut the vagina right off the dress and it will be perfect."

Holy cow. Had I just said vagina *aloud?*

"I meant the *rose*." I backtracked. "We'll cut the *rose* off the dress and it will be perfect."

Oh. My. God.

Basia burst into tears—again.

That seemed to snap Amanda out of her horrified trance. She hung the dress on the hook and rushed over to Basia.

"I am *so* sorry." She patted Basia on the back, helping her to her feet. "Don't you worry. We're going to make this right."

Basia staggered to a chair, grabbed the bridal robe

and sank into the chair. She snatched the champagne bottle off the table and took a swig without using a glass. Apparently after viewing *that* dress, only straight from the bottle would do. She took a few more swigs and burped. "I can't believe this. I totally can't believe this."

Amanda seemed genuinely concerned. "You ladies just sit here and relax. I've got to make a call and I'll be right back." She dashed out of the room.

Basia took a minute before she seemed to get it together enough to speak to me. I was too afraid to open my mouth again.

"Lexi, what are we going to do?"

Like I would know. What a total freaking disaster. But she was waiting for an answer and I was the maid of honor.

This time I chose my words carefully. "Amanda said they would make it right, so they'll make it right. If not, we'll find a new dress. This is a bridal dress store, right? There are lots of dresses out there. One of them has to be right for you."

"Lexi, wedding dresses have to be ordered months in advance. Custom-made dresses take even longer. I'm petite. I don't fit the ones that are off-the-rack. I'll *never* find another dress."

"Yes, you will," I said firmly. "The right dress is out there, probably right here in the store. I'm sure of it. We'll ask if we can buy one of the sample gowns that the brides try on. A few alterations, and *boom*, you've got the perfect dress."

Technically I had no idea what I was talking about since I knew exactly zip about wedding gowns, but I spoke with confidence on her behalf. I'd learned from her that sometimes confidence was half the battle. Besides, the odds were high there *was* a dress out there that *would* fit her. The unknown variable was whether or not she would *love* it. As that seemed to be an important—although subjective—criteria, I couldn't calculate the odds with certainty.

Basia drained the rest of the champagne from the bottle and set it on the coffee table. "I hope this isn't a bad omen about the start of my marriage." She looked at her ring and got all teary again.

I had to put a stop to *that* before the waterworks started again. "Don't be ridiculous, Basia. There are no such things as omens. Your wedding to Xavier is going to be perfect. This is just a small snafu with a dress."

"It's not just *a* dress, Lexi. It's *the* dress. The most important dress of my life."

"And we are going to deal. We've got this. It's just a minor setback, that's all."

"You think so?"

"I know so."

"Oh, God. This is so stressful. Can you pour me another glass of champagne?"

"Of course, I can." I grabbed a new bottle and unwound the foil. "When Amanda comes back, we'll find out what the options are for fixing the dress and then we can look for a backup one, just in case. We survived in a jungle for several days. We can survive the process of finding the perfect wedding dress for you, right?"

At this point, I was actually missing the jungle, which wasn't a good omen either, except I didn't believe in omens.

To Basia's credit, she inhaled a deep breath and nodded. "You're right, Lexi. I'm overreacting. Everything is going to be fine."

"Of course, it will be." Relief swept through me. "That's the spirit."

Feeling better, I pressed my thumb against the champagne cork. It popped out with the force of a speeding bullet. To my horror, it headed straight for Basia. Yelping, she ducked and fell onto the corner of the table. One of the tea lights toppled over and the oil and flames spilled onto the paper tablecloth.

Whoosh!

The entire table went up in flames as Basia staggered backward and narrowly avoided getting burned. In the small room, the sprinklers on the ceiling immediately went off. Water sprayed everywhere, drenching us and everything else in the room in a sudden cold shower.

Basia shrieked. I stood frozen, clutching the champagne bottle and looking about in disbelief as water sprayed throughout the entire freaking room.

Amanda dashed into the room and slid to a stop next to Basia. Right behind her were both FBI agents, storming the dressing room with their guns drawn. One of the agents tackled me, apparently with the intent of protecting me with his body. As we slammed to the ground, the slippery champagne bottle flew out of my hands and hit Amanda in the head. She spun once and collapsed.

The second FBI agent tried to catch her with outstretched arms like a football wide receiver. He caught her, but the leap caused him to accidentally discharge his weapon. The huge 3-D mirror shattered in a spectacular display of exploding glass.

"What the hell is going on here?" the agent on top of me roared. "We heard a shot."

I was squashed beneath him. Water dripped into my eyes and I couldn't breathe.

"I'm fine." I wheezed for breath. "It wasn't a shot. It was a champagne cork."

The second agent laid Amanda gently on the ground and was now beating out the fire with my bridesmaid's dress. The agent pinning me to the floor finally slid off, still looking around for a perpetrator. He came to a stand, water dripping off his hair and gun.

"Put the gun away," I said, sitting up and rubbing my sore knee that had been slammed into the floor. Dang it, now it hurt again. "We're fine."

"Fine?" He gave me an incredulous look. "You're telling me all of this happened from a champagne cork?"

"It went…astray."

"Astray?"

"Are you going to repeat everything I say?"

"Possibly."

I stood, pushing several wet strands of hair off my face and surveying the damage. The mirrors were shattered, the furniture soaked and the dresses ruined. The fire was out, but my bridesmaid dress was a goner. It still smoldered. The entire room was a complete loss.

"Wow," I said. "This is *so* not happening."

Amanda moaned and sat up, holding her head. Thank God for one miracle. At least I hadn't killed the bridal assistant.

Basia stood shivering from the cold water. She looked like a small, drowned rat staring in horror at the shattered mirror. "Seven years of bad luck. What. Just. Happened?"

I ran over to her, slipping twice. Putting an arm

around her, I glared at the FBI agents and pointed to the door of the dressing room.

"Go away. We're fine. This is a girl matter. We've got everything under control."

"This is control?" The agent shook his head, then helped Amanda up from the floor. "Are you okay, ma'am?"

"I'm...not sure." She wobbled a bit and looked around the room in a daze. The agent held her steady and pointed at the sprinkler on the ceiling.

"Can you turn those things off?"

She nodded and staggered from the dressing room. Realizing there was no immediate threat, the agents finally retrieved and holstered their guns, filing out after her. As the last agent was leaving, he stopped and stared at Basia's dress still hanging on the hook, water dripping off it.

"Hey, is that a vagina on that dress?" He pointed to the thing that was not a rose. "I've heard of weird fashion trends, but that's really taking things to a whole new level."

Basia started wailing.

SIXTEEN

"It's all going to work out perfectly," I said to Basia for the millionth time as we drove to Xavier and Elvis's house. "I'm so sorry. I'm the worst maid of honor ever."

"It's not your fault the cork got away from you, causing me to fall on the table and start the fire. And you certainly couldn't have anticipated the bottle squirting from your hands and hitting Amanda in the head when the FBI agent tackled you."

Oh, God.

"Well, at least the medics from the ambulance said she'd make a full recovery," I said with fake cheerfulness.

Yep, that was me—Susie Sunshine. Looking for the one bright spot in a sea of disaster.

"The mirrors," Basia whispered. "Three full-length mirrors. All shattered. If that doesn't spell seven years of bad luck, I don't know what does."

"That's ridiculous. Superstitions contradict natural science. They are nothing more than folklore, scary stories with no grounding in the real order of the universe. The mirrors mean nothing, Basia. Seriously."

She remained silent. I groped for more reassurances, but all I could come up with was another apology. "I'm really sorry about your dress, too. I guess it's ruined from the water."

"It's was already ruined. That dress deserved to die. That rose was hideous."

"It wasn't a rose."

"No, it wasn't. It's just so disappointing. It didn't look at all like the picture online."

"False advertising for sure."

We fell silent and I searched for a more upbeat tempo to the conversation. "Well, the good news is that Amanda says there's a good chance I can get another bridesmaid dress in my size delivered in a week or so. There will still be plenty of time before the wedding to do any alterations.

"Yes, there's that." Unfortunately, she didn't look cheered up in the slightest. "It's my dress that's the problem."

"I'm, ah, game for going back with you to try on different wedding dresses when you're ready. Amanda said she had a good idea of what you liked based on your online viewing selections, so she's going to place an order for a few of them that are already made and the dresses should be in next week. Yay. Right?"

"Right."

I paused. "Who am I kidding? It's a good thing that she still wants our business."

"I think she was too scared by the FBI agents to refuse us service."

I smiled a little at that. "I'm really sorry about what happened, Basia, but you've got this wedding thing down. You are going to find the perfect dress. You will be the most beautiful bride in history. The wedding is sure to be a day for all to remember. I mean that. This is just a little bump in the road. Something to remember and laugh about in our old age." My voice was so over-the-top cheerful that I wanted to duct-tape my mouth shut.

Jeez.

"It's okay, Lexi. You're right. I'd never have remembered a perfect fitting. This one is for the record books for sure. By the way, how's the planning for the bachelorette party on Saturday going?"

"Fantastic." I hoped I had sufficiently kept the panic out of my voice. "Totally awesome."

"Do you need any help?"

"Absolutely not." Biggest. Lie. Ever.

Basia wound her engagement ring around her finger. "Can't you give me a few small details?"

"You already know where it is going to be and who is coming. That's all the detail you get. You'll just have to wait and see. I want this to be the perfect surprise."

"Thank you, Lexi." She gave me a tremulous smile. "I know this is really out of your comfort zone, so I appreciate your efforts. I really do."

"It's the least I can do for my very best girlfriend. I'm honored you trust me with such a big responsibility. I've got this, okay? You don't need to spend a second more worrying about it. You've got enough other important details to focus on."

We pulled into the Zimmermans' driveway. Basia left the car idling. "Are you sure you don't want me to drop you off at your apartment?" Basia asked.

The FBI sedan pulled to the curb. One of the agents had been on the phone the entire trip to Basia's place. I had no idea what they were reporting back to headquarters. Well, actually, I might have had an idea, but I didn't want to know the details.

"No." I put my hand on the car door handle. "I need

some fresh air to clear my head. I'll be fine. Besides, if I want a ride I can hitch one with those guys." I jerked my thumb at the FBI sedan.

We got out and she gave me a hug. We were both still damp. "Love you, Lexi. Thanks for sticking with me."

I waited on the sidewalk until she walked to the front door. Xavier opened it almost instantly and ushered her in. He waved at me before they disappeared inside. When the door shut, I closed my eyes and *thwunked* my palm against my forehead.

I was *never* going to have a wedding. *Ever.*

I wasn't even the bride and I couldn't handle this kind of stress. It was a nightmare. Giant tears, roller-coaster emotions and vaginas on wedding dresses.

Someone just shoot me.

Of course, seeing as how someone had recently tried to do just that, I had to be careful what I wished for. But right now, it seemed like a sane alternative.

I walked home, followed by my FBI tail. They asked me twice if I wanted a ride because I was limping, but I shook my head. I needed to unwind after the wedding dress fitting from hell.

When I got home, the agents went through my apartment and declared it safe. I offered them my hair dryer so they could get dry, but they declined. After they left, I peeled off my clothes and pulled on a pair of dry sweatpants and a light blue T-shirt. I took a pain pill and checked my phone, discovering I had a text from Slash saying he'd be over soon.

I pressed a button on my phone and called Elvis.

"Hey, Elvis. It's Lexi. How's Basia doing?"

"Oh, hi, Lexi. Basia is…oddly wet. She arrived and they disappeared into Xavier's room a bit ago. I thought you were going to a bridal dress fitting, not swimming. What happened?"

I gave him a quick rundown of the events.

When I was finished he said, "Wow. I'm not sure what to say. Was there really an ambulance, fire truck and an insurance adjuster involved?"

"Unfortunately, yes."

"That's epic."

"Epic fail is more like it." I sighed. "Look, would you just keep an eye on her and let me know how she's holding up? I feel awful."

"Sounds to me like most of it was out of your control," he said. "Accidents happen."

"True, but it's a statistical anomaly that accidents seem to happen to me far more than anyone else I know."

"Nah. Anomalies are an integral part of statistics. You're just fitting in."

"And *that* is exactly why we are best friends."

He chuckled. "So, how's the bachelorette party planning going?"

"Probably about as good as *your* bachelor party planning. No, actually, it's probably worse. A lot worse. After this bridal dress fiasco, the pressure is on me to perform."

"Understood. I'm in panic mode, as well. What have you done so far?"

"Well, I found this store called Faylene's Bachelorette Parties and Supplies. Supposedly they do it all. I'm looking into it."

"Sounds promising. We're in a lot of trouble, aren't we, Lexi?"

"Oh heck, yes."

He paused and then spoke. "Well, good luck."

"You, too. Thanks, bud."

I hung up and slipped the phone back in my purse. I was in the kitchen making coffee when Slash came in, wrapped his arms around me and kissed me on the back of my head.

"Um…why is your hair wet?" he asked.

I turned around in his arms, ready to spill what happened, but his eyes were twinkling with amusement.

He already knew, the cad.

I glared at him. "Who told you?"

He chuckled. "When I pulled up in the parking lot the team was changing shifts, so I checked in to see what was going on. A shift change during the day is pretty unusual. I discovered the agents who had been watching you had to be relieved so they could change out of their wet and smoky clothes."

"Total accident." I lifted my hands. "I swear."

"The fault of a champagne cork, or so I hear."

"Unfortunate aim. I should have used a towel."

"And the ambulance?"

"Not my fault. If the overzealous FBI agent hadn't tackled me while I was holding a slippery champagne bottle, the bridal assistant would have been fine. Thankfully, she only had a mild concussion when the bottle squirted out of my wet hands and onto her head. The medics said she'd make a full recovery. The room, the mirrors and the dresses, however, were a complete loss. Luckily for Basia—not me—the bridal assistant said we could come back and try on dresses again *after* the insurance adjuster and cleaners finished fixing up the place."

A laugh rumbled from his chest and he pulled me to

him again. "Did you know they're actually considering adding trainees to your detail, so young agents can understand the concept of needing to be prepared for all contingencies?"

I twisted my damp ponytail around my finger. "That's really not fair. You have no freaking idea how stressful this maid of honor thing is. Do you have any idea what is involved in trying on a wedding dress? I had to toast a dress! Apparently this is just the start. Weddings are nightmares. I honestly found myself wishing the assassin would show up and put me out of my misery."

He trailed his fingers across my cheek, pausing at one of the diamond earrings he'd given me for Christmas. "I'm sorry things didn't go as planned at the fitting, but I'm confident it will all work out. Despite the trials, you seem to endure with ever-increasing frequency. Luck favors you."

I stiffened.

Slash pulled back. "What's wrong?"

I took a moment to compose myself. "Sorry, I didn't mean to have that reaction. Your words just triggered a memory."

"What memory?"

I didn't want to say it, but I didn't want to keep sweeping it under the rug either. "Quon. He said the same thing to me when…well, when he was asking questions about you."

Just hearing Quon's name changed Slash's mood instantly. He stepped away from me, a dark expression covering his face. Quon had said that phrase to me shortly before he'd started torturing me for information about Slash. That session was still a touchy subject with us. I hadn't talked much about it because I knew Slash would freak out. Slash hesitated to ask because he worried about upsetting me. I hadn't meant to bring it up, but it had caused a reaction I didn't want to lie about.

I reached out and took his hand. "I'm sorry, Slash. I didn't mean to upset you. It just jogged my memory. I don't want to suppress those memories because then they stay buried and it hurts worse. Okay?"

"You don't upset me. He does." Slash closed his eyes. "He hurt you."

"Yes, he did. But you didn't kill him, and you could have."

Slash cupped my face and looked into my eyes. "Don't think I'm a good guy for that. Do you want to know why I didn't kill him? Because I knew he'd endure much more pain and suffering if I kept him alive. *That's* the only reason he's still alive."

I'm not sure I'd ever seen him this angry, as if the violence within him was barely restrained.

He seemed to sense my unease and his expression softened. He kissed my cheek. "Anyway, I do have some good news for you."

Just like that the darkness vanished and I saw the warm, kind eyes of the man I loved.

"You do?"

"I do. We got a hit on the woman from the facial recognition software.

SEVENTEEN

"That's great news, Slash. Who is she?"

"Her name is Feng Mei. She came to the US three years ago on a special work visa. Guess who she's working for?"

I thought back to what I knew about the Chinese, about the Red Guest. "Sinam Tech?"

"Exactly."

It made sense. Sinam Tech was a Chinese technology company located in Silicon Valley that officially produced standard interfaces, communications and data architecture. Unofficially—thanks to certain unauthorized peeks into their network by Slash—they served as a front for cyberattacks, cyberintelligence and industrial espionage. Jiang Shi's uncle owned Sinam Tech, so the connection wasn't coincidental. The Red Guest was up to their freaking necks in this mess.

"Where is Feng Mei now?" I asked.

"Her official address is in Menlo Park, but she isn't there. Looks like she hasn't been there for a while. The executives at Sinam Tech claim Mei hasn't shown up for work in two weeks."

"But no one reported her missing."

"Apparently not. Her coworkers say she had talked about going for an extended vacation. Her boss said he thought she'd turned in her vacation slip, but he couldn't find it. An unfortunate oversight."

"We're supposed to buy that?"

"Not much we can do about it. We can't find any records of her flying or taking a train to Washington. We're running all train tickets paid for in cash, so it's still possible she might have come that way under a bogus name. Her car, a white 2014 Ford Focus, is missing from her apartment parking lot, so it's also a possibility she drove. We have an APB out on her and the car. But she rented a car to chase you down, so my guess is she ditched or parked her car somewhere and is paying with a bogus credit card and fake information for a rental. It's smarter, safer and she'll be almost impossible to find that way."

"Any luck on the kid in the bar who gave me the money?"

"Not yet. I doubt he knows much anyway. We're looking at nephews, kids, young male cousins of everyone remotely connected to Sinam Tech. He could have been a random pick, but for something this important, I doubt it. We'll find him. We need to know how many more hacks were ordered."

He sniffed the air, eyeing the coffeemaker. "That coffee smells good. You got enough in that pot for me?"

"Of course. I *made* it for you." I turned and poured a cup for him, handing it to him black.

He took a sip. "Hmm. It's strong, just how I like it. You made it just for me?"

"I did." I was working hard at this girlfriend thing. According to the book *Twelve Steps to Keep Your Relationship Alive and Healthy*, it was important to do little things for your significant other to make him feel important and cherished.

"It's a special Italian roast," I explained. "I'm planning to add a drop of it to my full mug of milk so I can manage to swallow it."

He laughed softly and kissed me on the head. "Ah, *cara*." He glanced at the clock on the stove. "We have a couple of hours until dinner. Are you up for some gaming? We could do Magic Shorn or another role-playing game. Your choice."

There it was. Now he was reciprocating and doing something nice for me. Maybe we were getting the hang of this relationship thing.

"Sounds great, Slash, but I thought you needed to work on the code."

"I do." He didn't quite meet my gaze. This was still not a comfortable or resolved subject for either of us. "Tonight I intend to take a small break and spend time with my girl in order to stimulate my creativity."

I poured a small amount of coffee into my mug already filled with milk. I stirred it with a spoon and took a sip, looking at him over the rim. "Okay, but after Shorn, I have *another* kind of role-playing game in mind."

He raised an eyebrow. "And that would be?"

"You'll have to beat me at Shorn before you can find out." I thought of the black velvet blindfold I'd hidden in my drawer, then grinned.

He set his coffee on the table and backed me against the counter, placing a hand on either side of me. "Details."

"Forget it. Intimidation won't work. You don't get a word until you prove to be a worthy opponent."

He took my mug from my hand and backed me farther against the counter, pinning me between him and the cold marble at my back. "It's not intimidation," he growled. "I'm a trained interrogator. I can *make* you tell me."

I raised an eyebrow. "I don't think so. I'm pretty talented at evasion tactics, if I do say so myself."

"Shall we see?" Keeping me trapped with the weight of his body and his eyes never leaving mine, he slid his hands down my shoulders and arms. He rested one hand on my hip while the other slid across the flat of my stomach and stopped just at the lower part of my abdomen. I could feel the heat of his hand through my shirt.

My breath caught in my throat. *Holy cow.*

"I'm going to venture a guess I have successfully exercised sexual innuendo," I said.

He leaned in and whispered in my ear, his breath hot against my cheek. "I *think* we need to play right now."

Yep. All indications were that I'd been effective. Hooray!

He nibbled on the sensitive spot just below my ear before whispering, "And, just so we're clear, *cara*, tease or not, I *will* beat you."

"Don't get cocky," I warned. "If you lose focus, you won't have a prayer."

"Don't make me crush you." He pulled me hard against him. "Game. *Now.*"

Gripping my hand, he pulled me toward the couch where my laptop sat. "Open it."

"You know, Slash, this teasing thing is kind of…empowering," I said, dutifully retrieving my laptop. "And sexy. I may need to practice more."

"All these epiphanies are putting me at a disadvantage," he grumbled, but I could hear a hint of humor in his voice.

He sat down beside me, opening his briefcase and

pulling out his laptop. He balanced it on his lap as he logged on. A few taps later, it was game time.

"Ready?" he asked, fingers poised over the keyboard.

"Ready." I positioned my fingers, then leaned over and kissed him on the cheek. "Good luck. You're going to need it."

"No worries. I am sufficiently motivated. I intend to win."

One hour and a fierce battle later, he did. Barely.

Later, lying in his arms, it didn't feel at all like I'd lost.

EIGHTEEN

IT SEEMED LIKE I'd just fallen asleep when my phone rang. I fumbled for it on the bedside table, but when I picked it up, there was no one there. At that point, I realized Slash was already talking to someone and I was holding my hairbrush.

I set the brush down and rolled over. I must have been sleeping like the dead. Slash had been coding. His laptop sat open and glowing on the bed. It was two twenty-seven in the morning. Who the heck called at two twenty-seven in the morning?

Slash snapped on the light and I blinked in the harsh glare.

"Give me the address. I'll be there in twenty." He snatched a pen and scribbled something on a scrap of paper.

Slash hung up and sat on the side of the bed, hanging his head and pushing his hand through his hair.

"Who was that?" I rolled over, shielding my eyes from the light.

He didn't speak for a moment, and when he did, his voice was unusually serious and something else. Anguished. "We've got a problem."

I snapped awake. Frowning, I sat up, clutching the blanket in my fingers against my chest. "What happened?"

He didn't answer right away or turn in my direction,

so I crawled across the bed and rested a hand on his bare shoulder. "What's happened? Slash? Talk to me."

The muscles in his shoulders were taut beneath my fingers. "I'm beginning to think this whole thing hasn't been about a hack."

I leaned closer, resting my chin on his shoulder. "I don't understand. It's not? Then what is it?"

"A hit."

I blinked in shock. "A *what*?"

"A hit. An IAD employee has just been shot and killed."

"Oh, God." My mind tried to process his words, but it was having a hard time. "Who?"

"Grant Durham."

"Grant Durham? As in, the Director of IAD I just met?"

"Si." He stood, pulling on a pair of underwear and his jeans. His face was grim. "He was just murdered at his home. I've got to get over there."

"I'm so sorry, Slash." My throat tightened. I'd met Grant only once, but there seemed to have been affection and mutual respect between him and Slash. I scrambled out of bed, spying my T-shirt on the floor. I snatched it, pulling it over my head. "I'm going with you."

He stopped, looked over his shoulder at me as he pulled his boots on. "Why?"

"Because I'm up to my neck in this, too. Please, I might be able to help."

I could see him weighing it. I figured he was concerned for my safety, but I also knew he didn't want to leave me alone right now, even in the custody of the FBI. Finally he nodded. "Okay. Stay close to me."

I didn't say another word, worried he might change his mind. After we finished getting dressed, we drove in silence to Grant's address, followed by our FBI tail.

It was a nice neighborhood and the houses were small mansions. The police had roped off the house at the base of a cul-de-sac. Slash pulled his SUV over to the curb and we made our way toward the tape. I saw a van, the coroner's vehicle and no fewer than four black sedans.

As we passed them, Slash commented, "The FBI is already here."

An officer standing near the tape saw us coming and held up a hand. Slash took out his ID and handed it to the policeman and then motioned that I should do the same. The guy shone a flashlight between our IDs and us before talking into his cell phone. After a moment he hung up. The two agents from our tail came up behind us.

"You're authorized to go to the side lawn and meet with your contact there," the officer said. "You'll have to be escorted to go anywhere else. This is a crime scene." He pointed to the two FBI agents. "You can wait here for them."

We retrieved our IDs before crossing the lawn. It was ablaze with light. The red, white and blue of the flashing police lights bathed the side of the house in a rainbow of color. A few neighbors stood on their lawns watching the show.

Slash took my elbow and we walked across the grass toward a lone figure. A police officer stood there waiting, along with Shawn Moore, the FSO from Slash's office. When he saw us, he asked the officer to give us a minute to speak privately. The front door to the house was open and spotlights had been set up, bathing the area in a blinding white light. Several people congregated in the doorway, while another group huddled around a black sedan in the driveway. All four doors and the trunk of the car were open.

Shawn held out a hand to Slash and the men shook. If Shawn was surprised to see me, he didn't say anything. "Before we go any further, let me give you a quick rundown."

Slash nodded. I hugged myself, trying to ward off a chill that had nothing to do with the temperature. I glanced at Slash and saw the angry set of his jaw and the hard glint in his eyes. He was back in that zone. He wanted payback. Revenge. As of this moment, the hack had not only become deadly, but worse, personal.

"Grant was murdered about eight thirty this evening," Shawn told us. "It was a professional hit. Staged and executed with precision."

Slash's fingers on my elbow tightened. "Where was Grant's security?"

"All present. Three are dead, one injured badly." Shawn swept his hand toward the front door. "Grant was headed to an event that was starting at nine. It was a…" He reached into his pocket and pulled out a small notebook. He flipped through it and found the page he was looking for, and continued, "…a charity gala. Grant's driver arrived right on time at eight fifteen."

"Grant has a driver?" I interrupted.

"Yes," Shawn replied. "A driver he's been with for twelve years. Grant was still upstairs, running late. One of his security detail opened the door and the driver shot him on the spot." He motioned toward the front door. "The agent who was in the basement monitoring the house surveillance equipment saw what happened.

She hit the alarm, drew her weapon and came after the driver who, by this time, was already in the house, presumably looking for Grant."

"Grant would have heard the shots by then," I said.

"Yes. Agent Moraites exchanged gunfire with the driver in the area of the foyer, was hit and went down. She's in critical condition."

"The driver didn't take time to finish her off," Slash mused.

"No, she wasn't the target," Shawn said. "Grant must have heard what was happening and took cover by barricading himself in the bathroom. He didn't go down easy and got off several shots at his attacker. In the end, he went down, too. In this case, the killer made sure Grant was dead. Three shots to the head—execution style."

My stomach heaved and I pressed my hand to my mouth. Slash glanced at me probably wishing I hadn't come.

"Is there any evidence Grant or the agent hit or wounded the driver?" Slash asked.

Shawn shrugged. "I don't know yet. The crime scene is still being analyzed."

I swallowed hard. "You said there were three dead and one in critical condition. In addition to the two agents and Grant, who else was involved?"

Shawn tucked the notebook back in his pocket. "The driver. The *real* driver, Henry Chang. We found him in the trunk of the car." He dipped his head toward the driveway at the black car.

I closed my eyes and Slash slid his arm around me. "How did security not recognize the driver?" he asked.

"The killer and the driver are a close physical match. Short and slight. It was dark and the killer wore a hat low across the brow, which should have raised a flag since apparently Henry never did."

"Complacence," Slash murmured.

I spoke. "You mentioned surveillance equipment. Do you have any of the killer?"

"We do. I haven't seen it yet, but the crime team has already reviewed it. We'd like you all to review it, too."

"Was anyone else in the house?" Slash asked.

"No." Shawn shook his head. "Grant lived alone except when his kids were visiting, which thankfully they weren't tonight. He's divorced. Work was his life. No surprise there. As you know, our line of work doesn't lend itself well to relationships." He dipped his head meaningfully at Slash, who looked away.

Someone from the front porch approached. A man who identified himself as J.P. Walton, the FBI Agent in Charge, shook our hands. "I'm glad you're here. The others have already arrived."

"Who are the others?" Slash asked.

"Sam and Charlie, as well as Marek from OSI. The party is ready to start."

"Where's Trevor?" Slash asked.

"Trevor is now Acting Director of IAD and is being debriefed at FBI headquarters as we speak. Your presence here has been requested from the very top."

He didn't say *who* at the very top, and what *top* we were talking about. No one asked for clarification, so I didn't either. Guess it didn't matter at this point.

"Please follow me," J.P. said, motioning to us. "Even though the area where we will be going has already been processed by the crime team, please don't touch anything."

"Where are we going?" I whispered to Slash as we followed along.

Slash leaned down and spoke softly in my ear. "They've got the surveillance footage from the front door queued and ready for us to review."

We followed J.P. around the lawn to a side door that was already ajar and guarded by an officer. He stepped aside and we slipped inside a laundry room, then through to a sitting area with a large screen television and pool table. It looked like it had been set up as a game room, presumably for his kids.

I'd met Grant only once, but he'd seemed like a nice guy. Slash had clearly respected him. Now there were three kids who didn't have a father. We passed through the room and down a small hallway until J.P. stopped at a small room to the left. Charlie, Sam and Marek stood in the hallway looking grim and shaken.

I peeked into the room. It was completely dedicated to house surveillance, both inside and out. It struck me that while Slash had to endure a detail following him around 24/7, the Director of IAD actually had a team of agents *living* in his house. How bizarre was that? I guess I'd never fully appreciated the sacrifices certain officials high in the government, my boyfriend included, made in the name of national security.

I swallowed as I stepped into the room. It was crammed with laptops, several large monitors, a couch, a mini fridge and a small table. A cup of coffee sat next to one of the monitors. The swivel chair had been pushed up against the wall, which made me imagine that whoever had been sitting in it had jumped up quickly.

"Do we know if the hit man ever made it down here?" I asked.

"It's doubtful, which is why this area was able to be so quickly processed by the crime unit. There was no time for that. Agent Moraites had already sounded the alarm and engaged the shooter on the front stairs. After the shoot-out with her, he went upstairs to find and confront Grant."

"Grant had barricaded himself in a bathroom and alerted 911, but the hit man managed to shoot his way in anyway. It wasn't pretty."

J.P. pulled the swivel chair over and sat down. "Let's take a look at the surveillance footage."

He tapped on the keyboard and a video popped up. According to the time at the bottom right corner of the video, the sedan pulled into the driveway at precisely eight fifteen. The driver got out and walked around the front of the car toward the door.

"No glances up at the security camera yet," Slash murmured. "He knew. He'd been here before and knew exactly where the cameras were. He knew there was surveillance on the door."

"The hat obscures his face," Sam said. "Look how it's pulled down over his face."

"He's about the same size as Henry Chang," Charlie observed. "That was clever. Someone had either been watching or did their homework."

The driver proceeded to the front door.

"He's going to have to look at the security camera at some point," Shawn said. "It's protocol."

The driver rang the bell and sure enough, for a fraction of a moment, lifted his head toward the camera and held up a hand.

"Freeze," everyone in the room yelled at the same time.

J.P. froze the frame. The hand he had lifted partially

obscured the man's face—on purpose, for sure. A closer inspection indicated the driver wore sunglasses.

"Sunglasses at night?" I said. "There's a red flag."

"Agent Moraites didn't notice?" Sam asked curiously.

"Yes. My guess is it happened in a nanosecond and she didn't notice," Shawn replied. "Or she saw what she expected."

"Can you magnify that frame?" I asked leaning over J.P.'s shoulder and staring at the screen.

J.P. tapped on the screen until the face was magnified. The face was blurry and slightly obstructed by his hand, but something seemed familiar about the shape of the face.

"Magnify it more," I said.

We were practically looking at pixels now, but I noticed something to the left of the screen. "What's that?" I asked, pointing to a dark shadow. It would have been near the left ear of the driver.

Everyone squinted and then Slash lifted his eyes and looked at me. "It's an earring."

The earring, the small shape of the hand, the chin and cheekbones. It all added up for me.

"Gentlemen, that driver is not a he," I said. "It's a *she*."

NINETEEN

"A SHE?" J.P. asked in surprise. "You know who that is?"

"I think her name is Feng Mei," I said. "She's the woman from the bar. The hacker who took the money and code and tried to kill me."

Sam looked at me in surprise. "How can you be sure that's her from just this glimpse?"

"I can't be a one hundred percent sure, but I feel comfortable with a 96.7 percent certainty. I have a photographic memory. The shape of her face, cheekbones and mouth is familiar. Too familiar to be a coincidence at this point."

"Even with the sunglasses obscuring her face?" Sam asked.

"Even with the sunglasses obscuring her face."

J.P stared at me openmouthed. "So, the woman you encountered at the hotel bar is both a hacker and an assassin? Of this level?"

I glanced at Slash and he nodded. "Apparently so," I said. "It's not a stretch. She did a good job of almost killing me. If Slash hadn't called the police while she was chasing me and showed up in time to save me, I'm sure I would have been dead."

Slash tensed beside me and I pretended not to notice.

Marek shook his head. "Chasing someone to kill them on the spur of the moment is a lot different than a hit of this magnitude. The planning and execution that went into this had to be a long time in the planning."

"Looks to me like they just needed a name and an address," I said. "Exactly what they stole with the hack."

"There had to be easier ways to get that than a hack into the NSA," Sam protested. "Come on, people, this is nuts."

"It's not nuts." I crossed my arms against my chest. "You can't just go poking around in databases at the NSA. You have to have a reason, a need-to-know for being in that particular database. Every name, every keystroke is logged. A hack is one way to circumvent that without arousing suspicion."

"A heck of an expensive way," Sam said.

I shrugged. "Whatever gets the job done."

"So, what are we saying here?" Charlie said, aghast. "That the hack was for murder?"

Slash studied the frozen picture of the driver. "Maybe. We can't rule it out."

Charlie unzipped his coat. Sweat beaded on his upper lip. "But it doesn't make sense. I'm with Sam. Why a hack? An insider threat at that level could have simply memorized Grant's address. It has to be something else."

"What if they didn't need or want just one address?" I offered. "Maybe they aren't sure who they are looking for, so they're going down a list. Or they intend to take out everyone in the department."

The room felt completely quiet, so I felt like I had to clarify. "I'm not saying this is what that is—I'm just throwing possibilities out there."

"So what *are* you saying?" Sam looked alarmed. "Are we next?"

"Possibly." I glanced at Slash and he lifted his eyes to meet mine. "It's as good a guess as any at this point."

"But why?" Marek asked. "What's the motive?"

"Revenge," Slash said, taking my elbow. "Come on, we've got work to do."

"Wait," Marek said. "What do you mean by revenge? Where are you going?"

Slash glanced over his shoulder at Marek, his eyes dark. "To put a stop to this. I'll report to Trevor later. We've got work to do."

To MY SURPRISE, we didn't drive to my apartment or Slash's. Instead Slash drove directly to the Zimmermans'.

"It's almost four o'clock in the morning," I reminded him as we got closer. "Normal people are often asleep at this hour."

"They're not normal. Neither are we. They're awake."

When we got to the driveway, sure enough, the lights were on in the house. Our FBI detail pulled up to the curb and turned off their headlights. I was *almost* getting used to them following us around.

Slash and I walked to the front door. Before we could ring the bell, Elvis opened it. "Did you get my message?"

"I did."

I glanced sideways at Slash, wondering when Elvis had contacted him and why.

We walked inside. Xavier was madly typing something on a keyboard in the living room command center. He lifted a hand in greeting and then pushed his swivel chair down a long table before checking something on another monitor. He made a notation on a piece of paper and stuck the pencil behind his ear.

"Hey, guys, thanks for coming at this hour."

"We were already awake," Slash said. "What have you got?"

"We've got a confirmed trail to the Red Guest," Elvis said. "Want to see?"

"Absolutely."

Elvis led us to a laptop hooked up to a large screen. He sat down and pulled up several windows. "Take a look at this. I worked backward from the data you gave me on the intrusion into the NSA. My focus was where did the information go once they were in and had gathered what material they wanted? What trail did they leave on the way out?"

He pulled up another window, shifted to another string of code. "I can tell you they left a very complex trail. I'm not done tracing that down yet and I'm not sure it will lead anywhere worthwhile. But what was more useful at this point was to run an exhaustive comparison of the extraction data to the code you gave me from last month's hack into the Transportation Security Agency. The hack you suspect came from the Red Guest."

"And?" Slash leaned forward intently studying the code.

"It's a match. I can say with near certainty that whoever followed the instructions for the hack worked for the Red Guest. There are other little nuances in the code that support that, but bottom line is, it's the Chinese."

Slash looked over his shoulder at me. "There you go. The Red Guest on a platter."

I blew out a breath, leaned against the back of a table. I didn't know what to say. What *could* I say?

Elvis spoke. "I've got more news."

"Good or bad?" Slash asked.

"I don't know," said Elvis. "I suppose it's all in your perspective."

"And that means?"

"Jiang Shi, the leader of the Red Guest, is here in Washington right now."

TWENTY

"WHAT?" I PUSHED off the table, incredulous. "Shi is *here*?"

"Yep. He's in Washington as part of an official Chinese diplomatic delegation."

"For what?" I asked.

"Don't laugh," Elvis said. "A special conference sponsored by the joint US-Chinese Partnership for Cybersecurity Peace or better known as PCP."

Oh. My. God. The irony.

"You have *got* to be kidding," I said.

"I wouldn't kid about something so ugly," Elvis said. "Slash was right. Apparently China is on a mission to spread peace and cyber cooperation in order to soothe the anger at all the high-profile hacks that have been traced back to them."

"By bringing their biggest hacker to the US in this capacity?" I couldn't wrap my head around this. "It's a slap in the face."

"Agreed," Elvis said. "Arrogance at its worse."

Slash who had been quiet up to this point, finally spoke. "It's all good."

"Good?" I threw up my hands. "What could possibly be good about Jiang Shi being in our neighborhood?"

"Saves me the trip."

"For what?" I asked.

Slash remained silent.

It took me a second to get there. "Wait. Slash. You're not thinking about snatching Jiang Shi. He's a Chinese citizen."

"So is Quon."

"That's different. Quon was caught in the act of kidnapping and torture," I argued. "Besides, he wasn't on US soil and he certainly wasn't part of an official delegation in the nation's capital."

"Jiang Shi is murdering people." His expression was cold, remote. "Even if he's not pulling the trigger, he's pulling the strings. Same thing."

"What?" Elvis said in shock. "Shi is murdering people? What the hell don't I know?"

Slash tersely filled the twins in about Grant's murder and my identification of Feng Mei as the probable hit woman.

Xavier blew out a breath. "Dude, that's unbelievable. A hit on the director of IAD? Unbelievable."

"You'd better believe it," Slash said. "That's what things have come to."

I needed to bring the testosterone down a level before things got more out of hand. "Regardless of what's happened, Slash, you can't go down this road." I reached over and brushed my fingers with his. "There are rules of engagement."

He didn't answer.

I shot an exasperated look at Elvis. "Tell him I'm right, Elvis. Please."

Elvis avoided eye contact. "I'm sorry, Lexi, but I can't do that in good conscience. We've just confirmed the Red Guest sanctioned the hack, which, by extension, includes the hit on Grant. Grant was a great guy— Xavier and I knew him personally. If the Red Guest is trying to kill you and killing employees at the NSA, then I'm with Slash. I'm not saying we *have* to do it, but I'm not taking it off the table either."

Had the freaking world gone crazy?

Panicked, I glanced at Xavier. "Xavier, please tell me you're not going along with this, too." My voice had taken on a desperate, pleading tone.

Xavier closed his eyes. "Man, this is beyond ugly. But Slash and Elvis are right. If the Red Guest is shacking up with Quodan and sanctioning hacks and hits on the NSA, I can't in good conscience say no. If it can be done with the approval of either the CIA or FBI, then I say do it. Cut off the head of the serpent and you hurt the body. It's been a historical option for thousands of years."

Slash finally stood, put a gentle hand on my back. "Breathe, *cara*. We're not saying we're going to do it. We're just not ruling it out. Okay?"

"But you will consider alternative courses of action, right?"

"Of course."

We spent the next few hours sorting through our options and discussing the technical parameters needed to construct the code. At some point, my phone rang. I pulled it out of my purse and looked at the number.

Faylene's Bachelorette Parties and Supplies.

I exhaled. "I'm sorry, guys. I've got to take this. I'll be back in a minute."

I pushed the answer button as I walked out of the living room into the kitchen for some privacy.

"Hi, Faylene. What's up?"

"I hope it's not too early to call."

I glanced at the time on my phone. It was already

after nine o'clock in the morning. "You're fine, Faylene. What do you have for me?"

"Well, I've put together a couple of package deals for you to choose between." The raspy sound of her voice, coupled with the heavy Southern accent, made it difficult to understand her. "You can choose the basic, the upgrade or the full deluxe."

"What's the difference?" I asked

"Well, you have more control and more options with the full deluxe, but it's more expensive. I can email you the details."

"Perfect. Shoot the info my way." I gave her my email address.

"There is also the matter of the menu, the goody bags, the games and the centerpieces." she said. She started rattling off a long list of options. I tuned out about a second after she started.

"Whoa, Faylene, please stop," I interrupted. I had no idea planning a party was so freaking complicated. "Look, to be perfectly honest, I have no idea what you are talking about. Can't you just do the regular thing? You know, whatever it is you do for everyone."

"There isn't a regular thing. Everyone is different. It might help if you tell me a bit about the guests and the bride."

I blew out a breath. "The problem is I hardly know anyone who's coming." Anxiety was feeding my irritability. "It's a bunch of the bride's cousins I've never met and a couple of our mutual friends. I would presume the women are normal. The bride speaks multiple languages, has a petite stature and is allergic to cat dander. How the hell do I determine games or a centerpiece from that?"

Faylene sighed. "Okay, I see I'm going to have to change my strategy. How about I provide you with some options and all you have to do is click the box with the option you want."

Oh, thank God. Boxes worked for me. Boxes were linear and logical. I could definitely handle boxes.

"Perfect, Faylene. Thank you so much."

She probably heard the relief in my voice, because she chuckled. "By the way, my son, Junior, will be helping with the party. He's a good boy. Got himself into a little trouble a few months back, but he's keeping his nose clean. He's excited to help me with the planning and setting up. You okay with that?"

"Sure." In my opinion, the more minds working on this party, the better.

"Great. I'll send you that checklist soon so you can read through it and decide what you girls want to eat, what games you want to play and what kinds of things you want in the goody bags."

It sounded like a heck of a lot to do when I was busy trying to save the US government from the hackers from hell.

"Oh sure, Faylene. I'm on it." I was so clicking the first box I saw on that sheet and leaving it at that.

I hung up and pressed the phone to my chest, partially relieved, but mostly traumatized. For me, planning a bachelorette party was equivalent to writing an automated code formatter in an obscure language while blindfolded. Except a bachelorette party was worse because it involved volatile variables such as giggling women, weird games, different kinds of alcohol and centerpieces. I needed an assistant, which, in my case, meant someone who could just take the damn thing over.

Who did I know that could do that?

Desperation caused me to flip through the contacts on my phone. My finger paused over one entry. Then, remembering I was desperate, I pressed the button. After two rings, she answered.

"Hi, this is Bonnie."

"Hey, Bonnie. It's me, Lexi. Hope I'm not calling too early."

Bonnie was Elvis's girlfriend. At this point, she seemed like the logical choice for the position of assistant, seeing as how her boyfriend was planning the bachelor party. They could bond over party planning. Perfect!

"Lexi?" Bonnie sounded surprised. "No, it's not early. I've already been at work for a half hour. How are you?"

I moved into the laundry room in case either of the guys came into the kitchen and I lost my nerve. I needed to sound poised without the slightest trace of desperation in my voice. Although, if I was honest with myself, there was a strong chance I might beg.

"I'm...fine." I didn't add the qualifier—as long as you didn't count that I'd been shot at, in a car accident, up to my neck in a matter of national security and at the scene of a murder all in the past forty-eight hours. I made a mental note to sound as cheerful as possible and not scare her off with vibes of extreme anxiety.

"So, to what do I owe the honor of this call?"

I considered what would be the right answer. I couldn't come right out and say, *Can you please take over Basia's bachelorette party? I'm totally desperate, have accomplished exactly diddly-squat so far and the party is this Saturday.* That might send her screaming in the other direction. Not that I'd blame her.

I could be honest and straight-out ask her to help me, but I was afraid that might give her the wrong idea. I didn't need her *help*, I needed her to *take the whole thing over*. How should I phrase it so I got an answer I could live with?

"Lexi?"

Shoot. I was taking too long to decide what to say. I shouldn't have called her out of desperation. That was stupid. I didn't have any conversation notes. I had no strategy, no index cards for handy reference or persuasion points, and no outline of the conversation.

But I had to start somewhere or she would hang up. The phone felt slippery in my hand. This party planning was making me a total wreck.

"Right. Uh, well, as you know, Xavier and Basia's wedding is coming up." Thank God I'd said something.

"Of course, I know." Bonnie sounded genuinely happy. "It's so exciting. I'm really happy for them. They're a wonderful couple. Perfect for each other."

"Yes, they are." Deep breath. "Elvis is planning the bachelor party."

She chuckled. "It's so out of his comfort zone, but he's really working hard to do it right. I admire him for that. Don't tell him I told you, but he asked me for help. I told him he had a duty to his brother to plan it by himself. It will mean so much more to both of them that way. Plus, he will have that important sense of confidence in his accomplishment."

I closed my eyes. Why in God's name had I introduced Elvis to a headmistress? She was all about building self-confidence and independence. While her sentiment was noble and would probably help Elvis gain the needed self-assurance, it also meant I was on my own. If she wouldn't help her own boyfriend, she certainly wouldn't help me.

I was as screwed as Windows 8.

"So, Lexi, why did you call?" she asked.

Great. Now I had to wind this up without sounding like a complete imbecile. "Ah, nothing, really. I was… ah…just making sure you are coming to Basia's bachelorette party on Saturday."

"Of course, I'm coming. I RSVP'd two weeks ago. Didn't you get it?"

I had. Shoot.

"You're right. I did get it. Well, nice talking to you."

I started to hang up when she suddenly said, "Hey, Lexi, wait a minute. Can I ask you something?"

Oh, no! If she asked me for any details of the party, I was in serious trouble. If I tried to make something up, she'd know. She was a freaking headmistress. Of course, she'd *know*. Then she'd tell Xavier, and Xavier would tell Basia. Then Basia would know nothing was planned and I totally sucked as a maid of honor. Major stressing out—above and beyond the major stressing out *already* going on—would commence.

Not. Good.

I swallowed my panic. "Sure, Bonnie. Ask away."

"You and Elvis are good friends, right?"

Okay, I hadn't expected that. "Um, yeah. Best friends, actually."

"Well, this is sort of an awkward question but I'm going to go ahead and ask anyway. I wondered if he had ever, you know, talked about me."

I paused. The question seemed forthright, but was there a subtext I was missing? Why did she seem nervous?

"Has he talked about you? Of course, he's talked about you, Bonnie. You're his girlfriend."

"I know *that*, but I mean in a way other than just a casual mention. Is he, well, serious?"

"Serious about what?"

"About me. About us."

I pondered the question and then the reason why she'd ask. Why would she think I knew the answer? "What do you mean by serious?"

Now she paused. "I mean, is he out for a good time or do you think he's looking for more in a relationship?"

I realized the question shouldn't—*couldn't*—be answered by me. "I really don't know, Bonnie. Why are you asking me? If you want to know, why not just ask Elvis directly?"

She was quiet for a moment, then blurted out, "I'm in love with him."

TWENTY-ONE

OH, JEEZ. TALK about dropping a conversation bomb. What the heck was I supposed to say to *that*?

I waited, hoping she'd laugh or clarify the comment, but she didn't. As the pause stretched on, it was painfully clear it was my turn to say something. "Ah, congratulations?"

She didn't respond. Apparently that was *not* the right thing to say. Why had I said congratulations? She hadn't earned an MBA or run a marathon. She'd just professed her love for a guy who happened to be my best friend.

I was pretty sure she wanted me to engage in some kind of girl talk about him, which would veer into totally uncomfortable territory for me for a variety of reasons. I didn't want to diminish her heartfelt declaration, but at the same I had no idea how to properly respond. For future reference, I needed to be better prepared for these kinds of situations. I made a mental note to create a spreadsheet of commonly asked relationship questions and have answers memorized for unexpected conversations like this one.

I liked Bonnie, I really did, but I was on boggy ground. "What I meant to say, Bonnie, is good luck with that."

No, I hadn't just said that. Oh, for crying out loud. That sounded worse than congratulations. What the heck was wrong with me?

"I just wanted you to know, Lexi."

The tremble in her voice made me feel guilty. Jeez. I tried to come up with a better response. "Well, you couldn't have fallen in love with a nicer guy. He's great, really."

"I know. Someday I hope to be as good a friend with him as you are."

"He's a good friend to have."

"Yes, I'm sure he is. God, Lexi, you're making this really hard."

Understatement. Of. The. Year.

I decided the best approach was the honest one. "I suck at girl talk. I can barely deal with my own relationship, let alone provide useful or supportive information on someone else's. It's a character flaw I'm working on. Sorry about that."

She laughed softly. "See, that's exactly what I'm talking about."

"What *are* you talking about?"

"You have a sincere heart, Lexi. I know why Elvis likes you so much. I do, too. Not only do I owe you my life, but I owe you for introducing me to him in the first place. I've never properly thanked you for that. Regardless of how things work out between Elvis and me, you've done me a favor I can never repay. Thank you so much."

I paused a moment to replay our entire conversation in my head. Why was she suddenly talking about me? What had happened to her declaration of love for Elvis?

After a few seconds of contemplation, I still came up empty. I had no freaking idea what she was going on about. "Um, you're welcome?"

To my amazement, she laughed. "Oh, Lexi, you're the best."

Now I was totally confused. This was *exactly* why I had only a few girlfriends. There was no logical way to anticipate what they would say next.

"Thanks for calling. I'll see you at the party on Saturday."

Bonnie hung up. I stared at my phone for a full minute wondering what had just happened. While the odds were statistically high I'd never figure it out, what *was* perfectly clear was I still didn't have anyone to help me plan the bachelorette party.

Sighing, I slid the phone back into my pocket and walked out of the laundry room. I crossed the kitchen and was just about to push open the swinging door into the living room when I heard my name. I stopped. Elvis was speaking.

"No, don't sit there, Slash. That's Lexi's chair. She always fusses if one of us adjusts the height. Sit somewhere else, okay?"

There was a pause and I worried that Slash might take offense. Then I heard a chair squeak and realized he'd sat in Xavier's chair instead.

"You know Lexi really well."

"Yeah," Elvis replied. "We're a lot alike, which makes it easy for me to understand her. Our friendship doesn't require much maintenance, thank God."

A board creaked above me. Someone was walking around upstairs. It must be Xavier. He'd probably left to go to the bathroom. That meant this was a private conversation between Slash and Elvis...except it wasn't because I was listening. I knew it wasn't right, but I couldn't bring myself to take a step forward into that room. Yet.

"You're a good friend for her to have," Slash said after a pause. "I'm happy for her…that she has you for a friend. You're important to her."

"She's a great friend. The best. You're a…lucky guy." Elvis cleared his throat. "Speaking of friends, a couple of days ago I came across this really innovative open source code that I thought you might be interested in. I've been meaning to tag you on it, but things got hectic at work and now…well, now isn't the greatest time to show you. But sometime soon, if you'd like to stop by, I'll provide the beer and the code, and maybe you can take a look at it. I'm curious as to your thoughts. I'm not sure what to make of it."

I held my breath. *Holy cow. Are Elvis and Slash making plans…as friends?*

"Sure. I'd like that," Slash said. "Sounds interesting."

I must have leaned too hard on the door, because it abruptly swung open. I staggered into the room like a drunken sailor, falling onto my hands and knees right in front of Slash.

Both men stared at me.

My knee was killing me and my face felt hot. "Ah… hi, guys."

"What…are you doing?" Elvis asked.

I searched for a plausible reason I'd been leaning against the door—one that didn't involve eavesdropping—when Slash's phone rang. It rang four times before he finally took it out of his pocket and answered it, his eyes still on me.

He frowned and listened for a moment longer before he spoke. "You've found the mole?"

TWENTY-TWO

I CAME TO my feet as Slash frowned, pressing the phone tighter against his ear. "You've got to calm down, Charlie. I can barely understand you."

Slash listened a bit more and then rattled off an address. "Okay. We'll meet you there. Thirty minutes. We'll be in a booth in the back."

He hung up and slid his phone into his pocket.

"What was that all about?" I asked.

"It's Charlie Hsu. He wants to meet with us."

"They found the mole?" I asked.

"No. He thinks he's being framed as the mole. We're going to go meet him."

We said a quick goodbye to Elvis and Xavier, who jogged down the stairs as we were leaving. I grabbed my light jacket, as Slash and I headed out into the bright sunlight. The FBI agents looked up when they saw us and started their sedans. Slash went over to talk to them while I climbed into his SUV.

"Which one is going to follow us?" I asked when Slash climbed into the driver's seat.

"Both."

Jeez. Talk about overkill on the taxpayer's bill. Not like I could do anything about it, so I refrained from commenting. "Where are we going?"

"Café du Pain. It's in Laurel."

"I know where it is. I've been there a couple of times."

Slash drove to the café in silence. I thought about the conversation I'd just overheard and wondered if Slash would bring it up.

He didn't.

Slash pulled into the café parking lot. The agents parked as well and while one agent stayed in the car, another one followed us in. The agent took a seat at a table near the bar with a view of the front door and the booth. Despite the fact that I was getting followed around a lot lately, I still wasn't getting used to being watched all the time.

We ordered coffee. I sipped mine, but Slash took one drink, winced and left it untouched. Ten minutes later Charlie walked in, looking openly distressed. Slash lifted a hand in greeting and Charlie saw us, heading straight for the booth. He slid into the seat across from us, anxious and upset.

"Thanks for meeting me. Hey, Lexi."

"Hey, Charlie."

"Look, I'm not going to waste any time." He glanced at his watch and then around the café. "I'm being framed. Someone set up a bogus account in my name and backdated it so it looks like it was set up three months ago. It's not mine, I swear."

"Where's the account?" Slash asked.

"An offshore bank in the Cayman Islands. I wouldn't even have known about it except I asked a friend who is in international banking to keep an eye out for me."

"What made you do that?" Slash picked up a spoon, examined it.

"Dude, you saw the way everyone looked at me in

that meeting. They think it's me because of my Chinese heritage. No one is going to believe I'm innocent. But I'm telling you—I'm not the mole. Whoever is doing this to me is trying to deflect attention from themselves."

"So, why did you come to me? Why not go to the top?"

"Because I don't know who to trust. I didn't know what else to do. You've got to help me, Slash."

"My advice is to turn yourself in."

"*What?* I just told you I'm not the mole."

"It doesn't matter. If you are evasive in any way, you become suspect. Go to Shawn. Tell him what you found. Be up-front and honest. If you're innocent, you have nothing to worry about."

"Nothing to worry about? What the hell is wrong with you? My friend said whoever hacked in to create the account did a flawless job. How am I supposed to prove my innocence with that? This was a totally professional job. I'm in serious trouble here. Besides, who knows what else is out there with my name on it? I have to start searching on my own, find out what I can, try to figure out who is doing this. I certainly won't have access to that kind of equipment if I'm in jail."

"You're not going to go to jail, Charlie. You'll be put on administrative leave."

"And detained."

"True. But knowing what's going on right now, that's not a bad place to be."

A wild look crept into Charlie's eyes. "You don't get this, man. There are millions in those accounts. I guarantee you, I'll be locked up by midnight with all the evidence handed to them on a silver platter."

Slash pushed his coffee cup aside and rested his arms on the table. "Charlie, listen to me. Calm down. Turn yourself in. Take yourself out of the equation. You've got to do it to protect yourself." Slash was cool and in control, his demeanor almost the exact opposite of Charlie's.

Charlie slid out of the booth and shot to his feet. He'd started sweating. "No way, man. No way. You wouldn't turn yourself in and hope for the benefit of the doubt. Tell me the truth. Would you?"

When Slash was silent, he continued. "That's what I thought. Look, I'll check in with you *after* I've had a chance to gather more facts and see what else might be out there." He slapped his hand on the table. "I'm out of here."

He turned around and nearly ran into two FBI agents in suits who had walked in the café. "Mr. Hsu, will you come with us, please?"

Charlie whirled around, stared at Slash in astonishment. His eyes were filled with hurt, betrayal and anger. "Tell me I'm reading this wrong, man. You didn't just turn me in, did you?"

Slash said nothing.

Charlie's eyes narrowed. "That was cold. Really cold. I didn't expect that from you of all people. I thought I could trust you."

"You can."

"Yeah, that's real obvious."

He turned around and was escorted by the two agents out the door. Our friendly neighborhood agent remained in his spot, interested by what was going on, but not interfering.

I shifted in my seat so I faced Slash. "Why did you do that?"

"It was for his own protection. If he's innocent, we'll prove it. He was about to do something really stupid. If he ran, he'd have lost his job even if he was cleared. Charlie is a smart guy, but he's running scared. Now he's safe and protected, as is his job, even if he's pissed at me."

"And if he's guilty?"

"Then he's right where he should be. It was a hard choice, *cara*, but it's the right one."

I felt a twinge of sympathy for him. Making tough decisions was not for the faint of heart. Still, I could see what the perceived betrayal had cost him and wondered how many times a week, day, hour he had to make them.

He stretched out a hand to help me out of the booth. "Let's get out of here. We've got work to do."

Before I could take his hand, his phone rang. Reaching into his pocket, he answered it. He listened. The sudden, violent expression on his face frightened me.

"Understood," was all he said before hanging up.

My anxiety heightened. "Slash, what's happened now?"

A muscled ticked at his jaw. He fought for control to answer me calmly. However, when he finally spoke, it wasn't anger I heard in his voice. It was pain.

"There's been another murder."

TWENTY-THREE

"*ANOTHER* MURDER?" My stomach took a dive. I was afraid to ask, but not knowing was worse. I steeled myself and asked, "Who?"

"Trevor."

"The deputy director of IAD? Oh, jeez. How?"

"A sniper. He was shot as he walked out of his house. Despite his considerable FBI detail and high alert, he… or she, got away. The timing, execution—literally—was perfect. Someone is providing inside information at the very top."

My stomach lurched. I pressed a hand to my belly, where the coffee now felt like it was burning a hole through the lining. "They're killing everyone in IAD, starting at the top. That's the end game. Who's in line after Trevor?"

Slash was silent for a moment before he finally spoke. "Me."

The breath whooshed out of me. For a moment, I was frozen. The directorship of such a senior position at the NSA was unthinkable for someone barely into his thirties like Slash. Then again, there was no one like Slash at the NSA, so it made perfect sense.

"You're…third in command at IAD?" My voice wavered.

He shook his head. "Not any longer. As of this moment I'm the acting director."

I let that sink in and tried not to let anxiety swamp me. A tight knot had formed in my throat, so I had to force the next words out. "What are you going to do?"

"My job. I'm going to bring down the Red Guest."

Now that he was in the crosshairs, I couldn't argue with him on that. The only contention would be exactly how we did it. Right now our options were a nuclear bomb in the form of a black code and kidnapping and/ or assassinating Jiang Shi. I didn't like any of them. But I liked Slash getting hurt even less, so I would deal.

I slid out of the booth. "Are we going to check out the murder scene?"

"No. I'm too high a risk now. The FBI and NSA are meeting at this moment to determine what to do next regarding better protection of the people in that data-base, starting with me. By extension, that includes you. I'm sorry, *cara*. We cannot return to our homes. You're going to have to go on an extended break from X-Corp. Shaughnessy is going to be pissed at me. Again."

"Oh, we're back to Shaughnessy now?"

"I don't see our so-called developing friendship on the fast track at the moment."

I looked over his shoulder at the FBI agent in the bar watching us. He was talking on his cell. Our eyes met as he hung up and stood. In a few steps, he'd reached us.

"I'm sorry, sir," he said to Slash. "I've been in-structed to bring you and Ms. Carmichael in."

Where *in* was, I didn't know. Looked like I wouldn't have any say in the matter anyway.

Slash removed his wallet and threw a couple of bills on the table. He paused and then held out his hand. Emotion, regret and concern flashed in his eyes. "Are you with me?"

As if I'd be somewhere else when he needed me most. I put my hand in his. "I'm with you."

He gave it a quick squeeze. "We'll get through this, okay?"

I managed a smile and squeezed back. "Okay."

"How long do we have to stay in this safe house?" I unpacked the backpack filled with my clothes into a dresser that wasn't mine. We'd been moved to a heavily treed residential neighborhood in northwest DC. The house sat at the end of a dead-end street and was fairly private, although two other large homes were a short walk away.

"Hard to say." Slash was not comfortable with the situation either. He hadn't bothered to unpack his duffel. He sat on a corner of the bed working off his laptop. "Long enough for me to write the code and figure out if we have one or multiple assassins."

I sat next to him on the bed, putting my chin on his shoulder. "You do realize this safe house thing is totally going to put a crimp in my bachelorette party planning."

"I'm sorry." He didn't look up from the monitor. "Can you outsource?"

"I've been working on that without success. I think I'm going to have to take it to a new level."

"Don't worry. We won't miss the parties even if it takes the entire damn FBI surrounding the clubs."

"That's good to know." I had no idea how the rest of the week would play out, but it was clear it wouldn't be the norm. "So, what did Finn say when the FBI agents told him I'd be out of commission for at least a few additional days?" I was a bit worried that Finn might be reaching the end of his patience with the government pulling me away for missions, but since it was out of my hands, there wasn't much I could do about it.

Slash paused his typing, flexed his wrist. "What could he say? He's just beginning to fully understand that you are on a perpetual standby loan to the US government. They have only to play the national security card and he's between a rock and a hard place. Knowing Shaughnessy, however, I'm sure he'll be in negotiations to figure out a way to get the government to compensate him for your time spent away, which I fully support." He paused, stretched his arms above his head. "I'm sorry. I know you didn't ask for this."

"This isn't on you, Slash. It's on me. I'm the one who sat down at that reserved table, not you."

"That wasn't coincidence. It was fate. There's a reason you sat in that chair."

"I don't believe in fate." I rolled my neck, working out the kinks.

"Really? Why not?"

"Because I believe in random occurrences and conscious choices."

He glanced up from the keyboard. "Why not include fate with those? Quantum physics offers plenty of evidence for the existence of both fate and choice. There's the theory that our conscious choice is already determined and shaped in advance by parameters of the known universe, contradicting the popular definition of free will. Therefore, it's actually grounded in science to say that fate—or if you are religious, a higher authority—is what guides us as we make our personal choices within predetermined parameters."

I thought it over. It *was* an intriguing concept. Were fate and choice intertwined?

"That's pretty interesting, Slash. It's hard to argue against a quantum physic understanding of existence in a deterministic and time-symmetric universe."

"Exactly. Consider it. If we want to take our understanding of reality to a new level, it will require us to seek out a balance in our own conscious understanding of the universe. Why must you believe in one or the other when it's perfectly logical to believe in both?"

"I have to think about that."

"You do that and we'll talk again. I look forward to it, and many more interesting conversations with you." He leaned over and kissed my cheek before he started typing again. I liked that he often kissed me for no other reason than the sake of showing affection. It was incredibly comforting.

His fingers tapped steadily on the keyboard. I squinted at the screen. I had assumed he was working on the dark code, but after watching him for a minute, I realized that wasn't what he was doing.

"Where are you?" I asked.

"I'm in the NSA rewriting an encryption code."

"What? Why?"

His fingers flew across the keyboard. "I have an internal chip that monitors my whereabouts and life signs. There's a good chance the mole knows that, too. Requesting the proper authorities at the NSA to turn it off will take too much time. So, I'm shutting it off myself."

"That's really going to make a lot of people mad."

"Only if they know I did it." He gave me a mischievous grin. "I won't tell if you won't."

"That's pretty naughty." I shook my finger at him. "Pulling one over on your employer isn't ordinary operating procedure."

"These aren't ordinary times." Slash pulled up another window and typed something in. "No one will get hurt, and, in fact, we'll be better protected."

"They wouldn't agree."

"They wouldn't understand."

I couldn't argue with that. I let out a breath. "Still, changing the encryption code won't last for long. This is the NSA after all. Someone will break it."

"I don't need long. A few days will be enough."

I wiggled my legs in front of me. My knee was sore, but still feeling a bit better. "Okay. Your call. Give me something to do. Can I help you finish it up?"

"You could. But I need assistance elsewhere."

"You do? Where?"

He pointed at a spot on the back of his neck. "Here."

"Your neck?" I stared at the skin on the back of his neck. "Are we still talking about the chip?"

"Maybe."

"Is that where you have your chip implanted?" When he didn't answer, I crawled onto the bed and examined the back of his neck with my fingers. "I don't see anything."

"Try harder."

I pressed and kneaded, but still felt nothing. "Nope. I got nothing."

"Use your mouth."

"*What*? Are you kidding me?"

"I would never kid about matters of national security." He kept typing, his fingers never slowing. He had about six windows open and was hopping back and forth between them. I was torn between watching him work and looking for the chip.

"The lips and mouth are among the areas on the

human body with the highest concentrations of receptor cells," he said after a series of dazzling moves. "Since there are a multitude of receptors on your lips, there is a greater chance you'll find it. Give it a shot. You might come up lucky."

Carefully, I pressed my lips to his neck. I nibbled around the back of his neck, up behind his ear and even down beneath his shirt across the tips of his shoulders. I came up empty.

"I can't find it."

He closed the laptop and stood.

"What are you doing?" I asked in surprise, sitting back on the bed.

"I'm done."

"That was fast. You broke and rewrote the encryption already?"

"I did." He set the laptop on the dresser, pulled off his boots and socks, and then removed his sweater. He wore only a tight black T-shirt and jeans. "I found myself motivated to finish quickly."

"But I didn't find your tracker yet."

He held up his left hand and pointed to his wrist. "That's because it's here."

"Oh, really. Then why was I looking on your neck?"

He grinned and pushed on my shoulders, gently pushing me so that I lay on the bed on my back looking up at him. "Why do you think? You didn't really buy that whole it's-hidden-in-my-neck thing, did you?"

"Of course, not. I knew you wanted a bit of necking…pun intended. It was fun playing along. After all, as you know, I'm in full support of activities that support our national security."

He laughed and brought my hand to his lips before kissing it. "And *this* is why I adore you."

I rested my hands on his shoulders. "So, does this mean no one can track you as of this moment?"

"It does."

"How much time do we have before someone notices the chip is off?"

"Oh, they've already noticed. But it will take them fifteen minutes to run the diagnostics to make sure it's not a software glitch and another fifteen to let the appropriate persons know it's not a glitch. After that I'd give them another twenty to inform the FBI and five minutes after that to inform our personal detail here. That makes a grand total of fifty-five minutes. Plenty of time."

"For what?"

He smiled as he lowered his mouth to mine. "More necking."

TWENTY-FOUR

FORTY-SIX MINUTES LATER there was a knock on the bedroom door.

I was in the bathroom combing my hair. I peeked out the door. "You were off by nine minutes," I said to Slash.

He shot me an amused look as he pulled on his sweater and opened the door. He was still barefoot.

Agent Daryl Knott, a big burly guy with a beard and gruff voice, stood there. He and FBI agents Cindy Clark and Jasper Mott had been assigned to us on the inside, as well as three roving agents who were stationed outside the house. They were pretty nice and tried their best to be quiet and nonintrusive. But there was no way around it. If I thought the fishbowl that was Slash's life was bad before—having six agents watch our every move was a hundred times worse. On the upside, seeing as how two NSA executives had been just been murdered by one or more clever assassins, being well protected sounded pretty good to me.

I stepped out with the hairbrush still in my hand and went to stand beside him.

"I'm sorry to bother you, sir," Knott said. "We've just been notified your tracking implant is malfunctioning."

"Really?" Slash said with remarkable calm. "Is it serious?"

"Ah…well, I'll be honest. Hell, if I know. All I know

is that it isn't working, so headquarters let me know I'm supposed to make sure you're okay." Knott shifted on his feet. I got the impression talking about technology made him uncomfortable.

Slash spread his hands. "I'm okay and she's okay." He slipped an arm around my waist. "See?"

"Roger that." Knott cleared his throat. "Well, let me know if you need anything. I'll keep you updated on the implant chip—you know, if they get it turned on or something."

"Thank you. I'd appreciate that."

After he closed the door, I whacked Slash on the shoulder with my brush. "Wow. Stellar acting. If this whole genius at technology thing doesn't work out, the theater may be the profession for you."

He chuckled and sat down on the bed, sliding his laptop onto his knees. "Knott doesn't have a clue. In ten minutes he'll be back in here with someone on the phone from the NSA who has a lot more knowledge about the chip. Then the fancy footwork will begin."

"They'll want to put a new one in you."

"Of course," Slash started typing. I admired his seemingly effortless ability to multitask despite everything that was going on. "But that takes time. This is the federal government. There are forms to be written, signatures required and budgets to be considered. In this case, that process works in our favor. Even if they sped it up, they wouldn't be able to locate, program and implant a new chip inside of seventy-two hours. We're good."

I sat down and started work on gathering as much information as I could find on Feng Mei.

Seven minutes later Agent Knott returned with his

cell. "Um, sir, it's Sam Nelson from IAD. He needs to talk to you about the chip. By the way, keep the phone. It's a loaner for the time being. They want to be able to reach you quickly."

Slash took the phone and clicked it on speaker so I could hear. "Hello, Sam."

"Slash. What are you doing?"

"Excuse me?"

"Your implant is disabled."

Slash exchanged a glance with me. "So, I hear."

"You can stop playing innocent." Sam's tone was anger mixed with exasperation. "What you're doing is dangerous. We need to keep track of you."

"If I'm not mistaken, I'm surrounded by six FBI agents. My every move is being closely monitored. I think I'm sufficiently protected."

"You know what I mean. It was a stupid move. You're safe now. We've caught the mole."

Slash raised an eyebrow. "You have?"

"Yes. Charlie is being held and questioned right now. They found a bunch of offshore accounts in his name. Looks like it was all about the money."

"That's nice, how it's all been wrapped up and tied with a bow." Slash's voice was mild, but his jaw tightened slightly. "Pretty convenient timing."

"There was nothing convenient about it. It was hard work tracking those accounts down. There were a lot of people at the NSA working on it."

Slash was silent.

Sam sighed. "Dude, I'm asking you to turn the chip back on. You know it's the right thing to do. We'll have it cracked in twenty-four hours anyway."

"Goodbye, Sam." Slash clicked the button off and set the phone on the bed.

The phone rang a few seconds later, but Slash didn't answer or look at it. I picked it up and turned it off. We needed to work and concentration would be key now.

We each retreated to our respective laptops and got down to business. Other than a few breaks for coffee and food, we worked steadily. When I went to the kitchen to get coffee for us, Agent Clark stopped me.

She was tall and thin with short brown hair and intense brown eyes. She'd taken off her jacket and wore a shoulder holster with her weapon in plain sight. Guess they weren't fooling around with this assassination thing.

"Hi, Ms. Carmichael. Sorry to bother you."

"You're not bothering me. Call me Lexi."

"Sure, thanks." She leaned a hand on the counter. "So, Lexi, I just wanted to let you know that we caught someone running surveillance on Slash's apartment."

"Really?" I paused in midpour. "You caught them?"

"Well, not exactly caught. We caught them spying electronically. We put a stop to it, but it means that someone has found his apartment. It's definitely not safe to return for the foreseeable future, okay? We are also pretty sure your place has been under surveillance by hostiles, too."

Hostiles. It sounded so ominous, which it was, given the fact that we were currently hiding in an FBI safe house.

"Okay." I supposed it was a good thing Slash was moving. I wondered if I would have to consider moving, as well. "Thanks for letting me know. I'll tell Slash."

I finished pouring coffee into our mugs. I added a lot of cream and sugar to mine and stirred.

"Appreciate it. There is something else. Kip Montgomery has been trying to reach you."

"Kip as in forensic artist Kip?" I took a sip of coffee. It was hot, but too strong. I added some more cream.

"Yeah, that's the one. You can call him back on my phone if you'd like."

"Do you know what he wanted to talk to me about?"

"I don't."

I glanced at the clock. "It's seven thirty. Do you think that's too late to call him?"

"We're the FBI. It's not too late." She grinned as she pulled up Kip's number, handing me the phone. "I'll be in the living room when you're done."

She disappeared and I pushed the call button. A couple of rings later, Kip answered.

"Hello?"

"Hey, Kip, this is Lexi Carmichael. I heard you're trying to reach me."

"I am. You are a hard woman to reach."

"These days that is not an understatement. What's up?"

"I wanted to let you know we got a hit on the young kid who passed you the envelope in the bar. You know, the one with the *Hack the Planet* T-shirt."

"Really?" My mood lifted. We really needed a break and maybe we'd just got one. "That's great, Kip. Who is he?"

"His name is Lin Yee, but he goes by the name Luke. He's a computer science student at San Jose University."

"That's near Silicon Valley."

"It is. Does that mean something to you?"

"It might."

"Well, we've also pieced together his whereabouts from his credit card statement and guess what?"

"He was in DC the day I met him."

"Bingo."

"That's great Kip. Good news is always welcome."

"I've got more for you. We got a copy of his student ID with a photo and a voice imprint. I'd like to shoot them your way and get your opinion. Want me to channel it through IAD?"

I thought about it for a minute. "No, it's a long story why, but can you send it directly to Agent Clark instead? To her phone is fine. I'll be able to get it from her."

"Sure, whatever you want."

"Thanks, Kip. Good work. Your department is stellar."

"We aim to please."

I returned the phone to Agent Clark and let her know that she would be receiving an important email for me. She promised to let me know when it arrived. I carried the mugs back to the room. Slash was pacing the room, a frown on his face.

I paused in the doorway. "Did I take too long with the coffee?"

He stopped, rolled his eyes at me. "No, I'm thinking." He walked over and took the mug from me. He took a sip and scrunched up his face in disgust. "My taste buds say this is five-hour-old coffee."

It didn't seem so awful to me, but then again I had completely diluted it, so how would I know?

I shrugged. "Unfortunately a quick run to Starbucks is out."

He set the coffee down on the dresser and pushed his

hands through his hair. "I'm sorry, *cara*. I didn't mean to be short. It's just I've hit a wall with the code. I need to figure a way through or around it."

I'd been in the same position many times. Writing code could be brutal. Think, rethink, write and rewrite. It was a never-ending battle between the magic and frustration.

"I'm a good sounding board." I perched on the corner of the armchair, sipping coffee and observing him. "What's the problem?"

"I'm not sure yet. That's the problem."

I wrapped my hands around the mug. The heat felt good on my fingers. "Well, before you get too lost in your thoughts, I have some news from the FBI and Kip Montgomery."

I gave Slash a quick update on everything Kip had told me.

Slash listened without interrupting. When I was finished, he strode over to the bed and picked up his laptop. "Silicon Valley? Let's see if Sinam Tech has an employee named Yee."

"With a son named Lin," I added. "Shouldn't take us long if we work together."

We sat down with our respective laptops. Twenty minutes later we had what we needed.

"Yee Bao." I read aloud. "He has two children. Lin, aged twenty-one and Hua, aged twelve. Bao is a network engineer at Sinam. That's another solid link to the Red Guest."

"It's where all roads lead right now." Slash looked up from his monitor. "No surprise there."

"So, that's what we know about the Red Guest, but

what's happening in terms of the hunt for the mole?"
I asked.

He stiffened. "Unfortunately the investigation is
going nowhere fast." A tug of emotion caught in his
voice and he cleared it. "I've got the short list from
OSI, but I don't see anyone on it as our mole." He hit
some keys and shifted his laptop so I could see the list.

I scrolled down through the names. Not surprisingly,
Charlie was at the top of the list. Slash remained on the
list, as did Trevor, Sam and six other names I didn't recognize. Based on the clearances and job descriptions
of those unfamiliar six names, all were high-ranking
systems or network experts within IAD, with top-level
clearance to have access to the required information and
systems needed for the hack.

"Well, they've narrowed it down, at least," I said.
"Even while keeping Charlie at the top. That's good,
I guess."

"It's not good," Slash insisted. "I don't think the
mole is on this list. I've personally worked with Grant,
Trevor, Sam and Charlie for four years. They are pa-
triotic, principled and dedicated. In regards to the rest
of the staff listed, I'm intimately aware of their capa-
bilities. They may be good at what they do in IAD, but
none of them have the mature skills needed for a hack
of this caliber. It's got to be someone else. Someone
we're not thinking of."

"Maybe someone on this list is hiding mad skills
you've never noticed before," I suggested. "You are aw-
fully busy."

"Trust me. I know. The mole may be in the NSA,
but is *not* on this list."

I opened my mouth to protest the sheer illogicality

of that statement, but I shut it before I said anything. My heart hurt for him because no matter what I said, he wouldn't believe it, *couldn't* believe it. Logic dictated that the people on that list were the only ones who would have both current knowledge, capability and access to the required systems in order to write the hack. He or she *had* to be on that list—there was no other explanation. Yet his passionate defense of his staff touched me deeply. For a man who showed so little outward emotion, he was fiercely protective of those he led.

"Sometimes, circumstances change," I said gently. "Things happen that make people change and cause them to make foolish or desperate decisions."

"Not on my watch," he said firmly.

Subject closed, he reached over and picked up the cell phone Agent Knott had given us. He swiped the screen and looked over at me. "Looks like we're in high demand. We have eleven messages."

He pressed a button and listened. The longer he listened the tighter his posture became. A dark frown crossed his face. After thirty more seconds he looked so angry, I set aside my laptop and went to stand beside him. I put a hand on his forearm, the muscles tensing under my fingers. I could almost feel the anger vibrating off him. Finally he pushed a button and turned toward me.

"What is it, Slash?" I asked. "What's happened now?"

His jaw was clenched so tightly I wondered if he'd be able to open it to speak. He finally did.

"Charlie Hsu is in the hospital."

TWENTY-FIVE

"OH, NO. CHARLIE?" I took a step back in surprise. "What happened?"

"I'm not sure. The message says he collapsed at the NSA during questioning."

"Is he going to be okay? Is it serious?"

"It's unclear. I've got to call in. But I don't like this. I'm not buying that this is an accident."

Slash pushed the call button and put it on speaker. After five rings someone answered.

"Sam Nelson."

"Sam, it's Slash. What happened to Charlie?"

"I guess you finally got my message. You took your sweet time to answer."

"Careful, Sam. The phone was off." Slash spoke in short clipped sentences. Everyone's nerves were on the edge. "We're working. What happened?"

"I'm sorry, man. We're all in disbelief here. I don't know what happened. He just collapsed. Stress, guilt, trauma, who the hell knows? By the time the ambulance came, Shawn was giving him CPR."

"Will he make it?"

"The last update I heard he was in critical condition."

Slash closed his eyes. "Listen to me. I want everyone in IAD to stay alert and focused on this case. We have to find out who is responsible for these murders. As acting director of IAD, I've already ordered every member of our division to have an FBI security team protecting them. The security details have already been cleared by Director Norton. They might skip me and move down the list of our personnel. You're next on that list, Sam. You are to take extra precautions. I advise strictly limiting your activities to work and home for the time being. Tell everyone else to remain on high alert and hyper vigilant at all times."

"Got it."

"Also I want you and the rest of the team to keep focus on plugging any holes in our system. The team priority at the moment, led by you, needs to be on defense. Am I clear?"

"Crystal. So, what do you think, Slash? Was Charlie the mole?"

"I don't know. At the moment, I'm leaving that determination in the capable hands of OSI and Marek. You focus on holding the line. I want every contingency considered and covered. I'm counting on you. I trust you to do this right."

"I will." I could hear the emotion in his voice. "When are you coming back?"

"When my work is done. It shouldn't be too much longer."

"What are you working on?"

"The offense. Don't worry about me. I'm covered. Just do your part and I'll be back as soon as I can."

Slash hung up and tossed the phone on the bed.

After a moment, he stood and hit a fist hard against the wall. "Damn it, I thought Charlie would be safe in custody. I had a hunch, so I played it. This is on me."

"Wait." I struggled a moment to catch up to his thinking. "What's on you?"

"I put him back in the lion's den. Charlie is a young guy. There's no way he just collapsed."

"Stress does strange things to people. It could have been too much for him."

"I don't believe so."

"What are you saying, Slash? That he was targeted while he was inside the NSA? That's nuts." Mole or not, it was hard for me to swallow that Charlie could have been hurt while in NSA custody.

"I think it's entirely possible and I made him stay." His face flushed with fury and I guessed the anger was directed mostly at himself. "He could have thrown his career away by avoiding coming in."

I exhaled a breath. "It was a tough call, Slash. You did what you thought was right. You tried to save his career."

"At what cost? If he dies, it's on me."

I didn't argue anymore because he had shouldered this responsibility for Charlie alone. Words from me, no matter how heartfelt or persuasive, weren't going to change his mind.

I shivered and rubbed my hands up and down my arms. It didn't help. The coldness had seeped into my blood. The noose was tightening around us.

Slash began to pace. His jaw had frozen in a tight clench. He'd disappeared into that zone—the one where he became unreachable. I didn't know what to do for him.

Honestly, at this point I couldn't even calm myself.

But I had to try. I stretched, tried to act casual. "I'm going to take a break. Want to game with me?"

"No."

"Watch television?"

"No."

He didn't even glance my way. At this point, I decided the best course of action was to leave him alone to work it out for himself.

I didn't feel like gaming alone and it was too risky to game with others while I was in hiding. There was no television in our bedroom and I didn't want to go out in the other room with the agents to watch. I could stream something to watch on my laptop, but I didn't feel like doing that either.

I wandered over to the bedroom bookshelf and pulled a well-worn paperback off the shelf. There was a picture of an impossibly good-looking guy without a shirt on the cover with rock-solid abs, a five o'clock shadow and dark, menacing eyes. A full moon blazed in the back of the dark night. The title was *The Vampire Who Loved Me*.

I flipped it over and read the back cover copy. A centuries-old vampire falls for a high school student. It sounded totally plausible.

NOT.

I was about to put it back on the shelf and then paused. It wasn't like I had anything better to do at the moment. Sighing, I sank into an armchair, opened the book and started to read.

Despite my initial resistance to reading the story, I was well into Chapter five before I realized Slash had stopped pacing and was now sitting on the bed watching me.

"So, how is it?" he asked.

"The book?" I held it up so he could see the cover.

He nodded as his eyes flicked from the cover to me.

I rested the book against my thigh, my finger holding my spot in the book.

"Well, for some reason a very old vampire that exists in the body of a hot male teenager is going to high school for—by my calculations—his four hundredth and sixty-sixth year. It's not clear to me why he's still in high school, but perhaps that's a plot twist that will be explained later in the story. I can tell you that by Chapter three the vampire hero—at least I think he is going to be the hero—has a perfect cleft in his chin, super strength and speed, and the body temperature of a Popsicle. The hero utters every word with a perfectly arched eyebrow and a smoldering look, which isn't that surprising since apparently he's had centuries of practice on unsuspecting and naive teenage girls. He doesn't need to hold down a job to survive and pretends not to be attracted to the heroine, for what purpose is yet to be revealed."

Slash said nothing, but lifted an eyebrow.

"Exactly." I enthusiastically pointed at his eyebrow. "The vampire does exactly that but with more of a sensual, brooding flutter of his long and sexy eyelashes."

"What the hell is a brooding flutter?"

I opened and closed my eyes trying, but clearly not succeeding, in demonstrating the flutter. "Well, according to the teen heroine, it's sexy when the guy flutters his eyelashes darkly while staring at her with a menacing, yet sensual, glare."

He rolled his eyes instead.

"Anyway," I continued, "Our heroine considers herself to be a perfectly ordinary girl, although secretly guilt-ridden because she inflicts deep longing on every male character in the book by being obliviously gorgeous."

"Is obliviously a word?"

"It is. Anyway, she's had a difficult home life, which apparently causes her to chew her lower lip every other sentence and forgive the hot vampire when he goes all postal and peeps into her bedroom window when she's sleeping. For some reason, she even lets him in her bedroom so he can snuggle with her, despite the fact he's as warm as a Fudgsicle. Did I mention he had great abs?"

I saw his lips twitch, but it wasn't a full-on smile yet.

"Anyway, our vampire hero has been waiting six-hundred-plus years of his life for this particular teenage girl because, after seeing her once, he was struck by some kind of supernatural lightning that imprinted her on him, whatever that means. That particular plot device is a little confusing at this point. As far as I can tell, *her* reasons for liking him remain quite shallow and focused on the physical—taut stomach, sculpted biceps and brooding good looks. I'm hopeful the author will provide a stronger motivation for her attraction to him—perhaps something other than the overused cliché of immortality—as the story unfolds."

"This has all happened by Chapter five?"

"I know, right?"

He finally gave me a full-on smile and stood, pulling me up into his arms. The paperback tumbled to the floor, but I didn't care. He held me tight and I wound my arms around his waist and closed my eyes.

"You're back," I murmured.

"I'm sorry," he said. "Thank you. You ground me."

"I'm worried."

"I'm worried, too. But we're going to stop them. I

needed only to regain my focus. You've helped me do that. You *always* help me do that."

I rested my head against his chest, worrying about this complicated boyfriend of mine. There was a lot of pressure on him...on us. How could I better help him?

The answer had to be in stopping the Red Guest. Hacker verses hacker. It was what I did best. It was what *Slash* did best.

"Let's get back to work," I said. "We can do this together. We can't let them distract us."

He glanced at the book on the floor. "What about your book?"

"I'm good for now." I reached down and picked up the paperback, returning it to the shelf. "Besides, I've got my own vampires to hunt."

TWENTY-SIX

AGENT CLARK BROUGHT me her phone about fifteen minutes later. I immediately downloaded the materials from Kip onto my laptop.

Agents Knott and Clark, as well as Slash, watched as I pulled up the kid's student ID and studied it.

"I'm 99.9 percent certain this is him," I said after magnifying the picture.

"99.9 percent?" Agent Knott said. "How can you be so sure?"

I tapped on the right corner of Lin Yee's lip. "See that scar here? The same kid who met me in the bar had that same scar in the same position just above his lip. You can corroborate this with Kip and the composite we created. I would say I'm one hundred percent certain, but there is a 1 in 945,700 chance another man this exact age with the identical facial characteristics could have this exact scar in the same place. But, obviously, it's not likely."

I looked up and saw Agents Knott and Clark staring at me in a weird way. "What's wrong? Do I have something in my teeth?" I picked at the front of them.

"No, you're fine." Agent Clark exchanged a glance with Knott. "How about the voice imprint? Can you give us your opinion on that?"

I pressed the play button and listened to a part of a conversation he was having with what sounded like a friend. Lin's phone had been tapped. They were talking about a class and, not surprisingly, some girl. But I recognized the voice, inflection and even the tone.

"It's him. The kid who passed me the money and the hack. One hundred percent certainty on this one."

Agent Knott opened his mouth to say something, but instead shut it. He walked out of the room, pulling his cell phone out of his pocket, presumably to alert the FBI of my findings.

Agent Clark thanked me and gave me a smile before she left. I was starting to like her. She and I seemed to have a lot in common—two women working in male-dominated fields and somehow holding our own.

Slash had continued to work on his laptop while I'd interacted with the agents. He'd apparently had a breakthrough because his eyes got this weird feverish look that hackers get when they are on to something exciting. That was definitely a positive development.

"Agent Knott thinks I'm a freak," I commented.

"He doesn't understand how our minds work." He kept typing. "Sometimes different can be scary or difficult to understand."

"I know that." Still, I liked how he implied *we* when referring to our minds. It was important to be included among my peers, even if we were misunderstood.

We worked for several more hours before calling it a night. When we finally crawled into bed it was one forty-seven in the morning. It was early by hacker standards, but we hadn't been sleeping much lately. We mutually decided to stop now and start fresh in the morning.

I dreamed I was in a giant fishbowl being chased around by a school of ferocious piranhas when one latched on to my arm. I tried to brush it off when I realized it wasn't a fish.

"Wake up." Slash had his hand on my upper arm.

I rolled over to my side, rested my head on my palm. "What's wrong?"

He held up a hand, motioning for me to be silent. A dog barked outside in the distance. Slash sat up. "Something's not right."

"How can you extrapolate that from a dog barking?"

He didn't answer, but slid out of bed and pulled on his jeans. "Let me check in with the agents in the living room."

He picked up his gun from the nightstand. "I know it's an odd request, but get dressed, okay? Keep it dark in here. I'll be right back."

He left the door ajar and I heard the murmur of voices from the living room. Light spilled in through the door. I had no idea what was going through his head, but I quickly pulled on my jeans, T-shirt and a sweatshirt. I was just tying the laces on my tennis shoes when Slash appeared in the doorway. He'd moved so silently, I jumped when I saw him.

"Jeez." I pressed my hand to my heart. "You almost gave me a heart attack. What's going on?"

"We're about to have company. The FBI agents outside aren't responding. We have to assume they've been neutralized." He now had a gun in each hand.

"Neutralized?"

"The police are on the way. But they aren't going to make it in time."

"In time for what?"

"In time to stop this." He cupped my cheek with

his hand. He was still naked from the waist up, but he didn't seem cold. I could feel the heat radiating off him.

"Hide in the closet." He pressed a gun in my hand. My fingers closed around it without thinking. It was cold and heavy.

"Why can't I stay with you?"

"I'm going to draw their fire and I don't want you anywhere near that. Crouch in the back and make yourself as small a target as possible. You can shoot through the closet door as needed, but it may affect your aim, so keep that in mind. Remember how we practiced using the gun? Hold it steady and aim straight. No hesitation. Listen to me, *cara*, shoot to kill, okay? This isn't practice anymore."

I couldn't believe I was having this conversation with my boyfriend. Most couples talked about the weather, who got to hold the remote and whether the vegetable lasagna was better than the meat-stuffed ravioli. But no, my boyfriend and I had discussions about the best way to kill intruders while in hiding in an FBI safe house. Still, he needed to focus and I didn't want him distracted or worried about me, so I sucked it up and nodded.

"Okay. What exactly are you going to do?"

He pointed to the far corner in the room. "I'm going to be over there so I can watch both the door and the windows." He flicked off the light in the hall and we plunged into darkness. It was silent from the living room and I had to assume the agents were taking their positions, as well. I had to trust they could do their job.

It took a few seconds for my eyes to adjust to the darkness. A little moonlight shone through the part in the curtain. Slash grabbed his shirt off the back of the chair and pulled it over his head, then shoved his bare feet into his boots.

There was a loud popping noise and a shout from the living room. Slash glanced at me. "Go. Now."

My heart thudding, I stepped into the empty closet and closed the door. I pressed my back against the wall. I could see through the slits in the upper half of the closet door. My hands were shaking so badly I hoped I wouldn't shoot myself by accident and save whoever was coming the trouble.

There was shouting and more shots. My heart thundered.

They were coming for us.

TWENTY-SEVEN

A BARRAGE OF shots came from the living room. *Holy war zone!*

I inched sideways so I had a partial view of the doorway through the door slits. A figure appeared there with a gun out. I stopped breathing. He was headed directly for the closet, as if he knew I was in there. I lifted the gun, but I was shaking so badly I couldn't keep a steady aim.

He had his hand on the closet handle when Slash shot him. The man dropped, rolled toward the bed and continued to shoot at Slash's position. Realizing Slash was trapped between the wall and the bed, I opened the closet door and fired at the guy's back.

Unfortunately, nerves, bad lighting and not enough practice in stressful situations, caused me to completely miss him. Instead I shattered a wall sconce beside him, startling him as glass rained down. As he pivoted to shoot me, Slash shot him in the back.

"Down," Slash yelled at me.

I dropped prone to the floor, the gun bouncing out of my hand just as another guy entered the room, shooting. His focus was on Slash, so he took one step and tripped over me. Terrified, I grappled with him, trying to keep the gun pointed away from me. Slash almost immediately fell on top of us, not daring to shoot. I got clocked in the left ear before the men rolled off me, grunting, punching and basically trying to kill each other.

I scrambled to all fours, panting. No idea what to do. There was no sound from the living room, so I had to believe the FBI agents were either down or killed. I had to do something to help Slash.

I spotted the gun that had belonged to the guy Slash had shot first. I grabbed it, rolling to my feet like an actor in a bad action movie. Unfortunately, the gun was completely unfamiliar. It was a big rifle-style thingy with a shoulder strap. I didn't have time to slip the strap over my shoulder so I braced it against my hip and hoped for the best.

Just as I lifted it, a third guy skidded down the hall and into the doorway, scaring the bejesus out of me. It wasn't an FBI agent. The ski mask and gun pointed at me gave him away.

Shoot to kill. No hesitation.

Before he even slid to a stop, I squeezed the trigger.

Rat-a-tat-tat-tat. Rat-a-tat-tat.

Holy machine gun!

The recoil knocked me backward into the closet door. Bullets sprayed across the doorway and up onto the ceiling. A huge chunk of the ceiling fell down, taking out the guy in the hallway. I continued to whirl around in a crazy dance with the gun. Slash and the bad guy he was grappling with took one look at me and both rolled for cover in separate directions.

I staggered around, spraying every freaking thing in the room. I tried to keep it away from Slash's direction as much as I could, but I wasn't entirely sure I succeeded. I shot the mirror, the dresser, two lamps, the remaining wall sconce, and made a circular mosaic on the wall before exploding both windows and sending glass flying everywhere.

Mother of God, would this thing ever stop?

Finally the gun fell silent and slid from my hands.

A single shot split the air. I staggered backward, touching my abdomen. No blood, no pain. No nothing.

Was I dying?

"Slash?" I whispered, my voice wavering. "Are you okay?"

TWENTY-EIGHT

THE WAIL OF a police siren sounded. It seemed as if hours had passed, but I figured the whole thing had had taken less than two minutes.

A dark shape lifted off the floor. "Slash?" I whispered louder.

Broken glass crunched and I heard a thud. "*Cara*, are you okay? Are you shot?"

"No, I'm fine, I think." I wiggled my legs and arms. Everything seemed attached and healthy except for the spots that danced in front of my eyes. My ears were ringing from the shooting and the hit to the head. "What about you?"

"I'm fine. Keep your voice down. You're shouting."

I was surprised by how calm he seemed in spite of the sheer number of bullets that had just been fired in one small room.

I blinked and saw the dark shape of him kneeling next to the man in the doorway.

"Did I...kill him?"

Slash stood. "No. He's still alive, but unconscious."

That was a relief even though the guy had been trying to kill me. "What about the guy you were just rolling around on the floor with?"

"He's dead. The guy I shot first is dead, too."

There was no remorse, no relief, no nothing in his voice. Just cold, hard facts.

I heard a snapping noise and realized Slash was cuffing the guy in the doorway.

"What are you doing?" I asked.

"This one will talk."

He suddenly materialized beside me. "What in the hell were you doing jumping out of the closet like that?"

My mind was still trying to process what had just happened. I couldn't believe I was still alive. "Well, you were trapped between the bed and the wall. I figured I could serve as a distraction so you could shoot him."

He pulled me into his arms and pressed a kiss against my forehead. "Don't you *ever* do that again. *Ever*. You will never risk your life for mine. Understood?"

"I can honestly say I hope I never have to do that again."

He pressed my head to his chest, holding me close. "But you did good. Cool under pressure, picking up that gun."

"I lost mine, so I picked his up. But that gun had a mind of its own. Are you sure I didn't hit you?"

"I'm sure. But you hit just about everything else." Despite what we'd just been through, there was a trace of amusement in his voice. "We need to spend some more time on perfecting your aim."

"I couldn't stop it."

"I know." He brushed his fingers across my cheek. Leaning over, he picked up the gun. "It's an Uzi. No wonder you had a tough time. Still, we're both still alive and unharmed, so that makes it a very good day."

If *that* was a good day, I'd hate to see his bad ones.

He handed me his gun and took the Uzi. "Stay here. I've got to make sure the rest of the house is clear." I heard a snap and realized he was reloading. "It's quiet now, but I have to check on the agents."

I stayed where I was. Although I strained to listen, I didn't hear him. He moved like a ninja. All I could hear was the fading ring in my ears, the rapid beat of my heart and the wail of multiple sirens, all of which were getting louder.

"Let's go," Slash said next to me. I jumped. I hadn't heard him enter the room again, let alone approach me. "The house is clear, but all the agents inside are down."

"Down as in dead?"

"No. It's a miracle, but they're all alive. Agent Knott is the most gravely injured, but there's nothing I can do for him at this point. The police and ambulance will be here shortly." He slung his duffel bag over his shoulder. "We've got to get out of here. Now."

I looked at him, stunned. "Whoa. Wait. Leave? Are you nuts? The police are coming."

"Exactly. We have to go. Now."

I dug in my heels, resisting his pull on my arm. "Slash, people are *injured*. People are *dead*. We're the only witnesses left who can tell them what happened. Not to mention, it's illegal to leave the scene of a crime."

"I assure you, we'll tell them what happened, but after we are safe. The police and FBI have a leak. That leak was high enough to tip someone off to our location. That means whoever is hunting us has a reach that extends way beyond the police department to the highest echelons of the FBI. Trust me, we are safer alone than in protective custody of the feds at this point."

I believed him, but I was pretty sure his bosses wouldn't see it that way. "The FBI isn't going to like this. The NSA won't either."

"No, they won't. But we're still going to do it."

Seeing as how I couldn't deter him from this course of action, I snatched my purse and laptop. Since I'd left my computer on the floor next to the bed, it had miraculously escaped being shot to pieces. Slash grabbed our jackets, tossing me mine. I put it on as we headed out the back door.

Slash led me across the backyard, his gun still drawn. I heard the screech of tires out front as we slipped into the neighbor's backyard and down the street. A dog barked and Slash took my hand, squeezing it.

"Where are we going?" I whispered, stumbling behind him in the dark.

"A couple of streets over. I'm going to hot-wire a car."

"Hot-wire, as in steal? Do I want to know *why* or *how* you can hot-wire a car?"

We passed under a spotlight and he glanced at me over his shoulder. "No."

Dogs were barking madly now, but we moved quickly. We tried four cars before we found one that was unlocked. It was a beat-up white, two-door Chevy truck that no one in their right mind would steal…except for us. Which was probably why they left it unlocked.

Slash pulled the passenger door open wider, motioning for me to get in. He wasn't kidding. We were stealing a car. I felt really bad about taking it, but hopefully, since we were doing it in the name of national security, the owner would be properly compensated.

Slash hopped in on the other side and reached under the steering wheel.

"Can you open your phone and aim it my way?" he asked.

I reached into my purse and pulled out my burner phone, shining it toward him. He pulled on some wires and pressed them together until the car started.

"Wow," I said impressed. "That was fast. Will you teach me that someday?"

"If you promise to use the skill only in the name of national security." He pulled away from the curb.

The comment brought a weak smile to my lips. I put my laptop and purse on the floor between my legs and fastened the seat belt. Leaning back in the seat, I tried to pretend I wasn't unnerved to have been stalked by armed intruders, stolen a car, and left the scene of a crime where people were killed and seriously injured.

Jeez.

My knees were shaking.

Slash noticed and put a hand on my knee, calming it. "*Cara*, look at me."

I turned my head and he took his eyes off the road for a moment. "I'm not going to let anything happen to you. Okay?"

"Okay."

"I mean it."

"I know. I believe you." I did. I trusted Slash with my life. But I had to admit it was a little disconcerting to see him in action. His focus in that room, and right now, was singularly dangerous and…violent. It was almost as if another version of Slash had taken over at the safe house and he was staying for the time being.

Slash drove down several small side streets and made a couple of U-turns until he was satisfied we weren't being followed. He kept a laser-focus on the rearview mirror and any headlights that appeared behind us.

"Where are we going?" I asked after the zillionth U-turn.

"Somewhere safe. But first I need supplies."

TWENTY-NINE

It was three thirty-three in the morning when we pulled into the parking lot of Jefferson's Self-Storage Facility in northwest DC. There was a bored guard at the gate watching something on a small television and drinking coffee. Slash showed his identification and the guy cross-referenced it with something on his tablet before he opened the gate and let us inside. Thankfully he didn't seem to care in the slightest that two people needed to get their stuff in the middle of the night. Slash pulled into a parking spot in front of the main building and we walked up to the front door. He used a key to open the door and we slipped inside.

The room looked kind of like a dimly lit post office with mailboxes of varying sizes lining the walls. Slash walked directly to one of the larger mailboxes and inserted a key. The door opened and Slash pulled out a large briefcase with a small keypad. He pressed a finger to the pad and activated it and then tapped in a code.

"What happens if someone other than you tried to open the briefcase?" I asked.

He smiled. "Kaboom."

The briefcase popped open and I jumped. His smile turned into a chuckle. I leaned closer, peering over his shoulder into the briefcase. I saw a laptop, some cords, a couple of passports, several large manila envelopes,

a small box, a cell phone and a couple of guns. Satisfied, he snapped it shut.

"Wow." I whistled. "That's some stash."

"I like to be prepared. Let's go."

I didn't ask where we were going. I trusted Slash
knew what he was doing.

We drove out of the storage area and a few streets
over before he turned into an underground parking garage for the District Hotel. A bored valet came out of
a small booth and took the key for the truck, handing
us a card with a number. We took our belongings and
exited the truck.

As we walked out onto the street toward the hotel
entrance, Slash said, "You've got everything? We aren't
coming back for the truck."

I nodded. The past few hours of activity had become
a surreal blur. The adrenaline had worn off and I was
facing a serious crash.

Slash booked us a room and paid in cash. This wasn't
a ritzy place or a dump, just an average hotel. Blending
in—that was the idea. Thankfully, Slash didn't even
have to show any identification. The hotel attendant
handed us a key card, not caring that we didn't have
any luggage. We took the elevator to the second floor,
the fourth room on the right.

When we approached our room, Slash stood still for
a moment, surveying the hallway.

"What are you doing?" I whispered.

"Reviewing the exits."

"Exits?" I stared at him openmouthed. "Wait. You
can't possibly think we've been followed. There's no
freaking way. We just stole a car and paid in cash for
this room. You made sure we weren't followed. You

disabled your chip. No one, I repeat, no one could find us. We didn't leave a trail. There is no way."

He pulled me to him, kissing the top of my head. "I love your optimism. Unfortunately, there's always a way. Trust me. I do think we're safe for the moment but we're going to take every precaution."

He slid the key card into the door slot and the door blinked green. We went inside. It was a pretty standard hotel room—two double beds with well-worn bedspreads, a couple of lame paintings on the wall, a single television, alarm clock and small desk. Nothing fancy. I put my purse and laptop on the dresser where the television sat while Slash checked out the double window. With a sigh, I plopped backward on the bed, holding my hand over my eyes.

"Now what?" I asked.

"Don't get comfortable," he warned. "We're not staying."

I bolted upright. "What? We just got here."

He sat on the corner of the bed, his laptop out. Without saying a word, he booted it up. Despite my exhaustion, I slid closer to him, resting my chin on his shoulder.

"What are you doing?"

"We need a couple of hours of decent sleep. Both of us. I'm going to hack into the computer system at this hotel and reprogram our key for a different room."

It took him four minutes to hack into the system. He booked the room under a false name, typed in the number on our keycard, marked the room as paid and then nudged me with his shoulder.

"Done. Two doors down, let's go."

He repacked his laptop. Keeping a hand on the gun

hidden beneath his jacket, he peeked out into the hall-way. Not surprisingly, it was empty. We walked down to the last room next to the stairwell. Slash slid the key into the door slot and the green light blinked. We entered and Slash flipped on the light. Same layout as the other room.

"Home sweet home," he said, fastening the dead bolt behind us.

"If you're certain we're staying this time, I'll go wash up first." I yawned. "I don't have any pajamas."

"We're going to have to sleep in our clothes anyway," Slash said. "As a precaution."

I shrugged. "Fine." We took off our jackets and laid them over the back of the desk chair. I dug a ponytail holder out of my purse and pulled my hair back. In the bathroom I washed my face and used the little tube of toothpaste the hotel had provided. When I staggered out, I saw Slash was busy typing away on his new laptop.

"What are you doing?"

"Sending a message to Shawn that we're okay and explaining what happened." After a moment, he stood, setting the laptop aside and handing me the gun. "Keep this while I'm in the bathroom, just in case."

I didn't want to know *just in case of what*, so I didn't ask. I sat on the bed holding the gun until he came out without a shirt on, his face freshly washed, his hair dripping.

"Everything okay out here?" he asked, looking around.

"All is quiet on the Western front." I held up the gun.

He grinned and pulled his shirt back over his head. He took the gun and put it on the bedside table next to him. Sat with his head against the headboard, then patted the bed.

"Come here, *cara*, but leave your shoes on."

"I bet you say that to all the girls."

"I only have one girl."

"Lucky me."

"No, lucky *me*." His grin faded. "Come."

Crawling on my hands and knees across the mattress, I settled into the crook of his arm as he lowered the lamp to its softest setting. He smelled like the hotel soap and toothpaste. His body relaxed as I leaned into him. He kissed the top of my head, resting his chin on the top. For a minute we sat in companionable silence, letting our minds and bodies unwind.

"Should I express surprise that you have a hidden briefcase with guns, a laptop and what are probably fake passports stashed away in a storage facility in DC?"

"You probably know me well enough by now that it shouldn't be that much of a surprise."

"I guess you're right." I tilted my face so I could look at him. "So, why do you do it?"

"In case I need to make a quick getaway."

"No, not that. Why do you take a job where you have to be prepared for a situation like that? Put your life in danger over and over again. Take the kind of risks that no one else will take. You could have a much safer and lucrative job utilizing your considerable skill at the keyboard in the private sector. Your simulation work is prime—I know that. You're a unique man, Slash. You could do *anything*. Yet you stay with the government and take on a lot more responsibility than just coding. Why?"

He leaned his head back against the headboard and

closed his eyes. I leaned against him, resting a hand against his chest. He covered it with his hand, squeezing it lightly. "I suppose it's because I believe everyone is born with God-given talents that we should use for the benefit of others."

I lifted my head so I could get a better look at his face. His eyes remained closed, but he kept a firm hold on my hand as if he didn't want to break the connection.

"Is that why you left Italy and came to the US?"

"Si."

"So, one day you decided that working for the NSA would best permit you to use your God-given talents for others? Explain that leap of logic to me. You were working for the Vatican, in some kind of top secret security organization that officially doesn't exist, and then you decide that the NSA is the place to go?"

He kept his eyes closed. "That's correct."

"Seriously? It couldn't have been that easy a decision, Slash. Why not stay in Italy? What was so important that you came here?"

Sighing, he released my hand and rubbed the back of his neck. "I never said it was an easy decision. It wasn't. But it was the right thing to do."

"Why?"

"Because there was a need and I have the talent needed. And because someone important asked me to do it."

I sat up straighter. "You were asked? By whom?"

"By a friend." He patted my hand. "A special friend. Someone who knew that important things awaited me here, including you."

"Me?"

"*Si*. I've never told you, but I considered the priest-hood very strongly."

I'd never in a million years seen that one coming. "You, Slash? The priesthood?"

He smiled. "I soon discovered it wasn't the right path for me. This is, no matter how difficult it may seem."

I took a minute to process this. Slash watched a myriad of expressions cross my face without saying anything. I tried to reconcile the many facets of this man who was abandoned as an infant, had a unique genius at the keyboard, was able to handle violence and killing with ease, to a man who had almost entered the priest-hood. A complex dichotomy, this boyfriend of mine.

He reached out, touched my cheek. "I've made you uncomfortable."

"Not true." I shook my head. "Just thoughtful."

"That's not what I meant." He studied me, thinking. He seemed conflicted, like he wanted to say something, but was weighing its potential impact on me.

"I meant that I've made you uncomfortable by my actions these past few days. Sometimes I see an expression on your face or a certain kind of concern in your eyes when you look at me. I don't like that. You are seeing that part of me—the person I must become to do what I have to do. It frightens you."

It wasn't a question and yet he waited for an answer. I fiddled with a loose thread on the bedspread. I wound it around my finger tighter and tighter while I chose my words. "I'm not going to lie to you, Slash. When you get in that zone, yes, it scares me. I can't reach you."

"I know." He hesitated, threaded his fingers with mine. "But it doesn't mean I don't have a conscience.

It doesn't mean I won't come back from the ledge. It helps to have something, *someone*, to come back to."

"I know you have a conscience, Slash, and that this struggle is not easy for you. I worry only that you give so much of yourself for the greater good, you've started to lose yourself."

A guarded look came into his eyes, a defensiveness. I didn't like that I was the one who put it there.

"You were the one who wanted me to share more about myself." His jaw tightened. "So, I shared."

"I'm not criticizing. Just observing." It was only a scratch on the iceberg that was the tightly raveled mystery of my boyfriend, but it had been a significant step forward. While I still needed to think about what it all meant in terms of our relationship, I appreciated the step forward. "Thank you for sharing. I appreciate it."

He pulled me back to the crook of his arm and rested his chin against my head. "There are a lot of things about me you're better off not knowing."

"Why?"

"Just because. Now, let's unwind. We're both exhausted and need to think about what to do next."

The subject was clearly closed, but he'd given me a lot to think about. I leaned into the warmth of him.

He stroked my hair. "Go to sleep, *cara*. Don't worry. I'm going to keep you safe."

"I know," I murmured as I closed my eyes. "Never doubted it."

THIRTY

I AWOKE FROM a dreamless sleep with a hand pressed over my mouth. Panicking, I started to flail and fight until I realized it was Slash bent over me. He was fully dressed with his jacket on, his duffel bag slung over his shoulder. He lifted his hand from my mouth and pressed a finger against his lips. He was holding a gun.

I nodded and he moved toward the door, motioning for me to grab my things. I slipped my jacket on and put both my purse and laptop straps across my shoulders. Taking Slash's briefcase, I hugged it to my chest with both hands. I had no idea what time it was or how long we'd slept.

Slash looked out the peephole before turning to me and mouthing the words. *One guy. Our old room.*

My skin chilled. How had they found us? We had taken every freaking precaution.

Slash pressed his mouth to my ear and murmured. "As soon as he goes into the room, we slip out and into the stairwell to the right. Go quickly, but quietly. He will need time to enter and clear the room. We'll use that time to get away. Once we are outside, go left and then right down the small alley. I'll take it from there. Okay?"

I nodded and he kissed my cheek.

He returned to watching the peephole. I held my breath, my heart racing. Suddenly, he pulled open the door, motioning for me to go. I slipped past him and into the stairwell. Keeping my footsteps as quiet as I could, I moved down the stairs. Slash was right behind me, walking backward with the gun out. I couldn't even hear him moving, but my breathing was so loud, I was pretty sure I'd given away our location to all life-forms on Mars.

It was just one flight until we were able to exit the hotel. It occurred to me that might be why Slash had requested a lower floor. He was always thinking of an exit strategy. When we burst out onto the street, it was still dark. The light from the streetlights made me blink. The streets were eerily empty but we were sitting ducks bathed in the light.

"Go," Slash urged.

I dashed left down the street with Slash right behind me. I took the first right I could, which led into an alley, and then stopped. Slash bumped into me.

"Keep going," he barked. "To the end of the alley and take a right."

I ran, holding Slash's briefcase close to my chest. As we came out onto another street, Slash tucked his gun in the holster and tucked my arm in his. We walked about a half block when he suddenly pulled me toward an open parking garage. There was no one in the guard booth, so we wandered down one row and through the rows of cars until he stopped and pulled me down between a black four-door Toyota and a dark green Buick.

I crouched, breathing hard from our getaway and balancing Slash's briefcase on my knees.

"There is no freaking way they could have found us. How, Slash? Could they have reactivated your chip?"

"No. It would have taken them a lot longer than a

few hours to figure it out, even using the fastest software. That's not it."

"Then what about your message last night? Maybe they traced it." It was a big stretch because Slash was far too good to be that sloppy.

"No. I was careful and that's my computer, not a government issue." He leaned a forearm against the car, thinking. "They didn't trace the message. They weren't able to unlock my chip—I'm confident about that. It has to be something else."

"Your phone?" I asked.

"No, I left all my phones behind as soon as we entered the safe house. I've got a burner, like you."

He suddenly turned his brown eyes on me. "It's got to be you."

"Me? I haven't even used my burner phone or laptop since we left the safe house." He stared at me as if the answer would magically appear. After a moment, he closed his eyes. "I should have thought of it."

"Thought of what?"

"Your earrings."

"My earrings? You mean the tracker in them? Who knows about them except for you and me?"

He was silent and I slapped my palm on my forehead. "Oh, no! My interns. Wally, Piper and Brandon. I bet they told the authorities about them."

The three high school students had helped Slash track me with them when I had recently crash-landed in Papua, New Guinea.

He sighed. "If you were an eighteen-year-old kid and officials from the NSA and FBI show up on your doorstep asking how to find us and claiming how important it is, wouldn't you help?"

"Of course. I'd give it up instantly." I sat back on my haunches. "They're just kids. They know you work for the NSA and I used to work there, too. They probably thought they were helping us."

"*Si.*" Slash had already removed the diamond studs from my ears. He tucked them beneath the front tire of the Toyota and grabbed my hand. "Time to go."

"But those were a Christmas present from you," I said, looking at them over my shoulder.

"I'll buy you a new pair. I wasn't satisfied with the prototype anyway."

We ducked out from the cars and headed for a stairwell. We took the stairs up two flights and then walked into a side alley. It was empty.

Slash took my hand and I looked at him. "Now what?"

"Now we find a safe place where we can work. I need to finish that code."

THIRTY-ONE

"STOP LOOKING FOR us, Shawn." Slash held the phone to his ear. "If you continue to try to track us down, you'll be leading them right to us."

Slash listened and then shook his head. "You know why I'm doing this." He clicked the phone off and tossed it in the trash can.

He leaned back in the creaky desk chair and closed his eyes. We'd hopped around to a couple of all-night diners until a decent hour of the morning before checking into a new hotel. It was nothing special and nothing bad. Just a middle-of-the-road hotel. Perfect for blending in. The important criteria had been that it had good Wi-Fi, which we desperately needed.

I sat down on the double bed with an ugly bedspread. The mattress was way too soft for my taste. "Well, that didn't go well. Shawn sounded really mad."

"Actually it went better than I expected. He has to save face, make an effort as part of his job. But he's smart enough to understand why we're not coming in."

"Does everyone else?"

"We can't worry about that now." Slash stood, stretched and flexed his arms and back. "It's out of our hands."

He was right. I went into the bathroom and splashed cold water on my face. I wasn't sure how long I'd slept, but it hadn't been more than a few hours. I had no idea how long, if at all, Slash had slept. We were running on fumes.

I came out of the bathroom, patting my wet face with a towel. "What did he say about the agents at the safe house?"

"The three who were outside are dead. Agents Clark and Mott are going to make it. Agent Knott is in surgery now. No one knows if he will make it."

I felt a horrible surge of anger at Jiang Shi and the Red Guest. How many more lives would he destroy if we didn't stop him?

"What about the guy in the house that you cuffed? You said he was still alive. Is he talking?"

"Unfortunately, no. He's still unconscious and has a neck fracture. The doctors don't know when he'll come around and what kind of shape he'll be in when he does. But when he does, hopefully he'll be willing to exchange information for leniency."

It was hard to feel sorry for him when he had hurt, and possibly killed, FBI agents and had been trying to do the same to Slash and me.

I looked around the hotel room. I was already feeling claustrophobic. I'd stayed out of sight when Slash checked in as Mr. Crowley. The authorities would be looking for a man and a woman checking in together, so at least we'd taken that out of the equation, although we both knew that wouldn't deter the authorities for long.

Since Slash paid in cash for the room, it would be a red flag the authorities would check out, regardless of how many guests were assigned to the room. But that was a heck of a lot of hotel rooms to cover in the Washington, DC metropolitan area, so Slash felt confident we had a bit of breathing room.

Slash had his duffel bag, but I really needed some clean clothes and underwear, so he went out and purchased a fresh pair of jeans, a couple of shirts, socks and underwear and basic toiletries for us. I wanted to go myself, but he didn't want me out there alone and together we'd be easier to spot. As he had experience with evasion and blending in he won.

He returned in just over an hour, bringing not only clothes for me, but also some food so we wouldn't have to leave the room. We needed to dig in and get to work.

After a shower, I changed into my new clothes. When I came out, he was already sitting at the desk at work on his laptop, sipping a cup of coffee. He glanced up at me and smiled.

"Everything fit?"

I slipped my hands into the black running jacket. He had bought me a black T-shirt and black socks and underwear, too. Guess color was not in his fashion palate for people on the lam.

"Yes, thanks. So, let me guess. You wear black because it helps you blend in."

He nodded. "Exactly."

"And all this time I thought it was because it made you look cool."

"That, too."

I sat down on the bed, combing out my hair with the brush he'd bought me. "So, I've been thinking. Why didn't the earrings pinpoint our room exactly?"

"It would have provided a general vicinity only. My guess is they took the location and matched it with the room paid for in cash and a general description of us, which I'm sure they solicited from the desk clerk.

When I hacked in and booked the new room, I left the old one as a decoy."

"That was smart."

"No, that was standard evasion. *They* were sloppy, which happens when you are in a hurry."

I fought with a tangle, wincing as I pulled it apart. "So what's the plan now?"

"The plan is you keep working on finding me something about Feng Mei."

I paused in mid detangle. "I'm at a dead end with her, Slash. Plus, there are already NSA agents working around the clock on her."

"And getting nowhere." He typed some commands and jotted something on a piece of paper. "You're better than all of them put together."

"Okay, I see. So, while I'm joining them in trying to track down information on her that doesn't exist, you'll be writing the black code."

There must have been something in my voice that made him look up from the monitor. He studied me. "You know, actually, scratch that. You're exhausted. Why don't you take a break and get some sleep?"

"Be careful, Slash." My eyes narrowed. "You're walking on pretty thin ice right now."

"*Cara*—"

"Don't *cara* me. In what universe do you think it's okay to give me a soft assignment or suggest sending me to bed like a kid so you can code alone?"

His eyes narrowed. "You're *not* working on this code."

I put my fists on my hips. "You have no idea how mad that statement just made me."

"I'm trying to protect you. I don't want you to be a part of this."

"I'm *already* a part of this. I thought we were a team."

"We are a team, but sometimes there are places I have to go alone."

Oh, heck, no. He did *not* just say that.

"Bull," I said between gritted teeth.

My emphatic statement startled him, which made me angrier because he'd really thought I'd fall for that crap. He had underestimated me and I didn't like it one bit.

"When Elvis was kidnapped and I was faced with impossible and ugly choices, you stood by me," I said.

"That's different. Your choice was noble—to save a life. Mine is to cause death and destruction."

"Of something that's inherently evil. The Red Guest has gone beyond standard cracking. They are *murdering* people. People we care about. They are trying to kill *us*. That's a big difference."

He stood, turning away from me and running a hand through his hair. "I know. But dark coding...it's different. The best way to support me is to stay out of this."

"It's way too late for that and you know it. Let's be perfectly clear, Slash. I'm not a novice. I've published four articles in the past year on this. I fully understand the dangers of black hatting. God knows I've skirted the edge enough times in my life. But Xavier is right. There isn't anyone else with our level of skill and knowledge of these particular circumstances to fight back. Sometimes, the dark choice is going to be the right one. If you choose this course, I'm coming along. You *need* me and you know it. Time is critical. Someone else is going to die if we don't stop the Red Guest right now.

It's likely to be someone else on your team. It could be you and I couldn't bear that. Please, it has to stop now."

I strode over to him and tugged on his arm, waiting until he looked at me. "Slash, look at me. I'm going to code with you. End of discussion."

He yanked me to him, putting his hands in my hair, his face in my neck. This hurt him, having to share this part of himself with me—a part he considered unclean. He held me tight without saying a word. I could feel his heartbeat against my chest. Finally, he pulled away, cupping my cheeks with his hands and studying my eyes.

"*Cara*, if this goes wrong…"

"It won't." I met his gaze evenly. "So, let's stop talking and get to work."

THIRTY-TWO

WE SET UP our respective laptops—Slash at the desk and me on one of the two double beds. Slash had obtained the required software we needed to get started using secret online channels. Using the software, we'd begun. Slash brought me up to speed with what he'd done so far and where he was headed. We had to borrow two additional pads of paper from the hotel concierge as we worked our way through a number of complex calculations. Soon papers were scattered across the desk and over the bed, spilling onto the floor. I had a pencil tucked behind my ear, one on the bed next to me and one on the bedside table to make sure I could find one the instant inspiration struck.

Malicious code was new ground for me. Even though the basics were the same, I'd never done it before. My emotions were running the gamut from disgust to a secret thrill. As much as I wanted to deny it, I was utterly pumped.

The attraction of the forbidden.

The power of the dark side.

I had to focus to keep it all in check before I started liking it too much. Slash hadn't been kidding when he said this kind of coding could change you.

Slash and I spent significant time discussing calculations and approaches before we'd actually started coding. We got so lost in our scripts before I knew it several hours had passed.

At one point, he stood and started pacing.

"What's wrong?" I said looking up at him from my laptop.

"I've hit a complication. I can't gain access to a critical military network. I haven't been able to compile enough information to detect or construct a pattern I can exploit. Without access, I can still inflict a serious blow, but they could recover. I've got to figure how to crack it before I can move forward."

"Need help?"

"Not at this point. I need to think it through. I want you to stay on your assignment. That's just as critical."

"Okay. But I need a break, too."

I set my laptop aside and stood to stretch. My fingers ached, my back hurt and my butt had fallen asleep.

I stretched my hands over my head and tried to touch my toes. "Ouch."

"You okay?"

"Just stiff."

I wasn't sure exactly how long we'd been working, but I think we were closing in on seven hours with just a few bathroom breaks and a couple of stops to brew more coffee. The last time I'd gone to the bathroom, I'd taken a quick peek behind the drawn curtains. It was a pretty day outside. Yet here we sat in the dark with our hearts and minds working on something even darker.

I rolled my neck, working out the tension. "Before you get thinking too heavily, you got a minute to look at something?"

"Certainly." Pushing aside some papers, he sat on

the bed and picked up my computer, setting it on his lap. I sat next to him, resting my chin on his shoulder.

"Start here." I tapped the monitor at the spot I wanted him to review. "I embedded this section into the official code. I need to know whether I should continue it within this node to increase security or if would that be too noticeable."

He studied it. "Can I see the full string?"

I pulled up another window and showed it to him. His brown eyes studied the code. Then without a word, he set my laptop aside and stood.

"What?" I looked at him in alarm. "Is it that bad? Does it totally suck?"

He ran his fingers through his hair. "No. It's good. Really good." He went over to the window and pushed aside the drapes. "Brilliant, even."

Thank God my coding didn't belong in the vacuous pit of suckitude. But I was puzzled by his reaction.

"If it's good, what's the problem?"

"It was…easy for you."

"Hey, that was *not* easy. I'm half-brain-dead right now."

He sighed. "I know. That's not what I meant. It just means you're a natural. I see where you're going and not only is it solid, it's clever." He returned to the bed and sat down. "But I'd end the string here." He tapped on the screen. "Begin a new node at this point."

"Here? Why?" I frowned. "How am I supposed to do that? Not all these nodes are online. Do you want me to improvise?"

He thought for a moment. "No. I know where to find more. Give me thirty minutes. In the meantime, can you run a scan and probe capability for me?"

"Sure. On what?"

"PLA Unit 61398."

"The Chinese military?" I stared at him. "Seriously?"

"Seriously. To be specific, it's the Chinese army. The Red Guest had a part in constructing their defenses. I want to get a feel for that defense. Probe the organization's firewall and find me a weakness or a uniqueness we can exploit while I pull up those nodes for you."

"No problem. But can I ask you something first?"

He lifted his gaze to me. "Of course."

"What if we don't use the code, Slash? Or don't have to use it. What happens to it? Do you turn it over to the NSA?"

He leaned back on the bed and blew out a breath. "No."

I lifted an eyebrow in surprise. "No? Doesn't the code technically belong to them?"

"Yes…and no. At this point, it's ours, *cara*. I'm not turning it over. They don't understand it. They can't. So either I release it or I hide it. I've built a fail-safe. I'll show you where, but you'll be the only one other than me who knows where it is. When we are done the code will reside there—hidden and protected—until the time is right to release it—if ever."

"Who exactly decides when the time is right?"

"I don't know. But I'll be the one who releases it. That's on me."

I wasn't sure what to think about that. But having a fail-safe backup and knowing where it was would make me feel a whole lot better.

He kissed me on the cheek and returned to his chair.

I poured myself some coffee and got the probe underway. While the computer started working, I sipped the coffee watching the data stream. "So, what exactly are Elvis and Xavier doing?"

"They're building the safety mechanisms."

"They can't plan for every contingency."

"I know. Let's just hope they are able to plan for the ones we need."

As promised, Slash delivered the nodes to me about thirty minutes later and we continued to work. Soon my eyes became blurry.

Slash shook my shoulder. "*Cara?* Wake up."

I blinked, looked down at the keyboard. "Huh? I was just thinking."

"For forty minutes with your eyes closed? Go to sleep. You did good work on the probe of PLA's firewall. I'm joining you shortly."

I glanced at the clock. It was already eight o'clock in the evening. Where had the day gone? Where had my mind gone?

He nudged my shoulder. "Go. We're no good if we're exhausted. We can't afford to make a mistake. I'm right behind you, I promise."

I considered arguing and then snapped my laptop shut. He was right. I was completely spent. It would be dangerous to code without my full faculties. I took a quick shower and brushed my teeth, drying my hair with the hotel dryer. Remembering what Slash said about staying dressed, I put my clothes back on except for my shoes. He saw me carrying them to the bed and shook his head.

"Leave your shoes off. I think we're safe for tonight."

"Thank goodness." It was the small things that made me happy these days. I crawled onto the double bed without papers and put my head on the pillow. I figured I'd wait for him to join me before I fell asleep but as soon as I closed my eyes, I was out.

THIRTY-THREE

I HAD NO IDEA how long I slept, but when I opened my eyes and saw the orange-and-brown bedspread, it took me a few seconds to become oriented. I was lying on my side and there was something heavy on my waist. I turned carefully, realizing Slash had thrown a blanket over me. Now he lay next to me, completely unconscious, his arm draped around my waist, and his nose tucked into the back of my neck. I wiggled out of his embrace, careful not to disturb him. I had no idea how long he'd been asleep and he needed a good rest.

For a moment I sat on the corner of the bed and stared at him. When he slept he was his most vulnerable. Now, he looked peaceful—a far cry from the man who could turn so cold and kill in an instant. Asleep he seemed defenseless and serene. He wasn't often like this. So far, whenever I woke him from his nightmares, he didn't want to talk about them.

Making sure the blanket was tucked around him, I rose and made a fresh pot of coffee with the last coffee packet. I poured myself a cup, adding sugar and creamer and, holding the cup with both hands, sat in front of Slash's laptop.

Studying his section of the code, it took me only about two minutes to realize he'd written something extraordinary. My breath caught in my throat. He'd come up with an elegant solution to the problem of cracking into the military network he hadn't been able to penetrate. Instead of focusing on getting in, he'd set a trap to identify and compile the information coming out. Brilliant. It was only a matter of time before he'd be able to spot and exploit the inevitable weak spots in the code. Once he had compiled enough information, he could turn it around and, boom, he'd be in. It required a bit more time than a straight crack, but I realized excitedly that I had a potential solution that might speed things up a bit on that front.

I read on. He'd already taken all the code I'd written and added it to his, weaving it into his beautiful string of complete and utter devastation. It meshed perfectly—two scripts, one mind.

I had no idea how long I sat there reading the code completely absorbed in the story. I scrolled on and on until I felt a hand on my shoulder.

"Well? What do you think so far?"

I jumped in my seat, feeling guilty I'd been caught peeking. I hadn't seen or heard him rise from the bed.

I shifted in my chair. "Slash, it's…magnificent." I looked up at him. "And, if I'm honest, terrifying. How did you even envision this?"

"You don't want to know."

"Actually I do."

He was silent for so long I wasn't sure he'd answer. Finally, he spoke. "My imagination, mostly, coupled with constant analysis and edit. And your coding inspired me to move in a direction I hadn't considered before. It fit perfectly. You have the most remarkable mind I've ever met, *cara*."

I felt the same way about him. Right now, though, I didn't want to dwell on the fact that not only had he dreamed up something as destructive as this code, but I'd helped him do it. More than that, I'd inspired him to go even deeper and darker. It made me more uncomfortable than I expected.

He put a hand on my shoulder. "For someone who has never written code like this, I'd say it was almost intuitive for you."

A part of me was flattered by his words while another part was appalled. I hadn't wanted to admit it to myself, but he was right. It was one thing to write defensive code while imagining all manner of invasions and penetrations, but it was a different beast entirely to code in a full-attack mode intended to cause widespread destruction and potential death. Yet my attack had felt... intuitive. What did that say about my inner character?

Unfortunately—or perhaps fortunately—this wasn't a time for inner reflection. There was work to be done. "I noticed one incongruence here, though." I tapped the screen. "What on earth are you doing in this spot?"

"Ah, you noticed that. I'm not done yet. I'm creating some special algorithms."

"It looks more like you're trying to calculate chaos."

"I am."

"You can't calculate chaos, Slash."

"Says who?"

"Says me." I narrowed my eyes. "There's no certainty in chaos."

He spread his hands. "Just the fact that there is no certainty *is* a certainty."

"That's *so* not an answer."

He looked at me with amusement and affection. "I've got this. I've actually got an idea—let me run with it. I'll show you when I'm done. Trust me."

I did trust him. I stood, went over to the coffeepot and poured him a cup, handing it to him black. "It's not the Italian roast, but it's all we've got. How long did you sleep?"

He scratched at the beard on his chin. "I came to bed right behind you. Mere minutes, actually, but you were out before I could even say good night."

"Sorry about that."

"No need to be sorry. It's been a hell of a few days."

"Speaking of days, that reminds me, I've *got* to do something about Basia's bachelorette party. I *really* need to make a phone call now. Is that okay?"

He looked like he was going to argue, but then he must have remembered his promise to Xavier that our activities wouldn't interfere with the weekend festivities. Of course, at the time he'd made that promise, he had no idea we'd be on the lam from assassins, the FBI, NSA and police. But one thing I'd come to understand about Slash is that a promise is a promise.

He walked over to one of the plastic bags he'd gotten from shopping yesterday and pulled out a burner phone, handing it to me.

"Who exactly are you calling?" he asked.

"Faylene's Bachelorette Parties and Supplies."

"Have you called the store in the past ten days?"

"Yes."

"Then you get to use this phone only once. More importantly, you'd better keep the conversation short. Short means less than four minutes. The FBI will certainly have her phone tapped."

"Really?"

"Really. Outsource everything to her and make it quick. Okay?"

"That's the plan." I was out of options.

He put on his jacket.

"Where are you going?"

"To buy more coffee packets and some breakfast food. I'll be right back. You know the drill. Don't open the door for anyone, no matter who it is."

"I know."

He pointed to the gun on the nightstand. "Use it if you have to."

"I will." I swallowed hard. "Just hurry back."

After he left I looked up Faylene's number on the internet and tried to plan my conversation so it would take less than four minutes. Finally, I took a deep breath and dialed the number.

"Hello, this is Faylene's Bachelorette Parties and Supplies. We do it all."

Thank God it was Faylene who answered the phone. I recognized the raspy voice. "Hi, Faylene. This is Lexi Carmichael. I'm sorry, but I'm in a big hurry, so I have to speak fast. I want the full deluxe package—or whatever it is you offer." I was so nervous all my sentences were all running together. "By that, I mean I want you to do and decide *everything* in regards to this party. Food, alcohol, entertainment and especially the centerpieces. I'm sure you are far more knowledgeable about these things than me anyway, so I'm putting it entirely in your hands. Just make sure it's all set up in time."

"Oh, hi, Lexi." Her drawl was thick and slow. "Are you sure, honey? Don't you want *any* say in the decorations or centerpieces?"

"None whatsoever. Please. Just go all out. Give me every bell and whistle. This has to be perfect. I want

Basia to have a totally unforgettable party. Can you do that for me?"

"Of course I can."

"Great! You're the best, Faylene." I gave her the location of the party, my credit card number for the retainer and hung up. After it was done, I felt as if a load had been lifted off my shoulders, even though I felt horribly guilty. I also had no freaking idea how much it would cost me. However, the fact that the party would go on, even if I didn't, made it totally worth it.

I dropped the burner phone in the trash and resumed coding.

Slash returned shortly with bagels, fresh coffee and fruit. The coffee smelled heavenly.

"How did it go with the party planning?" he asked, handing me a steaming cup.

"Easier than I thought it would. The call took three minutes and fifty-seven seconds and it's all taken care of. I hope."

"Excellent."

While we ate, Slash told me he'd received a message from Elvis. "What did he say?" I asked.

"He wants me to call him."

"Are we going to use another burner phone?"

"Yes, but we can use this one again. They'll be secure."

Slash dialed the number. After four rings Elvis picked up. Slash put the phone on speaker so I could hear.

"Hey, Elvis, it's me. Are we clean?"

"We're clean. No one can trace this call."

"Good. What have you got?"

"First things first." He paused. "Are you guys okay? How's Lexi?"

I leaned over closer to the phone. "I'm fine, Elvis. How are you and Xavier?"

"Good. We've been working hard. We're coding the hell out of the security shell for the dark code. I'm done with my part and Xavier is finishing up. Thanks to your earlier work and data, Lexi, I've been evaluating the two hacks into the NSA. I analyzed the style, methods and signature and cross-referenced them with the materials you provided, Slash, on the guys in your shop at IAD. I've come up with a plausible suspect for your mole."

"Bottom line?" Slash asked. He tensed, so I reached out to take his hand. I wanted him to know he wasn't going through this alone. It was hard for him, for all of us. When a hacker goes rogue, or worse, turns into an insider threat, it's a sick kind of betrayal, even if it isn't always personal. In this case, however, the mole's information had directly led to the deaths of several good people, caused serious injuries to others and had put us in the cross fire, as well. So, yeah, this time around it was personal.

Elvis exhaled. "You need to take a hard look at your vulnerability guy, Sam Nelson. His style matches the closest to those I've examined. He was careful, but I got an 87.6 percent probability. That's significantly higher than anyone else on your team I looked at."

"Sam?" Slash's fury was palpable. "Damn it. That can't be right."

"It doesn't look good, especially since that's not all I've got on him. Not surprisingly, everyone on your team, including you, Slash, has been under heavy surveillance since the hack. OSI is on to him, too. They have a surveillance photo of him with a time stamp that shows him in his home office talking on the phone about thirty-six hours ago. Problem is when they cross-referenced the home and cell phones of him and everyone in his family, there is no record of a call going out at that time. I double-checked them and it's good. No record whatsoever."

"He was using an unregistered phone," Slash murmured.

"Yes."

"That doesn't make him guilty," I pointed out.

"No, it doesn't, but Elvis is right." Slash's voice was tight, cold. "It's still suspicious. Where did you get the time-stamped photo, Elvis?"

"I hacked into the OSI database, of course."

OMG. Lines between light and dark were blurring all over the place. I was standing on shifting sand.

Slash stood, kicking the side of the bed. "They've got to be blackmailing him with something. I know Sam. This isn't political."

"It's always something," Elvis warned. "Whatever it is—watch him, Slash. That's all I'm saying."

I felt sick. My stomach churned from nerves, bad coffee and too much sitting around. "Did you have a chance to check out my analysis on the return path, Elvis?"

"I did. It led back to our Chinese friends, no surprise. I've determined a 99.4 percent certainty that whatever material was stolen from the NSA went back to the Red Guest. They are the guilty party here, no question."

"The final nail." The chill in Slash's voice made me shudder. "Good work, Elvis."

"The only thing is, Slash, I'm not sure it was sanctioned. It was shielded in a way that was not similar to other hacks in this style. I think they are keeping this private, even from the government bigwigs."

That was interesting. "That's pretty bold for Jiang Shi," I said.

"Well, technically we're doing something along the same lines," Elvis pointed out. "A black ops cyber mission. Although ours is officially *unofficially* sanctioned. Maybe it's the same on their end."

Slash shook his head. "Maybe, but I don't get that feel at all. The Chinese would certainly approve of such a hack, but not the end game. Not murder. This is a revenge quest."

Revenge. It was going to start a war between two countries with neither government having any control over it. Such were the times.

"Have you been able to tag Jiang Shi?" Slash asked Elvis. "What's he doing while he's here? Where's he going? Who is he talking to?"

I heard a whirring noise in the background at the twins' house—a printer probably. "Shi is being careful. From what I've been able to dig up, he's being watched by the FBI, but not to the extent you might expect. You've got to remember that following diplomats around is a sensitive business these days. Jiang Shi is on their radar, but they're not tight on him. They *can't* be tight on him."

"Well, we've got to know whose strings he is pulling." Slash rolled his shoulders. "He's the mastermind behind this, so we've got to believe he can lead us to Feng Mei."

"I'm in full agreement with you on that," Elvis said. "Which brings me to my next point. How do you guys feel about going to a party tonight?"

THIRTY-FOUR

"PARTY?" I ECHOED. "What party?"

"The Partnership for Cybersecurity Peace is having a black-tie affair tonight at the Chinese Embassy." Elvis shifted some papers around. "Here's your chance for a face-to-face with Quon."

"Are you nuts?" I jumped to my feet, shouting at the phone. "The Chinese are trying to kill us and you want us to waltz right into their embassy?"

I glanced at Slash for his support, but he remained silent. Apparently the opportunity didn't seem as completely insane to him as it did to me.

"Think about, Lexi," Elvis said. "They can't do anything to you in the middle of a party. They'll be the last to want to cause an international incident during a cyber peace conference. We have the advantage here. We know what Jiang Shi looks like, but he won't recognize you if you are in disguise. You can use this opportunity in two ways. The truth is right now Shi and Slash are the generals in this battle. It's time they met face-to-face to determine how far this is going to go. Maybe if Shi knows what's in store, he'll back off. It's worth a shot before we release the dark code."

Elvis had a point. A very good one.

"Even if we wanted to, how would we get in there?" My resistance started to weaken. "We can't just muscle our way past a bunch of Chinese security guards to see Shi."

"You don't have to," Elvis replied. "I've got an invitation for you guys. Your cover is Mr. and Mrs. Smith."

"Smith?" I repeated. "That's not cliché at all."

"It's actually legit. There really is a Mr. Ronald Smith who is an executive for the National Initiative for Cybersecurity Education, better known as NICE. You, Lexi, get to be Ronald's lovely wife, Emma."

"What about the real Smiths?"

"The real Smiths are temporarily out of the country in Sicily. Lucky them."

"No kidding. What if we run into any other NICE executives at this party?"

"I'll handle the conversation," Slash said speaking up for the first time. "We'll do it. I see where you're going with this, Elvis. Can you shoot the invitations my way?"

"You got access to a printer?"

"I'll take care of it. Thanks."

"My pleasure. It's coming your way shortly. Talk to you guys later. Be careful."

Slash hung up and looked over at me. "What are you staring at Mrs. Smith?"

"You do know there is a popular movie called *Mr. and Mrs. Smith*." I studied him. "It's about a husband and wife team who are spies."

"Really?" He lifted an eyebrow. "You don't say?"

He was enjoying the irony. In spite of myself, I smiled, too. "So, are we going to have to wear fancy outfits to this party?"

"I would say so. This is a black-tie event."

"Where are we going to get said outfits?" I did not

see how we would be able to go shopping for such outfits given our current situation.

As usual, Slash had it all figured out. "Ah, you'd be amazed at what you can find in a thrift store. I'll do all the shopping, no worries."

At least there was that. A silver lining in a sky of dark clouds. "This is all very James Bond-like. Tuxedos, gowns and an embassy party. I guess, as the guy, it means you get to be James Bond."

"Then you can be the delectable Honey Ryder."

"No way. I want to be Q."

Slash chuckled. "I'm afraid neither of us will be nearly as glamorous as either James or Honey. We're going in disguise. Remember? I'm going to be a middle-aged man and you are my middle-aged arm candy."

"Figures. I'm still going to be Q in my fantasy."

"We can work on that fantasy later if you want. I'll even let you try out your inventions on me."

A smile spread across my face. "Really?"

"Really." He swatted my bottom. "Come on, Q. Leave the fantasy for later. We've got a lot of work to do before tonight."

THIRTY-FIVE

I STARED AT my reflection in the mirror, peering closer at the crow's-feet Slash had created at the corner of my eyes. "Wow, will I really have this many wrinkles by middle age?" It was a fascinating experience to see myself age thirty years in a matter of a few hours. I wore a black, draped evening gown and some fake bling around my neck. The gown smelled, probably the scent of the previous owner. Seeing as how I had no washing machine and no time to drop it off at the dry cleaners, I did my best to ignore it.

My long brown hair was up in a bun and a pretentious fluffy white stole lay over the back of the chair. Slash had padded my butt considerably with some kind of funky underwear. I felt lopsided. I worried if I sat down too hard, the padding would shift and I would have a revolving butt.

Slash chuckled. "I gave you a few extra wrinkles just for fun. You're so pretty, I had to go overboard a bit to disguise you."

All the supplies and clothes Slash had bought had been thrift store finds or over-the-counter, but he had worked magic with the items at hand. I really looked about fifty years old. I turned away from the mirror, watching him as he added some padding around his stomach—giving him a wider girth—and buttoning his tuxedo shirt across it, holding it in place. His long hair was gray and tucked up and cleverly pinned to appear as if it was short. He had a thick gray mustache and matching eyebrows. I *knew* it was Slash and I hardly recognized him.

"Wait. You think I'm pretty?"

He looked up, surprised by my question. He slid his arms into a tuxedo jacket, buttoned one button around his middle with a bit of difficulty and strode across the room to me. He took both of my hands in his, his expression serious.

"You're the most beautiful girl in the world, *cara*." He pressed a kiss against the palm of my right hand while keeping his brown eyes on mine. His fake mustache tickled my skin. "Now and in thirty years."

His eyes were full of emotion. I had to clear my throat to remove the lump that had formed there.

"Well, you're not so bad yourself, James. I think you look quite distinguished with those gray streaks in your hair."

He smiled and leaned forward, this time carefully pressing a kiss against my lips so as not to mess up the makeup he'd carefully applied. I closed my eyes and kissed him, forgetting we were getting ready to undertake a dangerous operation inside the Chinese Embassy and simply letting myself feel cherished by a man I loved, but didn't always understand.

After a moment, he lifted his mouth from mine. "Are you ready for this, Mrs. Smith?"

"As ready as I'll ever be, Mr. Smith."

"Excellent." He slid the white stole around my shoulders, playing with it for a moment until it met his satisfaction.

We went outside and Slash hailed a cab to the Chinese Embassy. The cabdriver dropped us off in front and Slash paid him and got out first, extending me a hand to help me out. I resisted the urge to rearrange my butt and took Slash's arm instead. There were cabs lined up in front of and behind us with numerous well-dressed couples heading toward the lit-up entrance.

"Don't move so easily and quickly," he murmured in my ear as we headed toward the front steps. "Remember, you aren't twenty-five anymore."

My heart was beating in my throat, but Slash was completely calm and confident as we approached the entrance. My arm was safely tucked inside his arm, while his hand pressed against the small of my back, keeping us in contact. When we reached the steps, a man dressed in a tuxedo, with an earpiece and a cord snaking down his neck and disappearing beneath his jacket, politely requested our invitation.

Slash handed it over. The man took it and pressed a scanner against the small bar code in the corner of the invitation. After a second, there was a small beep and the man returned the invitation to Slash, who tucked it back inside his jacket pocket.

"Welcome to the Chinese Embassy, Mr. and Mrs. Smith," he said. "Please proceed to the welcoming line. We are pleased you were able to make it."

I would have responded with a thank-you, but his last words were perfunctory. He was already examining the invitation of the couple behind us.

I had a moment of panic when I realized we were going to have to go through a magnetometer. I tugged on Slash's arm until he bent down. "Where's your gun?" I murmured in his ear.

"At the hotel. It's okay."

I was thankful he was so calm because my heart was pounding. I put my purse on the conveyor belt and walked through the magnetometer. Slash followed without incident and we retrieved our personal belongings. I gripped his arm as we carefully climbed the steps and stood patiently in the receiving line that stretched out to the foyer to greet the Chinese ambassador and his wife. When we got close to the ambassador, another security guard requested our invitation.

Slash handed it over. The guy scanned the invitation again and passed it down to a woman standing next to the ambassador. She whispered something in his ear and he nodded. When it was our turn for the meet and greet, the ambassador bent slightly and shook Slash's hand.

"Mr. and Mrs. Smith," he said in accented English. "It is a pleasure to meet you. We are quite impressed with the ongoing activity of NICE and look forward to a lasting and fruitful cooperation between our countries on this very important matter of cybersecurity."

Somehow I managed to restrain myself from rolling my eyes as the ambassador shook my hand. I greeted his wife before being ushered by another man in a dark suit and an earpiece toward the coat check. After we handed over our coats, we were given name tags before entering the glittering ballroom.

Actually, glittering was an understatement. The entire room dazzled with sparkling chandeliers, large glass doors and gilded mirrors encrusted with crystals. Tuxedoed men and women in shimmering finery stretched as far as my eyes could see. I had no idea how we would find Jiang Shi in this crowd, but I kept my eyes peeled anyway.

A waiter dressed in a crisp white uniform offered

Slash and me a glass of champagne and some caviar. I took a champagne flute to give me something to fiddle with if people started talking to me. Slash declined both items, presumably to keep his hands free at all times.

Slash and I almost immediately got pulled into a conversation with a man who identified himself as Milton Hickman, a high-level cybersecurity official with the Department of Homeland Security. They were in the middle of a discussion about the Chinese efforts to fight corruption in the government and put an end to bribery, fraud and elitism among the ruling class.

"We applaud your efforts to streamline and clean up your house, so to say," Hickman was saying. "Now if only China would approach the issue of hacking with the same level of dedication, the problems between our two nations would be significantly lessened."

The Chinese official frowned. "I'm afraid making unfounded accusations is not only irresponsible, but unprofessional, Mr. Hickman."

"Which leads us to no progress on this front."

"I assure you, accusations and counteraccusations will not lead to a satisfactory resolution of the problem. China firmly opposes hacking. We have strict laws and regulations in place to prevent such activities from occurring."

Slash moved us on, but the exchange made me think. I wasn't naive. The US wasn't innocent by any stretch of the imagination—we were busy with our own hacking. Except I knew firsthand we played by legal and moral rules that China did not. Now that we'd been pushed against the wall, those rules were going out the window. We were going nuclear. What that meant in terms of the future of cyberspace remained unknown because we'd never gone there before. Once the bomb was dropped, so to speak, there was no pulling it back.

We continued to move about the room, Slash maneuvering me among the guests, his left hand almost always on the small of my back keeping me calm. We stopped a few times and chatted with people. Actually Slash did the chatting. I just stood and smiled, nodding my head on occasion. No one gave me a second glance, which was just fine with me. Since I didn't have to engage in meaningless conversation, I could actually do what we came for.

Find Jiang Shi.

Slash had stopped to speak with a Chinese man with a neatly trimmed mustache and sharp eyes. He identified himself as Liu Chunlin, Deputy Director of the Ministry of State Security. I smiled and tried to look invisible. It seemed to work because, after a brief nod of his head at me, Chunlin turned his full attention to Slash.

"So, Mr. Smith, what are your thoughts on the progress of cybersecurity between the US and China?" Chunlin asked. He inquired in a polite, perfunctory way, as if he'd been asking the same question to all the partygoers this evening.

"I think that's a difficult question," Slash answered. "Cybersecurity is a multifaceted concept. In many ways, it is not unlike the Cold War. Our countries— the clear leaders on this playing field—are reaching a level of hostility and belligerence that hasn't been seen in decades. There's an inherent danger in pursuing such deadly policies regardless of which side you are on."

His straightforward answer sparked a flash of surprise and interest in Chunlin's eyes. "That almost sounds like a warning. What might these dangers be, Mr. Smith?"

"Actually, I would enjoy hearing your suppositions first."

Chunlin took a sip of champagne and studied Slash and then me. "All right, then. Mass disruption, complete or partial shutdowns of the electronic highway, which in turn would mean a severe, if not complete, disruption in the supply chain resulting in food and water shortages. No electricity, no utilities, no functioning hospitals. Disease, death and eventually complete world chaos."

"Exactly." Slash nodded. "The cyber nuclear choice is a dangerous one. One that would be far more detrimental to the world than an actual nuclear bomb now that we are so tightly interconnected with one another."

Chunlin considered. "I'm in full agreement with you, Mr. Smith. Forgive me for being presumptuous, but it sounds like you are suggesting a policy of mutual assured destruction."

"It does, doesn't it?" Slash spoke mildly, but the significance of the words was not lost on Chunlin.

Chunlin assessed Slash thoughtfully. "So, then, what's your solution?"

"Cyber détente." Slash spread his hands. "A visible relaxation of tensions. We are both smart enough to know détente will not end conflict, competition or even confrontation between our countries, but it does offer us a less aggressive way to conduct our business with a shared goal as end game—mutual survival."

"Cyber détente," Chunlin murmured.

"Not such an unusual proposition. I assure you, there are still ways within this relaxation of tensions to pursue singular goals."

Chunlin stroked his mustache thoughtfully. "That's quite a thought-provoking analysis, Mr. Smith."

"Actually, it's fairly straightforward. I would go further to suggest you should keep a closer eye on certain cyber factions of yours that may be going places to which you aren't aware and may not approve."

"Factions such as…?"

"The Red Guest."

Chunlin visibly paled, but said, "I'm not familiar with this group."

He was totally lying. I'm not an expert on reading people, but even I could tell. His whole demeanor had changed and not for the better.

Slash tipped his head. "Just mentioning it."

Chunlin stared at Slash's name tag and then back at his face. "Mr. Smith, I would very much like to discuss this issue with you further. Will you be at the conference tomorrow?"

"I'm afraid not." Slash tucked my hand inside his elbow. "My duties take me elsewhere. But it was a pleasure making your acquaintance in person."

"In person?" Chunlin paused and stared at Slash. "We've met before?"

"In a manner of speaking." A smile touched Slash's lips. "Enjoy your evening."

Chunlin bowed slightly, watching us as we moved away.

"What the heck are you doing?" I whispered to Slash.

"Planting a seed," he murmured. "I'm not sure it will bear fruit, but I had the opportunity, so I took it."

"Okay, so while you negotiated world cyber peace, I found Jiang Shi." I nudged him with my elbow. "Straight ahead, to the right. The guy talking to the woman in the red dress."

"Good work," he murmured.

We moved closer and Slash effortlessly inserted us into the conversation. After a quick round of introductions, the woman in the red dress moved away, leaving just the three of us.

Shi looked bored and slightly annoyed that he was stuck with us. The way he watched the departing woman made me think we'd interrupted a conquest. Despite myself, I smiled.

Shi took a drink and glanced at Slash's name tag. "Mr. Smith. China welcomes the impact of organizations like yours on creating mutual beneficial cyber cooperation between our countries. The important strides we are making on this topic are of great interest to China."

Blah, blah, blah. He was spouting canned propaganda. It ticked me off more than it should have that he actually thought anyone at this party was stupid enough to buy it. In fact, Shi spoke so offhandedly, it bordered on rude.

"Important strides such as the recent hack into the TSA with Skylight?" Slash said pleasantly. "Or Mudsling at the DHS? Or perhaps we could discuss the multiple attacks on IAD and SIGINT at the NSA of late?"

It took a moment to sink in. Shi blinked and then stared at Slash and me in astonishment. After the initial shock subsided, he cocked his head. "Slash? Well, well. I'm certainly surprised to see you here."

THIRTY-SIX

"I UNDERSTAND YOU'RE looking for me." Slash spoke calmly although I could imagine he had vivid fantasies of smashing his fist into Shi's face. Those fantasies certainly played through mine.

"Indeed." Shi turned his gaze on me. "I presume you are Ms. Carmichael."

I didn't respond.

"Clever coming here." He glanced around the room. "Although I'm afraid it's not a good place for a productive dialogue."

"Depends on your definition of productive."

"Somehow I have a feeling our definitions would be at odds."

"You'd be right. I came here for one reason, Shi. A last chance. Call off your dogs or this is war. It's a place you don't want to go and something you can't stop."

"Your empty threats don't concern me." Shi snorted. "Your government doesn't have the stomach or the talent for a war of this kind."

"I wouldn't be so sure about that."

"You took my brother." He leaned in close, his teeth clenched. "Release him or you will be sorry."

"You shouldn't have sent Quon to get me in the first place," Slash said coolly. "That's on you…and the Red Guest."

"Where is he? Let him go."

"Why would I want to do that when he's being so co-operative?" Slash smiled tightly. "Have you considered that maybe he doesn't want to rejoin the Red Guest? Perhaps his older brother was a bit too controlling, too demanding. Couldn't see his real talent or let it shine through. We aren't making that mistake. We can offer him a lot more than you ever did."

"You're lying."

"Am I? Then how did I know about Skylight or Mud-sling?"

Fire flashed in Shi's eyes. "Does your government know what you're doing?"

"Does yours? Murder is pretty ugly business for a hacker. Especially when it involves high-ranking NSA officials. You were careless, Shi. You left a trail a mile wide leading right back to the Red Guest. I'd be excep-tionally worried if I were you."

"I don't know what you're talking about."

Slash waved an arm. "We're done here, Shi. I'll say it *one* more time. Back down or suffer the consequences."

"Don't you dare threaten me." He grabbed Slash's forearm. "I will annihilate you. Completely."

Slash looked at Shi's hand on his arm and then raised an icy gaze to Shi's face. Whatever Shi saw in it caused him to quickly release Slash's arm. I maneuvered be-tween the two men, pressing a hand on each of their chests.

"Gentlemen, not here," I said in a low voice.

A quick look around the room indicated the Chinese ambassador was looking our way and two Chinese se-curity guards with earpieces were heading toward us.

Shi stepped back. "This isn't over," he hissed and turned to walk away. "You're a dead man."

"Let's go," Slash said, taking me by the elbow. "We've got to disappear and quickly."

We collected our coats and walked out into the cool spring air. We'd gone partway down the sidewalk when we collided with someone in a trench coat and a fedora.

"Pardon me," the figure said and then whispered, "Take a left at the next corner and meet me on International Drive. I've got a car waiting. You've got at least one tail on you, possibly more."

"Elvis?" I murmured in surprise as he walked past us.

Slash yanked me forward and we kept walking in the opposite direction. I tried to spot our tail, but I didn't notice anything out of the ordinary.

"Act normal," Slash said.

"I *am* acting normal," I said.

"Then quit looking around." He pulled me sideways into a café. We passed through the tables and people sitting outside enjoying coffee under the lights and night air and went into the store.

"What are you doing?" I hissed, "Elvis said to take the next left."

"We've got company. I'm taking a shortcut."

I hadn't seen anyone, but apparently Slash had. We went right into the café and straight through the back, ignoring the yell of the astonished manager. Slash pushed opened the back door of the café and we entered an alley. His grip on my arm was tight.

We came out onto the street where he took a hard left. The next block up I saw Elvis standing under a street lamp.

"Hurry," Slash urged even though I was already nearly running to keep up with his long strides.

We crossed the street and were almost to Elvis when someone ran at us from a side street, taking us off guard and tackling Slash. I nearly went down with them, but I slipped off the curb and caught myself with a hand against the trunk of a car.

Slash was grappling with one of the Chinese security guys from the embassy. To my right, his partner ran toward us, yelling something and brandishing a gun. To my surprise, Elvis reached under his raincoat and pulled out something dark and elongated, hurling it at the figure.

The object hit the guy in the head hard and he went down without a sound.

"Get in the car," Elvis shouted at me as he ran to try to help Slash.

"Are you nuts?" I shouted and bolted after him. "When have I ever done that?"

As I ran, I glanced about for some kind of weapon. I saw what looked like a piece of tailpipe lying in the gutter. I grabbed it and ran back to where the three of them were now rolling around fighting.

I waited until the most opportune moment and swung the pipe like a baseball bat. The pipe connected with the Chinese guy's skull. He went down in a heap right on top of Slash. Elvis and I dragged him off, both of us panting from the excursion.

"Wow." Elvis looked at me in surprise. "Remind me never to piss you off."

"Noted and likewise. What the heck did you throw at that guy?"

"Nunchucks." He puffed out his chest. "I'm taking karate."

"Really? That was a really good shot."

"Thanks."

Slash rolled to his feet. He had a bloody lip and nose. "Let's get out of here."

We bolted for the car. Slash had just opened the driver's door when Elvis shouted a warning.

Slash and I whirled around. A man in a black jacket ran toward us with his gun out and pointed at Elvis. Before I could move, he fired.

It happened so fast I wasn't able to react. But Slash was already in motion. He threw himself in front of Elvis, taking the shot instead.

"No!" I screamed as Slash went down.

THIRTY-SEVEN

THE GUY WHO'D fired kept running toward us before coming to a screeching halt about twenty feet away from us. Elvis had a gun.

"Don't come any closer," Elvis warned. "I'll shoot you. I mean it."

Thankfully it was dark so he couldn't see the way Elvis's hand was shaking. I dropped to my knees next to Slash. My chest was so tight I couldn't breathe. I rolled him over, bracing myself for what I expected to see except... I saw nothing. No blood, no trauma, no nothing.

"Slash?" I said, patting his cheek. "Are you okay?"

He tried to focus on me but his eyes rolled backward and he went limp.

"Slash!" I shouted, shaking him.

There was no response, but he was still breathing. I pressed my hand to his neck and felt his pulse, strong and steady. I had no idea what was going on.

"Look, don't shoot me," the guy was saying to Elvis. "We're the good guys. I'm with the FBI. We're instructed to bring you in safely. No one gets hurt. Just put the gun down and come in with me."

My fingers brushed against something hard on Slash's side. I yanked it out and held it up to the light.

"A dart?" I shouted at the FBI agent. "You shot him with a dart gun?"

"I told you, we don't want to hurt you. We just want you to come in, okay? Let us keep you safe."

I set Slash down on the ground and stood. "Like you did at the safe house?"

"We won't let that happen again. I promise."

I took the gun from Elvis, pointing it at the agent with a lot more confidence than Elvis. In fact, I was pretty mad right now. Shooting him was totally on the table.

"Elvis, get Slash in the car and climb in," I said. "We're leaving."

"We'll find you," the agent said. "Don't be dumb, Ms. Carmichael. How far are you going to get without him?" He jerked his head toward Slash. "He'll be out at least twenty-four hours. Let us help you. You can't do this alone."

"I'm not alone."

Elvis looped his hands beneath Slash's armpits and pulled him into the backseat.

"Are the keys in the ignition?" I asked Elvis.

"They are."

"Good. Get in the back with Slash and buckle up."

A steadying determination and calm had settled over me. I had a photographic memory and I'd watched Slash enough times now to know the procedure. At least in theory. But sometimes theory was all you had until you put it into practice. No better time than the present to find out.

"Throw your gun behind you," I instructed the agent. "As hard and far as you can."

When he hesitated, I tightened my finger on the trigger. "I don't have a dart gun. These bullets will hurt. I won't kill you, but after I take out your kneecap, you won't walk for six months. Rehabilitation will be extremely painful. In fact, you may not ever be able to return to fieldwork. You'll be stuck behind a desk for the rest of your career. Your choice."

I hoped I sounded confident. Statistically, the odds that I could hit his kneecap at this distance in the dark with only a couple of shooting lessons were not high, but he didn't have to know that.

The agent tossed the gun behind him. I got into the car and started the ignition, peeling away from the curb and down the street.

"What are you doing, Lexi?" Elvis asked me from the backseat.

"Saving us, I hope," I said, taking a hard right. "Whose car is this? It's nice."

"It's mine," Elvis said. "I traded the pickup for this car yesterday."

"Great timing. Jeez. I hope I don't dent your new baby."

"No worries. I've got insurance."

We'd gone only a few blocks when I glanced in the rearview mirror and spotted a tail. FBI, Chinese or police, or who knew? It wasn't like I was going to stop and ask.

The black sedan screeched around the corner coming close to my back bumper, the headlights nearly blinding me in the mirror. They weren't even trying to be sneaky. I punched the accelerator and we shot around another corner, my tires squealing. Slash and Elvis were flung around in the back.

Adrenaline shot through me as I accelerated down a straight stretch of road before yanking the steering wheel to the left and down a smaller street. The sedan roared right behind me. It was clear I'd have to get creative if I was going to shake them.

I suddenly had an idea. I punched the gas heading for the spot I had in mind. Until we got there, I needed only to keep them on my tail and hope they didn't pick up any reinforcements. I'd driven this stretch of road many times and it *might* work if I could get the timing just right.

Two minutes, I thought. I just needed two freaking minutes.

I pushed hard on the gas, as we got closer to my destination. To my dismay, a police car fell in behind the sedan, lights and siren blaring. I had no idea if they were FBI reinforcements or just some random cop who was chasing the sedan and me for speeding. Either way, it was bad news. I'd just have to deal.

"Lexi, you got a plan?" Elvis asked from the backseat.

"I do. Brace yourself and Slash."

To his credit, he didn't ask for what. The object of my plan was just ahead. My breath was coming in hitches, my heart dancing a wild tango in my chest.

Hold the course, Carmichael. Think, plan, execute. You've got this.

I calmly calculated speed and velocity and adjusted accordingly. It was time to find my confidence behind the wheel. My earlier escapade with the Asian woman had taught me a valuable lesson. I needed to approach this as a mathematical problem like most of life. Calculate, concentrate and control. Still, my hands were slick on the steering wheel.

"Ready, Elvis?" I asked grimly.

"Ready."

We zoomed toward the curve. "Hold on tight. It's showtime."

THIRTY-EIGHT

AT ABOUT ONE hundred feet from my destination, I did a mental countdown in my head. On exactly the count of one, I jerked the steering wheel hard to the left and careened around a sharp curve. The car fishtailed slightly, the back wheels scrambling for purchase before they finally gripped the asphalt, shooting us forward.

The sedan behind us and the police car behind them weren't so lucky. They slammed on their brakes, but they were going too fast to compensate. Both cars slid off the road and into the ditch. I pressed on the gas and we sped away. I took several turns and twists until I felt sure we weren't being followed anymore.

As soon as I felt safe, I slowed down, willing my heart to calm down before I gave myself a heart attack.

It was silent in the backseat, so I adjusted the rearview mirror and dared a glance back. "Elvis, are you guys okay back there?"

"Where did you learn to drive like that?" Elvis said, his voice as shaky as a loose bolt in a hubcap.

I pulled off my wig and tossed it on the seat beside me. My hair was soaked with sweat. "Mostly from observing Slash. Today you can add in the desperation variable. It's a good motivator."

"That was...incredibly frightening. What now?"

"I'm sorry, Elvis. I can't take you home. They'll be looking for you, especially since it's likely they got the license off the car. You'll have to come to our hotel. I've got to finish the code and figure out how to track Shi. What were you doing at the embassy?"

"Watching out for you guys, of course. Good thing, too."

"Yes, it was. But you shouldn't have risked yourself like that."

"But it's okay for you to do it?"

Jeez. Now I sounded like Slash. What goes around comes around.

I pressed my hand to my forehead. "You're right. Thanks, Elvis. A lot. That's the appropriate answer."

"You're welcome."

"How's Slash?"

"Alive, but completely out. They must have shot him with some kind of heavy sedative. The agent said he'd be out at least twenty-four hours."

I glanced in the rearview mirror again. "I'll be honest with you. I'm not sure we have twenty-four hours. I have a feeling someone—either the FBI, the NSA or the Red Guest—is going to find us before that."

"I take it that means Jiang Shi was not receptive to the olive branch."

"He basically told us he was going to annihilate us."

"So much for détente."

"No kidding."

Remembering how Slash had checked for cars following him, I took several more detours before pulling up at the curb near the hotel. "Let's get him up to the room and then I've got to park your car somewhere away from this hotel and hard to find. I'm sorry, Elvis."

"I understand."

We got Slash out of the car and carried him between

us to a side door of the hotel. I had no idea how heavy he was in terms of deadweight. We struggled, mostly dragging his legs as we headed for the elevator. One curious female patron gave us a curious look.

Elvis shrugged and said, "My buddy drank too much."

Somehow we got Slash up to the room and onto the bed. We both sat for a moment panting from the exertion until I stood, scooping up my jeans, T-shirt and socks and headed for the bathroom.

"I'm going to change and then go hide your car somewhere."

Elvis nodded as he yanked Slash's boots off his feet and slid a pillow under his head.

I pulled off the dress and the padding before washing my face and pulling my hair into a ponytail. It was nice to look like myself again. In thirty years, I'd probably look back on this moment and wish I could do the same thing.

I came out of the bathroom and handed Elvis his gun back. "I forgot to ask—since when did you start carrying a gun and nunchucks?"

"About a month ago. They came in deadweight handy, right?"

Couldn't argue with that. "Right. You can fill me in later. For now, don't let anyone in."

I slid my arms into my black running jacket and took Slash's hotel key card, slipping it in the back pocket of my jeans.

"The black code is there," I said pointing at Slash's laptop. I rattled off the login and password info. "He's not done with it, but I think it's going to be up to you and me to take it across the finish line. But first, I want you to find Jiang Shi."

"How exactly am I going to do that?"

"At the party I noticed he's got a dWatch."

"One of those new digital watches?"

"Yep. See if you can hack in and find him."

"Excellent idea."

I went to him, wrapping my arms around his waist, hugging him hard. "Thank you, Elvis. For everything."

He hugged me back and then stepped away. We both looked down at Slash. He was still made up to look like a middle-aged man with the streaks of gray in his hair and the wrinkles on his face. He was breathing regularly, but his nose had dried blood crusted around it and his lip had swollen and was split on the left side. I needed to clean him up, but I had to hide the car first.

I leaned down and pressed a soft kiss on his forehead. "Don't worry," I whispered. "I've got this."

Elvis sat on the opposite bed, his elbows braced on his knees. "That's the second shot Slash took for me. He could have been killed both times, but he did it anyway. Who does that?"

I leaned over and brushed away a piece of hair from Slash's cheek. "He does."

THIRTY-NINE

I CHOSE A residential area to park Elvis's car. It was about two miles away from the hotel. I'd circled around until I saw a town house that looked like the owners were on vacation. A few newspapers were lying in the driveway untouched and there was only one light on in the house. I parked the car and jumped out, circling around the back to look inside the house. The kitchen was spotless, no dishes in the sink or on the table.

It was as good a place as any to leave the car for now. Tromping through the backyard, I spotted a folded-up tarp. I snatched it in a moment of inspiration. I drove the car along the curb and covered it with the tarp. It wasn't perfect, but would hopefully do the job for a bit.

Giving the tarp a final pat, I jogged back to the hotel and entered from the side door of the hotel again, using Slash's key card. Elvis was working on Slash's laptop when I came in.

"How did it go?" he asked, looking up.

"Fine. I parked it about two miles away in front of someone's town house under a dark blue tarp. Looks like they're on vacation. It won't fool anyone for long, but we only need a day or two." I handed him the car keys and he slid them into his pocket.

"Good enough, then."

I wet a washcloth in the bathroom and came back, sitting on the bed next to Slash. He was still breathing evenly and deeply, his chest rising and falling. I checked his pulse and it seemed normal.

"I think he's okay, but I worry about him becoming dehydrated."

"That's inevitable without an IV," Elvis said. "But we only need twenty-four hours. He'll be okay."

Although theoretically Elvis was right, it was still hard not to worry. Was any of this worth risking his life? I had only to remind myself that bringing Slash in, especially when he was this vulnerable, would be worse. I had no idea who might be able to get to him in the hospital while he was unconscious. As much as I didn't like it, this was the better solution. I dabbed at his lip and nose until his face was clean of blood.

"Elvis, I forgot to tell you not to use your phone. Did you?"

"I'm not stupid. I didn't. It's turned off. Don't worry. I got a message to Xavier in my own way. He knows we're okay. By the way, he's almost finished with his piece of the code. As soon as he's done, he'll shoot it my way and I'll add it to mine."

I exhaled a breath. "Great." I pointed at my laptop. "How's that going?"

"Well, I've started the hack on the dWatch. While that's been running, I've been reviewing Slash's code. He's really, really good, Lexi. It's both spectacular and twisted. What's in his head…man, I don't even want to know."

I didn't tell Elvis that part of the code was mine.

He continued. "I think Slash is probably the best wizard in the US right now, maybe even the world. This kind of talent across the board—it's pretty rare."

"Except for yours and Xavier's."

"No." He shook his head. "This is different, Lexi. Sure, I can write dark code if I have to, but not like this. Not with such…flair. I don't have the stomach or aptitude for it. This kind of mastery of dark coding is organic. You either have the skill or you don't. Slash clearly has it in abundance, which is why he's so good, as well as dangerous."

I stuffed my hands in my exercise jacket to prevent Elvis from seeing them shake. What had Slash said to me earlier?

"I'd say it was almost intuitive for you."

Slash had seen that in me—one coder to another. It hadn't been false praise. either. He'd been right. It had flowed out of me easier than I'd ever expected. I wasn't sure I wanted to know how or why it had been that easy.

I pushed aside that line of thinking for another time. "Can you access your part of the code from here?"

"Of course. But we have to finish what Slash started first. I'm just trying to get up to speed and figure out where he's going with it."

I put my hand on his shoulder. "You don't have to. I know where he's going with it. I'll do it."

Elvis looked up at me, surprised. "*You* want to finish coding this, Lexi?"

"I don't want to do it, but I can." I had no hesitation in my head or heart. At some point—although I'm not sure when—I'd made my peace with this, perhaps much in the same way Slash had.

"You'd be comfortable doing that?" Despite my confidence, he didn't look convinced.

"Not comfortable, but capable. Elvis, there's something you should know. He didn't write that code alone. Part of it is mine."

"Yours?" Elvis stared at me, giving me a clearer look into his blue eyes. "Lexi, are you sure about all of this?"

I wasn't sure if his question referred to the code, my life or something else entirely. At this point I wasn't sure it mattered.

"It's weird, but I'm sure, Elvis. Whether I like it or not, I've got the talent, too. But no worries. Despite my former escapades skirting the line with illegal hacking, I'm not going to give in to the dark side. So, abdicate, okay?"

He held my gaze for a long time before he finally rose. "It's all yours then, Dark Princess. I'll work off your laptop."

"That would be great." I sat, my fingers poised over the keyboard. "Thanks, Elvis. You're the best."

"No worries. You need anything, let me know."

"Okay. I will."

While he started our first pot of coffee in what promised to be a long, long night, I lowered my fingers to the keyboard and dived into the darkness.

FORTY

"I'VE GOT HIM." Elvis raised a fist in the air. "Yes."

I glanced up from the computer and the six windows I had open. My vision was blurry from staring at the screen. I'd been coding for hours. Calculations were strewed all over the room.

I set my computer glasses aside and rubbed my eyes. "Who's him?"

"Jiang Shi. He bought the watch four months ago in Beijing. Even better, he's got the Find Watch feature turned on so he can locate it if he loses it or it gets stolen. That's perfect for us because we can see not only where he is now, but where he's been, too."

"That's great news." My mood buoyed. I leaned back, took a sip of my stone-cold coffee. "We needed a break. So what do we know?"

"Well, it looks like Shi is staying at a rented town house on Connecticut Avenue, a couple of blocks from the embassy. He's been in and out of the Walter E. Washington Convention Center, presumably for the conference. However, he's spent quite a bit of time at a house on Upton Street in northwest DC, also not too far from the embassy. My initial scan marks it as a private residence owned by a Marcus Grover and rented, a month ago, to one Margie Chen.

"Who is she?"

"Well, my guess she's the Asian woman who's been after you."

"Feng Mei?"

"Possibly. She could also be an embassy employee, a girlfriend or someone completely random, although that possibility is low on my list. I'm going to cross-reference the list of Chinese Embassy employees to see if I can find her. If I come up empty, I'll see what I can pull up on Margie Chen from the DMV and other sources. It's definitely a thread to pull."

"Good work, Elvis."

"Thanks. How's the coding going?"

I stared at the string I'd just written. I hadn't had to think too hard about it. It was solid, even good.

"I'm not sure since I've never done this before. It's… a different kind of thing." That was an understatement, and Elvis knew it, but it was what it was.

"Want me to review?" he asked.

"Not yet. Soon. How's it going on your end?"

"It's going."

We worked for another hour and a half until I finally pushed back from the desk, exhausted, but exhilarated. "Okay, that's it for me. I can't go any further until I'm sure I'm on the right track."

Elvis tapped a few more keys and set the laptop aside. "I'm finished, too. Mine and Xavier's section of the coding is pretty much done except for a bit of fine-tuning. My head is pounding. I need some ibuprofen and whatever food you've got in those shopping bags over there. But first things first. I've got a hit on Margie Chen."

"Really? Excellent. Who is she?"

"Margie is bogus. All the data she provided on her rental application is fake. Margie Chen doesn't exist.

But—and you're going to love this—I've got a photo of her."

"How?"

"Well, as soon as she rented the house, she put in a top-notch security system, including external cameras. Unusual, right? Well, I hacked into the security system and caught her exiting and entering her own property. Want to see?"

"Oh, boy, do I ever."

He leaned over and brought up a new window. A minute later I was looking at a grainy photo of the woman who had met me in the hotel bar at HACK CON and then subsequently tried to kill me.

"That's her," I said tapping the screen. "One hundred percent certainty. That's Feng Mei."

"Well, then, we've got a lock on the assassin *and* proof that she has a connection with Jiang Shi." He pulled up another picture of Shi entering the house.

"That is such good work, Elvis. You're da bomb."

I stood and walked around in circles, swinging my arms and trying to get the blood flowing, before sitting on the bed next to Slash. I picked up his hand, pressing it between mine. It was warm.

"I wish I could tell him what's happening." I lifted his hand to my cheek.

"He'll wake up in a matter of hours," Elvis said. "He'll be proud of you, of course. He's got it really bad for you."

"You think so?"

"I know so." He looked down at his hands. "Can I ask you something, Lexi? It's totally unrelated to coding or the situation we're now in."

"Of course. You know you can ask me anything."

He thought, apparently formulating his question while I waited. Finally, he spoke. "How did you know that entering a serious relationship with Slash was... well, the right thing to do?"

His question surprised me, but I took a moment to answer. "That's the weird thing, Elvis. I can honestly say it's the first decision I've made where I led with my heart instead of my head. Not that I didn't have a list of pros and cons—I did. But in the end, I kind of just went for it. It felt right." I held out my hand for his water and he handed it to me. I took a drink and handed it back. "I knew Slash was a good man at the core, even with his flaws."

"Wait. Slash has flaws?"

I laughed. "By the way, speaking of love and relationships, there's a certain headmistress who is really into you."

"Really?"

"Really. I think she's good for you. If my door swung the other way, she'd probably be good for me, too. You might want to talk to her about how she makes you feel and where you want it to go. I think she could use a little clarification in terms of the level of interest you have in her."

"Really? How do you know this?"

"She might have mentioned it."

"When?"

"When I thought about asking her to help me plan Basia's party. Well, technically I wanted her to do the whole thing. But before I could ask, she told me you'd already asked her and she said no. She thought it would be good for you to organize and accomplish the party by yourself. Give you confidence. So I didn't even ask."

He sighed. "I'm worried Bonnie is too honorable for me. After all, here I am on the run from the FBI and NSA while supporting a black hat hack. Not to mention, a lot of my normal work involves breaking rules. Bonnie is all about rules and stuff. Those kinds of opposing forces could be relationship breakers. How do you and Slash deal with it?"

I lifted my hands. "I don't know, Elvis. We're making it up as we go along. Somehow we deal. It's important to both of us to find a way to work it out."

He raised an eyebrow. "You know, I'm pretty surprised you've been engaging in girl talk. I never would have thought it of you."

"Don't rub it in." I narrowed my eyes at him. "I mean it, Elvis."

He laughed and pulled me into a hug. The tension of the day eased. Elvis and I—we were good. We'd *always* be good, because that's the kind of friends we were.

FORTY-ONE

WE SWAPPED LAPTOPS and started our peer review. Two hours later I stood and walked over to the counter above the mini fridge where we'd set up our coffee station. I poured myself some coffee and drank it halfheartedly. It was burning a hole in my stomach.

Elvis looked up and decided to take a break, too. He stood, stretching his back. His hair was disheveled and his shirt had ripped during the fight with the Chinese guard. Exhaustion tugged at his eyes. For the first time I noticed the bruise on his chin. He must have been hit during the fight.

We were all hanging by a thread.

"I'm done with the review," he said. "Shall we switch laptops again? I really have no suggestions to fix anything. The code is damn near perfect. Seriously disturbing, but prime. I didn't know you had it in you, Lexi."

"I didn't know I had it in me either," I said. "But we are who we are."

"So, what do you want me to focus on next?"

I set my coffee on the dresser to consider. If I was honest with myself, I was exhausted from coding, worried about Slash, terrified we'd be discovered any minute, scared Feng Mei was plotting the murder of another NSA employee and not sure what the heck to do next. I did *not* have this field agent thing down. It sharpened my admiration for Slash a lot more than I expected.

How could he juggle all these options and choose the right one—often in a split second? Then he had to live with those decisions and the resulting consequences. Maybe the FBI agent had been right. I couldn't do this without him.

I glanced over at the bed, but Slash still hadn't moved. This was on me to figure out.

A noise came from the bed. Was it my imagination or had Slash moaned?

"Did you hear that?" Elvis said.

It hadn't been my imagination. I hurried over to the bed and sat down next to Slash. Gently I cupped his scratchy jaw with my hand.

"He might be coming around." I spoke more with hope than realism, but I didn't see the harm in positive thinking at this point.

Elvis reached out and patted Slash's stomach. "You know, he's got some special padding here around his middle as part of his disguise. The dart may not have penetrated as deeply as a result."

"Yes, and I pulled it out fairly quickly, too." My voice hitched with excitement. "How many hours has he been out already?"

Elvis glanced at his watch. "Just over nine hours."

Wow, had we been working that long? No wonder my butt throbbed and my wrists and fingers were sore.

I picked up Slash's hand and squeezed it. "Slash, are you there? Come on—wake up. We really need you."

He moaned clearly and I exchanged an excited glance with Elvis. "I think he hears me."

"Maybe. Keep talking to him."

I patted his cheek and his dark eyelashes fluttered,

but didn't open. "Come on, Slash. You can do it. Wake up."

I thought he might have squeezed my hand, but then it went limp. I swallowed my disappointment. "He's not awake yet."

"It's okay. It still means he's coming around and that's good." Elvis patted me on the shoulder. "In the meantime, you need to take the code across the finish line."

Elvis was right. The code had to take priority.

"Okay." I rubbed my eyes. They were gritty. "I'll fix us something to eat if you'll make more coffee. There are some bagels in the shopping bag along with a small first aid kit. We need fuel to keep us going."

We drank more coffee and ate dry bagels and apples while working. Another two hours had passed before Elvis suddenly spoke.

"Lexi, we've got a problem."

FORTY-TWO

I LOOKED UP from my code. "Why? What happened?"

"I just got a message from Xavier."

I stood and walked over to Elvis, leaning over his shoulder. "What did he say?"

"He's been monitoring your home server. He intercepted a message for you last night. It was heavily encrypted. He's been working on the encryption all night and just broke it." He looked up concern in his eyes. "It's from the Red Guest."

My heart skipped a beat. "They sent me a message? How does he know it's from the Red Guest?"

"They didn't try to hide where it came from."

My mouth had gone dry. I leaned closer to the screen. "What does the message say?"

"That's what's weird. It says 'a brother for a brother.'"

"What?" I stepped back, horrified. "What does that mean? Jiang Shi is threatening my brothers?"

"I don't know." Elvis had a worried expression. "I bet he thinks Slash can get his brother released in some kind of swap."

"Could he?"

"Possibly." Elvis considered. "As acting director of IAD, he carries a lot of weight with the CIA and FBI. But I doubt he would do it, just as I doubt the CIA or FBI would agree to a trade."

"Even if it meant the life of one of my brothers?"

"Good point. For you, Slash might circumvent procedure. Might even try something stupid and try to whisk him out of custody. Shi would know that—play on it. Can you call your brothers to check on them? Maybe it's just an empty threat."

I didn't believe that for a moment and the pounding of my heart confirmed it. Despite the fact that Rock's phones were certainly tapped, I called Rock's cell and home. No answer at either location. I tried his office at *The Washington Post*. Nothing.

Oh, God.

Heart in my throat, I called my brother Beau's cell. No answer on his cell, which wasn't unusual because officers have to turn off their personal cells when on duty. I called his office at the Baltimore PD, which was less likely to be tapped. After four rings, I heard his voice.

"Robbery. Detective Carmichael."

I closed my eyes. "Beau, oh thank God, you're okay." My voice shook.

"Lexi?" Beau heard the distress in my voice. "What's going on? Are Mom and Dad okay?"

"Mom and Dad are fine." I took several breaths to calm down. Hysteria helped no one. "It's Rock. When was the last time you spoke to him?" I swiped at the tears on my cheeks.

"Funny you ask. I tried to call him earlier this morning, but he isn't answering either of his phones. Why? Is he okay? Are *you* okay?"

"Can you keep trying to reach him, Beau? Please."

"Of course I can. Lexi, what's happening?"

"I can't explain it now. Just trust me. Try to reach Rock. If you reach him, tell him to stay somewhere safe. Also, it's important you stay at your office at the PD for at least the foreseeable future. Don't go anywhere alone. I'll call you back shortly. Don't call my cell, I don't have it."

Before he could question me further, I hung up, tossing the burner phone in the trash.

Elvis put a hand on my shoulder. "Are you okay, Lexi?"

"No. I'm not. I wish Slash was awake. This is a lot to handle. How does he do this kind of thing all the time without breaking?"

"I don't know. I'm sorry I'm not a bigger help. What can I do?"

I took a steadying breath. I had to hold it together. I had to think. Logic would save me now, not panic.

"You *are* a big help, Elvis. More than you know." Thank goodness I wasn't alone. I would have fallen to pieces. "Just stay focused on the safety mechanisms for the code, it's the final piece."

"What are you going to do?"

I thought for a moment. "I have an idea."

IT WAS A risk to make the call and I used our last burner phone, but I was 85 percent certain the NSA and FBI wouldn't have his phone tapped. I had to risk the other 15 percent. I located the number by secretly accessing my hard drive at home, then sat down on the edge of the bed with my back facing Elvis. I punched in the number. It rang five times before someone picked up.

"Who is this?" The voice was deep, male and curt.

I took a deep breath, steadied myself. "Hey, Hands. This is Lexi Carmichael."

Hands was a Navy SEAL and a friend. We'd been to hell and back on a recent mission for the US government in Africa. Our time spent together had created a special bond, the kind formed when people go through life-threatening situations together. Plus, he was an all-around good guy, even if I had no idea of his real name.

"Keys?" I heard the surprise in his voice. "I didn't recognize this number. How the hell are you?"

Keys was his nickname for me. He'd named me that because when I first met him I'd been working on my laptop, banging on the keys. I couldn't ever remember him calling me by my first name.

"This isn't my regular phone." I blew out a breath. "You got a minute to talk?"

"For you, Keys, I'll make time. What's up? You okay?"

"Well, I'm alive, which—as you well know—makes it a good day. Where are you?"

"I'm in DC visiting Gray. We were just talking about you. It would be great to see you again."

Grayson Reese was a CIA agent who had helped Slash and me bring down a cyber mercenary. The two of them had sort of hit it off during our mission and apparently had continued to see each other. I smiled.

"Yeah, I'd like that." I really meant it. "How's she doing?"

"She's as sexy and complicated as ever. Just how I like my women." He laughed and then paused. "Nah, she's good. *We're* good. Taking it slow, but steady. Neither of us is very experienced at this relationship thing, but we're giving it a go. She's pretty special. So, why are you calling? From the tone of your voice, I'm going to guess this isn't a social call."

"No, it's not." I wanted to word this carefully. "I need your help. It's a long story."

"Give me the condensed version."

I did, providing the necessary details, but leaving out any classified information.

He listened without saying a word but when I was done he whistled. "Wow, Keys, you sure know how to find trouble, don't you?"

"Other way around. Little black cloud. It finds me no matter how hard I hide."

He laughed and I was beyond thankful he hadn't hung up on me. Yet.

"So, what do you need?" he asked.

There was no easing into this. It would be better to be up-front, honest and swift. "I need you to check out a house in DC without attracting attention. Slash is still unconscious, so he can't do it. I think this leader of the Red Guest, Jiang Shi, might have taken my brother there, perhaps in an effort to conduct some kind of exchange. I need confirmation of my brother's presence, if possible, as well as intelligence on how many people are in the house. I know you've got the special equipment to do that."

"I do. You're sure you can't go to the authorities with this?"

"I'm sure. The NSA has a mole, the FBI has a leak and the Red Guest isn't playing by our rules. My brother's life is at stake here." I closed my eyes. It made me sick just thinking about it.

"Okay."

"Okay?" I opened my eyes. "That's it? Just okay? No more discussion necessary?"

"Your request is enough for me."

"I'll be honest with you, Hands. I'm feeling conflicted even asking you to do this. I don't want anything to jeopardize your career. But my back is against the wall. This is my brother."

"Shut up already. Just give me the damn address of the house."

Gratitude swept through me as I rattled it off.

"You got a picture of this brother of yours?"

I searched my mind for options. I didn't have my own phone or laptop. Where could I get a picture of him?

I snapped my fingers. "*The Washington Post* website. Look under the staff bios. He should be listed there with a photo."

"Roger that. Give me an hour. Lucky for you, I've got the next two days off. By the way, I have a permit to carry concealed, so I'm not going in empty-handed."

"Jeez. You're just looking through some windows, okay?"

"Okay. And these guys are just playing house with your brother. Just so we're clear."

I wavered between doubt and gratitude. I was asking a lot of him. Too much, but he still came through for me. "Thank you, Hands. I'm sure Slash would thank you, too, if he could."

"That guy sure has his hands full with you." He chuckled and then paused. "Lucky him. Can I call you back on this phone, Keys?"

It was risky to use the phone more than once, but we were out of burner phones and I was out of time and options. "Yes."

"Good. Over and out."

He hung up and I sat on the bed, closing my eyes and pressing the phone to my forehead. I was exhausted. Mentally, physically, emotionally. We desperately needed a break, something to go our way.

"Lexi?" Elvis spoke. There was a strange catch in his voice.

"What, Elvis? I swear I can't take one more piece of bad news." I stood and turned, tossing the phone on the bed.

Slash was sitting up on the bed, looking at me.

"Cara?" he asked in a soft voice. "What's going on?"

FORTY-THREE

"Slash!" I nearly knocked him over in a hug. "Oh, my God. Are you okay?"

He put an arm around me, steadied himself and blinked a couple of times. "Water," he said.

I went to the shopping bag and pulled out a bottle of water. I unscrewed the top for him. He took the bottle, gulping the water. I sat next to him on the bed, my hand on his thigh.

"How do you feel?" I asked.

He lifted the bottle from his mouth and massaged his temples. "I've got a wicked headache. I could use a couple of ibuprofen and a strong cup of coffee."

"Coming right up." Elvis stood and went to get them.

"What happened?" Slash asked me. He looked around the room. "We're in the hotel room. How did we get back here? My memory is a little fuzzy."

I gave him a quick rundown from the moment he'd been shot with the dart to my conversation with Hands.

He shook his head as if trying to clear it. "You evaded the FBI? In a car?"

"Well, I think it was the FBI. It could have been the Chinese or the NSA. I didn't stop to ask. There was also a police car chasing us, too."

He opened his mouth to say something and then just rubbed the back of his neck instead. "How long have I been out?"

I glanced at the clock. "Just over eleven hours."

"That long? Damn. The code?"

"I finished it. Elvis is adding the safety mechanisms and then it's done."

"You...finished it?"

I kept my eyes on his and nodded. "Yes."

Slash glanced between Elvis and me, but didn't say anything. Elvis handed him the ibuprofen. Slash swallowed them with another slug of water. He stood, swayed a bit. I stood and put a hand under his elbow to steady him.

"I think you should take it easy."

"No time for that." He took a sip of the coffee Elvis handed him. "When is Hands doing his reconnaissance?"

"Right now. Hopefully, he'll be able to let us know if Rock is there. I've got to call Beau soon."

"Can you hold off on that for a bit? I need a shower, more coffee and fuel before I can think clearly. What do we have to eat?"

"Our menu consists of some dry bagels, peanut butter, a couple of power bars and an apple. I haven't been shopping since you've been out. I can go get something fresh."

"No. That'll do. Give me fifteen."

"Are you sure you're okay?"

"I'm good." He finished off the water in his bottle. On the way to the bathroom, he bent over the plastic shopping bag and snagged another bottle. "Carry on."

The shower turned on. I began pacing as Elvis worked to finish adding the safety mechanisms. After several minutes, he stood and stretched.

"Okay. It's done. Heck of a job, Lexi. Seriously. I

never thought I'd say it, but you and Slash think alike. I couldn't tell where his code ended and yours began. True sorcery. It's going to make a heck of a boom."

I swallowed hard. "That's the idea."

"I guess it is."

My laptop beeped. I looked at Elvis. "What was that?"

Elvis sat back down, tapped on the keys. "It's a message from Xavier."

"What does it say?"

He read for a moment. "It seems like the NSA and FBI are funneling messages to you and Slash via Xavier. I presume they correctly deduced that since I'm with you, Xavier would know how to reach me."

Slash exited the bathroom in jeans and a T-shirt. He was barefoot. His hair was wet, his eyes clear and more alert. He rubbed his hair with the towel, looking a lot better than he had going into the bathroom.

"What's going on?" he asked us, tossing the towel in a corner.

"Xavier just sent a message," I said.

Elvis peered at the screen, reading. "Sam Nelson has just been arrested by OSI. Xavier just passed me the OSI report."

Slash leaned over his shoulder, reviewing the message, a frown on his face. "Damn it, Sam," he murmured.

Elvis tapped the keyboard. "Apparently they found an illegal offshore account under the name of his eldest son who is twenty-two. The son had no knowledge of it, but the OSI took the kid in for questioning anyway. Shortly thereafter Sam confessed."

"He was framed," Slash insisted. "He had to be. Just like Charlie."

I'd already scanned to the end of the report. I put a hand on Slash's arm. "He confessed, admitted he'd gotten himself into debt—one hundred and ninety thousand dollars' worth. He was facing immediate bankruptcy and his wife was threatening to leave him. He says he didn't know anyone would get hurt. I don't know what to say, Slash, except sometimes desperate people make bad choices out of fear and despair. Really, really bad choices."

Slash silently read to the end of the document and then stood, walking over to the window, pushing aside the drape and staring outside. Elvis and I remained quiet. I knew he was hurting, but I didn't have any way to ease the betrayal.

After a moment, he let the drape fall back into place and turned to face us. His expression was normal except for a slight tick of his jaw. "Did he finger the Red Guest as the source of the requested hack? I didn't see it there."

Elvis scrolled through the message and report again. "I don't know. It doesn't say. They want you and Lexi to call or come in. That's all."

"We're not doing that," I said resolutely.

"Agreed." Slash nodded. "Not yet. We've got other more pressing matters to attend to."

For the next hour or so, Slash ate and drank several more bottles of water while we updated him on everything that had happened while he was out. He was particularly interested in how we traced Jiang Shi to the house on Upton Street via his dWatch and where I believed Rock might be held, so we spent significant time examining the layout and location of the house via

Google Maps. We were examining the records on the house when my burner phone rang. It was such a startling sound, we all jerked our heads toward it.

I picked up the phone, punching the button to answer and putting it on speaker so everyone could hear.

"Lexi?"

"Hi, Hands. I'm here. What's up?"

"I have a visual on your brother at the house. He's sitting on a couch in what looks like a family room in plain view from a sliding glass door at the back of the house."

I let out a breath I hadn't known I was holding. "Oh, that's great, Hands."

"The house is fairly secluded with trees and a high wooden fence, so they don't seem too concerned about discovery and didn't even bother to pull the drapes."

"They have no idea we even know about it," I said.

"Well, I counted three men and a woman—all of Asian descent. The woman has long dark hair and seems glued to a cell phone."

"Feng Mei," I murmured.

Slash sat down on the bed next to me. "Hands, this is Slash. What can you tell us about her brother's condition?"

"Hey, Slash." Hands's voice perked up. "About time you got up from your nap. You good, man?"

"I'm good."

"Well, from what I can see, his condition is normal." There was a beep in the background and the sound of a faint siren. He was calling from his car. "He's tied up, though. Someone had to feed him. In terms of layout, there are a couple of outdoor security cameras, so it's likely they have an active security system. Good news is I didn't see any guards strolling the grounds. No overt evidence of weapons on the inside either, but I'd bet you a pricey bridge in London they're packing. Not a big party, but big enough. What's the plan?"

"You've done enough, Hands," I said. "Thank you so much. I don't want you involved any more in this mess."

There was silence and then a squeal of tires. "Don't piss me off, Keys. What's the plan?"

"You sure?"

"Keep talking like that and you and I are going to have serious words."

"Fine." I kept my eyes on Slash's when I spoke. "I've got an idea. It requires the involvement of my brother Beau and…all of us. It's risky, but it might work."

Slash leaned forward and took my hand. "Okay, *cara*. Let's hear it."

Taking a deep breath, I told them.

FORTY-FOUR

THE PLAN WENT into effect at dark. Since I wasn't on a regular sleeping and eating schedule anyway, time had somehow ceased to be relevant. Now it was just a matter of hours. Everyone seemed calm except for me. It was my plan, but I'd second-guessed myself at least twelve times before I talked myself into staying the course.

We had carefully reviewed the blueprints that Elvis had obtained of the house. Although blueprints of residences are typically impossible to locate, this house had been recently remodeled, so Elvis was able to find and hack the contractor's server in order to locate useful spec sheets providing us with a decent layout of the inside of the house. Hands had contacted Beau and brought him up to speed. Slash had made a few minor modifications, but essentially it was my mission. They had faith in me, so I needed to act like I had some in me, too.

Now it was game time. Elvis would stay behind to do his part. While Slash pulled on his jacket, I slid my laptop bag and purse over my shoulder. I turned and gave Elvis a big hug.

"Thanks, bud. I couldn't have done this without you."

"Yes, you could have." He hugged me back. "But I was happy to help."

When I stepped back from the hug, Elvis held out a hand to Slash. "Before you go, I want to thank you.

You took that shot for me. It's the second time you've done that. You keep saving my life. Thanks. I'm not sure why you do it, but I want you to know I appreciate it. I owe you big."

I saw the surprise flash in Slash's eyes. After a moment, he took Elvis's hand and shook it. "You're wrong, Elvis. You don't owe me. That's just what friends do, right?"

"Well, only *damn* good friends," Elvis said, but smiled. "But, yeah, you're right. Glad I got you on my side…friend."

I couldn't keep the smile off my face as Slash and I left the hotel. I made Slash wait at a spot nearby while I hoofed it the rest of the way to the house where I'd left Elvis's car. Slash wasn't happy about me going it alone, but he needed to preserve his strength for the mission.

Thankfully, Elvis's car was still at the curb under the tarp. I pulled off the tarp and got in the car. Remembering what Slash had told me, I took countersurveillance measures so when I picked him up, I was reasonably confident that we weren't being followed. Slash insisted on driving. We headed to our predetermined rendezvous spot keeping close to residential areas. When we got near, he parked the car along a neighborhood street and we hoofed it another three blocks before approaching our meeting spot in an empty parking lot near an urban elementary school playground.

Slash had me wait out of sight a block away while he circled the area twice to make doubly sure we hadn't been followed before coming back to get me.

"The van is already there with two occupants," he said. "I didn't see anyone else so I think we're in the clear."

"Are you sure you're up for this, Slash?" He seemed steady on his feet, but being out for eleven hours straight because of heavy narcotics had to leave residual side effects on even the most rugged and determined of men. Whatever they were, he wasn't showing them. He seemed solid and alert, but I knew better.

"I'm fine. How are you?"

"If I'm honest, horribly nervous. Here we go. Again."

"You've got this, *cara*." He kissed me on the top of the head. "Let's go."

As we approached the van, the passenger side door opened slowly and a hand extended waving us over. Slash took the lead, approaching the van, his hand beneath his jacket. When we got close, Hands stepped out of the van and I released a breath of relief. My brother Beau got out of the driver's side and strode over to greet us.

Beau enveloped me in a tight hug, "You okay, sis?" Concern and worry made his voice sound strained and tight.

"Not really." No sense in lying to my brother. He knew me too well anyway. "How about you?"

"Not so good either. But we're going to get Rock out safely."

"Yes we are. Thanks for coming, Beau."

Hands walked over and gave me a one-armed hug. The olive-colored duffel bag he had slung over his shoulder dug into my hip. "Hooyah, Keys. How's my favorite soldier?"

"Trying to hold it together."

"Welcome to the pressure of a team leader. My advice—embrace the power."

I knew he was trying to cheer me up, but my nerves

were jangling. I glanced over at Slash, but he had started a deep conversation with Beau, presumably updating him on the forthcoming operation.

Figuring I had a few minutes, I decided, perhaps foolishly, to broach a topic with Hands that might have been better left for another, saner time. But seeing as how my life never seemed sane anymore, I decided to throw caution to the wind and go for it.

I shoved my hands in the pockets of my jeans and kicked a pebble on the sidewalk. "Hey, Hands, this is kind of awkward, okay *really* awkward, but can I ask your advice about something?"

He was on one knee, pulling items from his bag and checking them. This brought back a sudden memory of our last operation together where he'd checked and rechecked everything. This comforted me, knowing that Hands was confident in my plan. I knew he'd leave nothing to chance.

"Sure." The easy way he said it made me think he expected an operational question.

I swallowed hard. "Um, it's not a question regarding what we're about to do. It's something totally different. It's about a person." I cleared my throat. "A guy."

He stopped what he was doing and looked up at me. "A guy?"

I closed my eyes. "Okay, fine. It's Slash. I'm trying to figure out something about him."

Hands glanced over his shoulder at Slash and then back at me. "And you're coming to me about this because?"

"Because you have to deal with this same kind of thing."

"Which is?" He frowned and stood up, brushing his hands off on his pants.

"Violence and darkness and keeping sane with it." I struggled with the right words. "It's hard to explain but sometimes, especially in dangerous situations, Slash turns into a completely different person. He can hurt people, kill them, without blinking an eye. When it's done, it's like nothing happened—he just moves on. How does he deal with that? And, as his girlfriend, how do I deal with that…with him?"

He took me by the arm, turning me away from Slash, lowering his voice. "Look, this is the first time I've ever met Slash in person, but it's clear from the way he talks and moves he's had some military or paramilitary training. In life-and-death circumstances, our training takes over. Completely. It's what keeps the people we are protecting and ourselves alive. At this point, it's as natural and instinctive to him as breathing. He couldn't turn it off even if he wanted to. It will be a part of him until he dies. It's a sacrifice people like Slash and myself accept as soon as we say yes to the service, be it the Navy SEALs or an intelligence operative. You'll either have to accept that as an integral part of him…or leave him because of it, Keys."

I was silent, thinking, so he spoke again.

"I'll say one more thing. You can't change this about him, so don't even try. His training, his reflexes, they are a part of him now. The hard truth is that it takes a special kind of person to love a man like him…like me. That may, or may not, be who you are. But let me give you a perspective from his side. When we do finally find someone who can love us—even knowing that dark side of us—that person is a treasure worth keeping."

Hands raised his arm at something over my shoulder. I turned around. Slash was waving us over. Hands slapped me on the back and picked up his duffel bag. "Speaking of single-minded focus..."

"I know, I know. Mission time."

"Don't worry, Keys. You've got this."

I wasn't sure whether he referred to the mission, the situation with Slash or both. I'm not sure it really mattered at this point.

"You've got the comm gear?" Slash asked Hands as we approached.

Hands opened his duffel and pulled out the equipment. Slash handed them to us and showed Beau and me how to insert them into our ears. We did a quick check, making certain we could all hear each other.

Hands spent a few minutes showing us how to work them, before putting a hand on my shoulder. "Perfect. You've got it down. Just like old times."

"This is little different, of course," I replied grinning.

"Of course." He laughed. "God, I've missed you. Bet you're going to like this. Just promise me no screaming or falling down."

Slash glanced at me and raised an eyebrow. "Obviously there are more nuances to your operational experience and technique than I was aware of. Perhaps you can fill me in later?"

I rolled my eyes, but it made me smile. They were putting me at ease, which I greatly appreciated.

Hands opened the back doors of the van and I hopped in.

I whistled. It was set up with the necessary electronic equipment I'd requested on a small card table with a folding chair. All it needed now was my laptop and brain.

"Excellent job, guys," I breathed.

"Your brother secured most of it."

"Hands and the Zimmerman brothers guided me," Beau said. "Couldn't have done it without them."

He pulled back a cloth covering a rack of additional equipment such as batons, ropes, flashlights, cuffs and other assorted boxes.

I glanced over at my brother. He lifted his shoulders. "Courtesy of the Baltimore PD."

"You checked this out?" I said in surprise.

"Not exactly."

I didn't want to know, so I didn't ask further.

I climbed in and inspected the equipment, plugging in some cords and making sure everything was properly connected.

"Your part is critical, Lexi," Hands warned. "We're relying on you to be our ears and eyes."

"Understood."

Slash looked over at Beau. "You've got the Tasers?"

I came out of the van to watch. Beau returned to the front seat and came back with three Tasers that looked more like guns and three fat rolls of duct tape. He handed one of each to Slash and Hands and then held up his own Taser.

"This X3 Taser series offers the highest takedown power available. The blast, which is fifteen feet, will temporarily override the central nervous system and can bring down a three-hundred-and-fifty-pound male with one blast. The stream hurts like a mother, though, so they'll scream like a baby while going down. There is also a stun gun backup, which means you can also stun on contact as needed." He pointed and then fired the Taser. "Perhaps most important, the X3 can fire three times instead of just once per weapon. This gives us nine shots to subdue everyone in the house."

Slash and Hands studied the controls, holding them out to get a feel for them. I climbed back into the back of the van and began running a check of my own.

After completing my setup, I called Elvis. He answered on the first ring.

"I'm ready," I said. "Take me in, please."

Elvis took control of my laptop and within two minutes I was inside the house on Upton Street's security system. There were five camera views. Rock sat on the couch, his hands were secured behind his back and his body anchored to the couch by a rope. A guy in a gray-hooded sweatshirt and dark pants sat comfortably in an adjoining armchair watching television. I was so relieved to see Rock alive, tears formed in my eyes. I took a moment to get control of myself, then took a thorough look through the rest of the rooms serviced by the security cameras.

When I finished, I went outside to report to the guys.

"Okay, we've got three guys and one woman, for a total of four, in addition to Rock, in the house as far as I can see," I said. "I don't have an angle into every room, so you're going to have to be prepared for contingencies. Right now the woman is in the living room with Rock and one other guy. They are watching television, but the woman is on the move, walking around and talking on a phone. There are two more guys moving around in the kitchen. Watch the woman. She's personally taken down at least one NSA employee, probably two. Good news—the house alarm is not activated. My guess is they set it when they are out or asleep. That should aid our access into the house."

Hands pulled out the diagram of the house and spread it out in the back of the van while everyone huddled around, looking at it.

Hands pointed to the kitchen. "Slash, Beau, you guys take the two in the kitchen. I'll take the two in living room, here, including the woman." He tapped on the spot. "Lexi, guide us the best you can so that we bring them down as simultaneously as possible. Trust me, as soon as the first person goes down and starts screaming a merry tune, the party will be underway. Everyone in the house will know we're there."

My heart was pounding, but I nodded. "Understood." I had to be calm for everyone. Right now, my two brothers, boyfriend and friend were all at risk if I didn't do this right.

Hands looked at me. "Are we ready, Keys?"

I steeled my nerves. This was my plan. These were my orders.

"We're ready. Let's go, team."

FORTY-FIVE

Beau drove us a block away from the house on Upton Street, parking along the curb across from the house and down the street a bit. Before exiting the van, Hands handed out SEAL night-ops masks. They weren't true masks, but they greatly reduced exposed white skin and made individual faces hard to distinguish. After a final communications check, Slash hopped out and slapped two magnetic cameras on the outside of the van so I could monitor street and pedestrian traffic. They headed for the house while I took position in front of my laptop in the rear of the van. I reviewed the cameras again, confirming the new exterior cameras were working, my eyes hopping back and forth between the views on my laptop, trying to keep track of everyone's movements.

I gave my first report as they approached the yard and hunkered down near some bushes. "There are still three in the family room—Rock, one guy and the woman. Rock is alone on the couch. The other guy has remained in the armchair near the back sliding glass door. The woman is walking around the room and still talking on her cell."

"Roger that," Hands said.

"There are two men in the kitchen. One guy is sitting at the kitchen table now. He's facing the opening into the kitchen from the living room and the back door to the kitchen. The other guy is doing something at the stove, probably cooking. His back is to the guy at the table. Both men appear to be wearing shoulder holsters, so I would presume they are armed. The kitchen back door is out as an entrance because of the guys in the kitchen and the sliding glass door entry is out, too."

"Okay, team," Hands said. "Given the location of the hostiles, looks like we're going to have to stroll in through the front door."

Oh, God, it was crazy that the front door offered the safest option, but there you had it. I swallowed hard.

"Should we knock or ring the bell?" Beau joked.

"Hilarious," Hands said. "Hey, hotshot policeman, you got that lock pick set handy?"

"Yes, sir," my brother answered. "Official law enforcement grade."

"Good. Lexi, confirm the alarm system is off."

"Confirmed."

"Let's move out, then," Hands said.

I held my breath, waiting for them to appear on the front door security camera. Moments later they streaked across the lawn and crouched down by the front door. Thankfully the porch light was not on, which gave them the barest shred of cover.

I checked all the security cameras to confirm that no one had changed location. No one had.

I heard a small clink and assumed Beau had opened the lock pick kit. Hands and Beau started whispering about which would be the best tool to use when Slash reached up and turned the knob on the door.

It opened.

"First rule," he whispered. "Check to see if the door is open."

Hands swore under his breath as I checked the camera view in the foyer. The area was empty.

"Foyer is clear," I said, but my heart took a dive. "I've lost the woman. Repeat. She is no longer in the family room or the kitchen."

I checked all the other cameras, but she'd vanished. "She might be upstairs or in the bathroom. It's hard to say."

The front door remained ajar. They waited there exposed. The chance for discovery grew greater with every moment they hesitated.

"We're going in," Hands murmured. "React as needed. Whoever finds the woman, consider her a target of opportunity."

I wasn't sure exactly what that meant, but apparently everyone else did, because they slipped into the house without another word. They disappeared from my front door camera view, so I switched to the foyer view. Hands peeled off to the right, heading for the family room, while Slash and Beau went left, slipping into the dining room en route to the kitchen.

I temporarily lost sight of everyone. Concerned, I rechecked all the views. Rock and one man were still in the family room watching television. The two guys remained in the kitchen—one still at the table and the other at the stove.

"There's still one guy at the kitchen table," I murmured. "Beware. He has a clear view of both entrances into the kitchen."

To my surprise both guys in the kitchen went on alert, as if they'd heard something in the backyard. The guy at the table stood.

"Uh-oh. The guys in the kitchen are on the move," I warned.

Worried, I checked the back door camera, but saw nothing in the yard. When I popped back to the kitchen view, both men were peering out the back window. It presented Slash and Beau with a clean entry and clear shots at their backs.

"Go," I ordered, but Slash and Beau were already in motion.

At that moment a scream came from the family room. My heart leaped to my throat as I switched over and saw the guy in the armchair was down and twitching. Hands was on one knee beside him, ripping off chunks of duct tape with surprising efficiency. Rock was untouched, although clearly terrified.

Screams now came from the kitchen. Both men were down there, as well, and Slash and Beau were working on subduing them with duct tape, but with considerably less effectiveness and a lot more swearing under their breath.

I examined the other cameras for the woman, but still nothing. She had to have heard the commotion. Where was she?

I kept my voice calm. "Still no visual on the woman. Remember she is armed. Take no chances."

I caught a sudden glimpse of movement in one corner of the foyer camera, but when I pulled up the full view, no one was in sight. I was about to say something when I noticed Hands had disappeared from the family room. Now, I had no idea whether the movement was from Hands, the woman, or someone else in the house we didn't know about.

I glanced back at the kitchen where Beau and Slash

were talking quietly while wrapping the feet of the last man. Suddenly, at the bottom corner of the camera at the entrance between the dining room and the kitchen, I saw an arm extend with a gun.

"Gun!" I shouted, just as the arm with the gun disappeared from view.

Slash and Beau whirled around, paused and then stood up carefully, facing the door to the dining room. I couldn't see what they could, but my imagination was filling in the blanks with the woman holding a gun on them and slowly squeezing the trigger, milking every amount of terror out of her victims.

Suddenly Hands stepped into the kitchen, dragging the woman by her collar. She was still twitching uncontrollably. He dropped her on the floor, nodded silently at the duct tape and disappeared again, presumably to make certain the rest of the house was clear.

Slash trussed her up as Beau stood guard. A minute later Hands returned.

He turned toward the security camera and gave me a thumbs-up with his gloved hand. "Mission accomplished."

"Good, finish it off," I said. My hands were still shaking. "Police have been notified. Their ETA is approximately two minutes."

Hands went into the living room and cut Rock loose from the rope tethering him to the couch and his cuffs.

"You're safe now," I heard Hands say gruffly as Rock stood on shaky legs. "Just stay here. The police are on their way. Tell them these folks were holding you hostage and threatening your life. You were rescued by some mysterious people you don't know, and who didn't say anything."

"How do I thank you? I don't know your name."

"No thanks necessary. Just make sure these guys spend a lot of time in jail."

"Trust me. That won't be a problem," Rock said rubbing his arms.

"Get out of there, guys," I warned. "You first, Hands. I don't want you anywhere near this place when the police arrive. Beau, follow him out."

Hands opened the sliding glass door and he and Beau slipped out, dashing across the backyard. Slash was about to follow when I gasped. A quick glance at the street view camera showed a car pulling into the driveway of the house. It stopped and the driver hopped out.

"Guys, we've got a problem," I said as calmly as I could. "Jiang Shi is here."

FORTY-SIX

HANDS SWORE SO loudly through my comm link, I winced. My thoughts raced. What should I do? Slash could take Rock with him, but that meant the people in the house who had kidnapped him would go free. On the other hand, if we left Rock behind, Shi might hurt him.

What should I do?

Slash hesitated at the sliding glass door. He, too, was clearly conflicted for the same reasons.

I made an executive decision. "Hands, get out of there. You, too, Beau. Proceed as planned. I repeat, do not divert from the plan. Slash, stand by."

I focused on the outside camera view. Shi had exited the car and was headed toward the front door.

Shi inserted the key in the lock of the door. I had exactly one second to decide what to do. Whatever happened, this was on me.

To my great relief, the solution abruptly presented itself as a police siren suddenly sounded from just a few blocks away. Shi paused trying to get a sense of the direction when it became clear that the sirens were getting louder. A few moments later, a police car squealed into the driveway, its lights spotlighting Shi at the front door, his keys still in the lock.

"Police are here," I said to Slash. "Go. Go. Go!"

Slash left, closing the sliding glass door behind him and disappearing from view. Rock yelled after him, clearly not recognizing Slash and thoroughly confused by the events going on around him.

At the front of the house, Shi turned in astonishment, blinking at the bright lights, as police jumped from the car shouting orders and brandishing their weapons at him. Shi held up his hands, anger and confusion showing on his face.

"Hurry up, Beau," I urged.

"I'm hurrying," Beau answered. I heard some huffing and puffing and figured he was running.

There was a noise at the back of the van and Slash hopped in and closed the door behind him, pulling off his mask and gloves and tossing his roll of duct tape in the corner.

He joined me at the laptop, peering over my shoulder.

"What's happening?" he asked.

"Two policemen have entered the house. They just encountered Rock. One of them is talking to him and Shi, while the other one is going through the house, checking things out and presumably finding the others trussed up like turkeys."

After another couple of minutes, the outside camera showed another car pulling up and parking across the street as the driveway filled up with cars and flashing lights. Beau hopped out, still obviously winded. He'd taken off his jacket, mask and comm link, so now he wore only a white T-shirt, dark jeans and tennis shoes. As he approached the house, a policeman got out of one of the cars and stopped him.

"Hope he's persuasive and can tell a good story," Slash said.

"He can."

We watched as Beau flashed his badge and started

talking. After a moment, the two of them entered the house and we followed them into the living room where Rock was still giving his statement to the other policemen. Beau and Rock hugged and I smiled. My two brothers were earnestly talking to the policemen when yet another police car drove up.

"And so the real party begins," I said leaning forward with a full-fledged smile as Slash put his hands on my shoulders. "Now we wait."

IT WASN'T SAFE for us to leave with so much police activity going on nearby, so we waited. I was glad because it let me keep an eye on Rock and Beau.

I called Elvis and put him on video. "Hey, Elvis, did you see what happened?"

"I sure did. I watched the whole thing unfold on camera, just like you. When I saw Jiang Shi drive up, I almost crapped my pants."

"Join the club," I said.

"Man, that was an unexpected variable," Elvis said. "Will his presence change anything about the plan?"

Slash had grabbed a bottle of water and now sat on a duffel bag, resting against the side of the van. "Absolutely. All kinds of US agencies must now get involved in the investigation, which actually turns out to be a stroke of luck for us. This situation becomes even more high-profile than we could have hoped for now that Shi is directly involved. It was a clever plan."

"Even if they won't be able to link him to anything that happened in that house?" I asked.

"Even then." Slash stretched his legs out in front of him. "I assure you, the fact Shi was caught entering the house won't go unnoticed by the Chinese government.

He'll have a lot of explaining to do, especially since we believe the Chinese government doesn't know most of what Shi is up to, including murder."

"What about Rock?" Elvis asked.

"Beau will fill him in on what happened later," I said. "For now the official story is that Beau received an anonymous tip about Rock's kidnapping and location. Since Beau happened to be in the area at the time of the tip, he alerted the police that he was on his way to rescue his brother. However, by the time he got to the house, he found the police already on the scene and all the kidnappers tied up and restrained. His brother, Rock, had apparently just been freed by a mysterious group of apparent do-gooders who must also have been the source of the tip to Beau. Rock will be able to innocently and accurately corroborate Beau's story."

Slash took a drink and lifted his water to me in a toast. "Even better, as soon as the FBI and NSA discover Feng Mei is involved—and I've already helpfully provided a tip to that effect—they are going to be all over this and, by extension, Shi."

"How can we be sure something will happen to Shi?" Elvis asked. "Given his skill, he has to be considered an asset by the Chinese government."

"Only if his usefulness continues to outweigh his liability," Slash said. "I wouldn't count on Shi coming out of this unscathed, especially after we destroy the Red Guest with the dark code."

I leaned forward in my seat. "Speaking of Shi…he's coming out the front door now. It looks like he's going to make a phone call."

Slash quickly rose to his feet. "Magnify," he ordered leaning over my shoulder.

I magnified the view as Shi raised the phone to his ear.

"Can you record the conversation?" he asked me.

I tapped a few keys. "It's recording, but we've got visual only. What's the point? We can't hear what he's saying.

"No, but we can read lips."

"Not helpful if he's speaking in Chinese."

Slash grinned at me. "We're the NSA, *cara*. We have an app for that."

We watched as Shi spoke, becoming increasingly furious. After a few minutes and several explosive hand gestures, he hung up.

"He probably called the embassy," I said. "Someone has to come vouch for him."

"I don't think so." Slash leaned over me and tapped on the keyboard, retrieving the file and sending it somewhere. "Either way, we're about to find out."

"How long does it take the app to work?" I asked.

"It's pretty fast. It is not always accurate, but you generally get the gist of what they are saying. Stand by."

After a couple of minutes, the results were back. I scooted over in the folding chair so he could have half of it.

He typed in a few commands and the file popped open.

"What's it say?" I asked.

Slash was silent for a moment and then spoke. "Shi is instructing someone to release a code against us."

"A code?" My eyes widened. "What kind of code? A black code?"

Slash raised his eyes from the monitor to meet mine. His expression was grim. "*Si*, and it appears we have one hour to release ours first."

FORTY-SEVEN

"WHAT ARE YOU DOING?" I asked Slash as he climbed to the front of the van and slid in behind the wheel.

"We're leaving."

"Is it safe?"

"We don't have any choice. We'll have to risk it."

I pulled up the front door camera. There was still a lot of police activity in the driveway, but the street was not blocked off and no one seemed to be watching the street.

"Okay. Let's do it. I don't see anyone who will stop us."

I pulled up video as Slash pulled away from the curb. "Elvis, are you there?"

His face came into view. "I'm here."

"Have you been listening?"

"I have. What do you want me to do?"

"Well, we've got to make sure the police can't track this raid back to us and we've only got one hour to release our code before they release theirs."

"Don't look at me to release the code." Panic crossed his face. "I don't have a clue where or how he intends to release it. Man, that's all in Slash's head, not mine."

"I know. Get started on erasing the security video starting about ten minutes before our appearance and up to just before Beau's arrival. Make sure to leave Shi's phone call."

"Ok, I'm on it. Shouldn't be an issue. All of the video is shipped off-site for cloud storage."

I peered at the monitor. "Slash, is there any way for us to release the black code from this laptop?" Even as I asked, I sincerely doubted it. The black code would require specific release architecture and protocols that were not present on my laptop.

Slash shook his head. "No. We've got to get back to the hotel room and quick."

Swallowing my panic, I turned to Elvis. "We're on the way back to the hotel. Assemble the code and do a final check, okay? It's got to be ready to go."

"Understood. Anything else?"

"Watch for any escalation or preparation for an attack. Pull in Xavier to help monitor."

"Got it." He clicked off.

I leaned forward, my hands on the back of Slash's seat, looking out the front window. "Is anyone following us?"

Slash glanced in the rearview mirror. "Not yet."

"Well, there's that at least."

"*Cara*, listen to me carefully. There is something I need you to do right now."

"What?"

"Get to the keyboard. You need to send a message."

I scrambled back to the chair, the laptop nearly sliding off the table as Slash took another corner hard. "Hey, take it easy. We almost lost the laptop."

"Sorry."

"To whom am I sending this message and from what account?" I asked.

"Get an anonymous account. I'll provide the email."

"An anonymous account is going to take time." I

blew out a breath of frustration. "Time we don't have. Not to mention, all I've got is a weak signal."

"Do your best. Just get me something."

I dived into the web, hopping around with the speed of a sloth until I finally had something to work with. "I've got something. Not perfect, but it should do."

"Is it traceable?"

Panic was combining with irritation. "*Anything* is traceable, Slash."

"You know what I mean."

"We're good for now. I can work on fixing it later. It doesn't really matter, does it? They will know you sent the message, right? Just give me the address."

He gave it to me and I typed it in.

"Now what's this message supposed to say?" I steadied the laptop as it slipped sideways. I was practically typing one-handed in order to keep the laptop steady.

Slash spoke clearly and deliberately. "We have indisputable evidence that in less than one hour, the Red Guest will release a malicious code called Nightfall. At this time the US has elected *not* to respond preemptively. That may change if action is not taken to stop this. We *will* respond to any attack. Do not doubt that we have the capability. This is one last chance at a stalemate and an understanding that the ability for mutual assured destruction is so terrible neither of us should use it. If Nightfall is released, it will be a cyber catastrophe for both countries, and by extension, the world. We do not have the luxury of time as we just became aware of the pending attack. If we don't hear from you within the next forty-five minutes or see any evidence of an escalation leading to an attack, we will respond accordingly."

I typed the final letter and then sat back, my mind reeling. We were teetering on the brink of cyberwar. History in the making in the back of a van with *my* fingers on the keyboard.

"Do I press Send?" I asked, my voice wavering.

"Immediately."

I sent it and then double-checked to make sure it went. "It's gone. To whom did we just send it?"

"I've been cultivating an online relationship with a certain Chinese official."

"That guy at the embassy? Chunlin? The one with whom you were talking about cyber détente?"

"He's the one."

"Wait. We're trusting *him*?" I sat back in stunned surprise. "You do understand that he is the Minister of Security. That means he's in charge of the secret police and does, you know, democratic suppression and all that."

"I'm well aware of that fact."

"Well, what if it's his *very* department that's financing the development of China's black code. He could be the money mind behind the very operations of the Red Guest. How can you possibly believe he's trustworthy?"

"I'm not certain he's trustworthy." Slash maneuvered forward, barely squeezing between a few cars that had pulled over to let us past. "But Chunlin isn't stupid. He understands the consequences of a war at this level. It's just a hunch. Sometimes you have to operate on faith."

"That's *so* not logical."

"True. But sometimes it's all you've got."

Before I could respond, we came to a screeching halt. I fell out of the chair, twisting my body so I protected the laptop that fell with me. My head clunked the side of the van.

"Ouch!" I sat up, rubbing my head. "That hurt. What happened?"

When Slash didn't answer, I scrambled to my feet and looked with horror at the line of cars stretched ahead of us.

A horrible, impossible Washington, DC, traffic jam. We'd never make it in time.

FORTY-EIGHT

"Oh, DEAR GOD," I said. "How are we going to get to the hotel in time?"

Slash slammed his hand on the steering wheel and let out a long stream of words in Italian. I was pretty sure he wasn't referring to kittens and unicorns.

Behind us I heard the wail of sirens.

"What's going on?" I asked.

Slash looked in the rearview mirror. "Fire engines coming up behind us. There's probably an accident ahead."

My mind raced. "Wait. Beau borrowed this van from the Baltimore PD, right? It's a *police* van. Quick, check under the seat to see if it has a portable flashing beacon light. Hurry. I'll look back here."

I started going through boxes when I heard Slash say, "I've got one. I think I know where you're going with this."

Slash rolled down the window and slapped the blue flashing beacon on top of the van. It was already spinning and flashing.

"I guess it would be too much to hope for a siren," I said.

"We won't need one," he said. The fire engines screamed as they got closer.

I leaned forward to the front seat so I could see the

passenger-side mirror. The traffic was pulling over to make room for the fire engines.

"Ready?" I asked him.

"Ready."

As soon as the fire engines passed, Slash yanked hard on the steering wheel, falling in directly behind the engines.

"It's working," I shouted as the traffic parted as we moved forward on the tail of the engines.

It took us seven minutes to get to the scene of the accident. As we blasted past the scene and shot forward, we got surprised looks from the police on the ground.

"Good thing they're too busy to follow," I said. "I hope."

Slash didn't answer. We raced down the street, weaving through traffic and turning down side streets so he could keep us moving. We kept the light flashing so people stayed out of our way and no police cars started chasing us.

Yet.

"Time?" Slash asked curtly.

I glanced at the laptop. "We have thirty-seven minutes left."

"Check the account. Anything?"

I pulled up the account from which we had sent the email. "Nothing."

We were still at least twenty minutes from the hotel. I called Elvis, using the video cam. "How's it going?" I asked when he popped up.

"What kind of question is that? I'm sitting on a nuclear bomb. I'm nervous as hell. When are you guys getting here?"

"We ran into some traffic. Is the code ready?"

"As ready as it can be. You do realize Slash didn't even have time to review what we did."

I swallowed. That was the truth. That meant he had to trust we did it right. If we didn't, the mistake would cost the world more than was imaginable. My mind raced through all sorts of doomsday scenarios until I shut it down. I couldn't dwell on that now. Strain was evident on Elvis's face. I figured I had the same look.

"Time?" Slash asked again.

I looked at the computer. "We have twenty-four minutes. Slash, we don't even know if the Red Guest is going to release it exactly on the hour or whether they'll just let it go whenever it's ready."

"We can't worry about that now.

"Any answer to our email?"

I checked and shook my head. "No. No response yet. Elvis, any evidence of escalation?"

"None that we see. We're in a holding pattern."

I glanced at my watch. "We'll be there as soon as we can. Stand by."

"Trust me," Elvis said. "I'm not going anywhere."

I clicked off. Slash had made good time, but it was going to be tight. He rocketed down the streets, going through red lights and stop signs. I closed the laptop, put it in its bag and looped it over my shoulder.

Within minutes we were coming up on the hotel. "I take it we are not going to park in the garage," I said.

"Hell, no," Slash said, turning the wheel hard, causing me to slide to the other side of the van. In the back, the folding table hit the side of the van and collapsed.

"You ready to hop out?" he asked me.

"I am." I glanced at my watch. "Seven minutes."

"It's enough if they don't jump the gun."

"I hope you're right." I squeezed the laptop to my chest.

He screeched to a halt. He'd pulled up to the curb near the hotel. I scooted to the back just as he wrenched open the door and extended a hand.

"Let's go," he said.

We dashed across the street and into the hotel lobby. I pushed the button, waiting impatiently for the elevator to arrive.

Just as it dinged its arrival, a voice said, "Don't move. FBI."

FORTY-NINE

I WHIRLED AROUND and saw Slash and an FBI agent pointing guns at each other. The agent was young, dressed in a jacket and tie with a shock of blond hair and flushed cheeks. Definitely right out of freaking college. His hand trembled as he held the gun on Slash, but he tried to look authoritative. He failed miserably.

"*Cara*, get on the elevator," Slash said in a calm voice.

I stuck out a hand to stop the elevator from closing when the agent shouted. "I said don't move."

"Here's the situation," Slash said evenly. "I could shoot you before you got a shot off at me. Even if you were faster on the trigger—which we both know you aren't—you can't shoot us both. You have to trust me when I say that we are in the middle of an important matter of national security. So, she's going to get on that elevator and you and I will have a discussion after she leaves. Do you understand me? Go. You know what you have to do."

I took a step into the elevator, bracing for a shot that didn't come. The elevator door shut and I pressed the button for our floor. My hands were shaking. As soon as the door opened, I sprinted down the hallway to our room.

"Elvis, open up!" I shouted, banging on the door. "Hurry."

The door opened and I ran past Elvis, tearing the bag off my shoulders and pulling the laptop out of the bag.

"Where's Slash?" Elvis said, looking bewildered.

"We've been had," I said putting my laptop on the table and opening it. "The FBI is downstairs. We've got to do this without him."

"What?"

I signed in and shoved my laptop at him. "We have three minutes at most. Check this email account one last time to see if we got a response." I rattled off the information so he could find it. "I'm going to send the code."

"You?"

"No, Kim Kardashian. Yes, me."

Elvis sat down, his fingers flying across the keyboard. My hands were shaking as I started the necessary protocols.

"Are you sure you know what you're doing?" Elvis asked.

"Unfortunately, yes."

We fell silent a moment, each working as quickly as we could to get things underway. My heart was pounding.

"Elvis, what do you have from the account?"

"It's loading slowly." He tapped on the keyboard. "The good news is that Xavier just reported in that there is still no evidence of any escalation or a launched attack. If they are preparing an attack, they aren't using any of their standard protocols. Just give me a minute on the email."

"We don't have a minute."

Someone hit the door hard. "FBI. Open up."

"Oh, no!" Elvis exclaimed. "They're here."

I finished the protocol and my finger hovered over

the send button. "This is it, Elvis. It's ready to go. Should I send it?"

The door crashed open. Elvis leaped from his chair to stand in front of me like a shield.

"Do it," he commanded.

Everything seemed to move in slow motion after that. Perhaps as evidence of divine intervention or fate, my laptop spun toward me when Elvis jumped up. On the screen—from the mail account where I'd sent the original message of warning—was an answer in all caps.

THREAT NEUTRALIZED. STALEMATE. STAND DOWN.

Holy Armageddon! Did I trust the message was legit or press Send?

The blood thrummed in my ears as the FBI agents crowded into the room with their weapons drawn. They were shouting something, but my focus was so insular I couldn't make it out. Elvis still shielded me and shouted something back.

Taking a deep breath, I made my decision. I typed the command to activate the fail-safe on the code and sent it into deep hiding before an agent grabbed me by my arm, dragging me from the chair and cuffing me.

Elvis's gaze met mine as he was forced down on the bed and cuffed, as well. "Did you send it?"

I gave him a weak smile. "Didn't have to. Apparently we came to a stalemate at the last minute. The world is safe for another day."

Elvis closed his eyes, relief washing across his face. "Damn, that was close."

"Isn't it always?" I answered as the FBI gripped us under our armpits and hauled us out of the room.

FIVE HOURS LATER, Elvis, Slash and I walked out of an unmarked office building together in northwest Washington, DC. Two FBI agents followed us at a discreet distance—Slash's regular detail. We headed for the underground parking lot where an SUV, on loan to Slash, was parked.

This was first time all three of us had been reunited since being taken into custody by the FBI. The FBI had just released us and we'd met up in the lobby, exhausted and drained. Slash told Elvis he'd drop him off at home and then Slash and I were headed to his place.

"Well, I'm glad *that's* over," Elvis said as we walked. "I can cross exhaustive questioning by agents of the NSA and FBI using good guy/bad guy techniques off my bucket list. That was seriously grueling."

"I suppose that's the idea." I rubbed my eyes. I, too, was exhausted mentally, physically and emotionally. "I'm just glad we're off the hook for now."

"You're sure we're off the hook?" Elvis asked. "Totally?"

Slash nodded. "We're still working through things, but essentially, *si*."

Elvis gave an audible sigh of relief and I patted his shoulder. "So, Slash, the Red Guest never released their code, right?"

"Right," Slash answered. "No blips, no escalation, no nothing. It looks like it was a true stalemate. It was a good call, *cara*."

"Technically, it was *your* call. It was just *my* finger

on the nuclear button, which I might add, was a totally nerve-racking place for it to be."

"Cool head under pressure," he murmured.

"I still can't believe your hunch was right." I blew out a breath. "It was a huge risk."

"More often than not, that's how diplomacy works." He tipped his head. "Just don't tell anyone."

I rolled my eyes. "How can you be so sure it's safe to return home?" I fiddled with the strap on my purse as we walked. "Do the FBI and NSA really believe we are no longer under a threat?"

"They do. They, and I, believe we have all the major players under wraps right now."

I trusted him, so I tried to relax. "So, what happened in the lobby with that young agent after I left?"

"Yeah, spill," Elvis said, pushing the glasses up on his nose. "When Lexi barged into the room without you, shouting the FBI had found us, I thought the world was ending."

"Well, it sort of was," I said, with a small smile.

Slash held out a key fob and pressed a button. A black SUV about four cars down beeped and flashed its lights. "Nothing much happened. I talked him out of getting himself shot before his reinforcements showed up. I would have taken him down if he shot at Lexi or me, but he was too green, too indecisive. I was counting on that. I was pretty sure he'd been told to bring us in alive. I also knew he wasn't alone, so I was simply buying us—you—some time without anyone getting hurt. Looks like the plan worked."

We'd reached the car. Before he opened the door, Slash paused with one hand on the side of the car and turned to look at us. Elvis and I stopped in our tracks.

He paused a moment, assessing us. "Before we leave here, there is something I want to say to both of you. You did well—better than well. There are only a few people who know what you did and sacrificed, and I'm one of them. Your work on the code, on everything, was nothing short of genius, as was your dedication." He leaned over and brushed a kiss on my cheek, murmuring in my ear, "I'll thank *you* later."

He straightened and turned his gaze on Elvis. "I'm not overstating it when I say the security sheath was spectacular, and your support of Lexi while I was incapacitated, invaluable. I don't know how to best express my deep appreciation to you, Elvis. So, thank you... friend." He held out a hand to Elvis.

After a moment, Elvis reached out and took it. As they shook, I threw my arms around them both so we were locked in a group hug.

"Hey, don't forget Xavier," I said, my words muffled by Slash's leather jacket. "He wouldn't be happy to hear we've excluded him from the group hoorah."

When we pulled back, Slash was smiling. "True. Guess that means I'll have to come up with a damn good wedding present for him."

FIFTY

I BRUSHED MY hair one more time, setting the brush down on the sink when I finished. "Slash, I think I'm ready," I called out. "How do I look?"

I glanced at myself in the mirror. I wore a black skirt, a shiny gold blouse Basia had bought me for my birthday last year and a knee-length black sweater. It seemed overkill, but I'd never been to a bachelorette party, let alone thrown one, so what did I know about the dress code? Basia had told me dressy and this was as dressy as I was going to get.

Slash walked in from the bedroom, dressed in a gray sweater and black jeans. He looked relaxed, happy and healthy. I caught a whiff of his cologne as he dropped a kiss on my cheek. He stepped back surveying me.

"You look stunning. You're sure there are no men coming to this party."

"I'm sure. Well, except for Junior, Faylene's son."

Slash narrowed his eyes. "He'd better not look twice at you."

I punched him on the arm. "You can ease up on the alpha male posturing. Junior is helping his mom with the party. I seriously doubt you have anything to worry about."

"I'd better not." Grinning, he walked over to the sink and picked up his toothbrush.

"How come you don't have to dress up?" It seemed

patently unfair that Slash could go to his party in jeans and a sweater and I had to wear a freaking skirt.

"We're men. Dressing up would be counterproductive to an evening that will certainly involve a lot of alcohol, minor debauchery and most likely cigars."

"Gross."

He laughed.

I leaned back against the sink and looked around the bathroom. "You know, this is a weird thing to say, but I'm going to miss this bathroom. Well, mostly the showerheads, but still. When is moving day again?"

"Next Wednesday." Slash put the paste on his brush and ran some water over it.

"Are you going to show me your new place?"

"Of course." He pointed the dripping toothbrush at me. "You, *cara*, are first on my list to see it. Actually, you are the *only* person on that list."

"I'm honored." I watched him as he brushed and spit. When he was finished, I asked, "So, did we ever find out what happened to Shi?"

Slash shook off his toothbrush before wiping his mouth on a towel. "He was questioned and released. Feng Mei was arrested on suspicion of murder. The others in the house are being held for Rock's kidnapping. The kid, Lin Yee, was arrested yesterday and is undergoing questioning by the FBI. Unfortunately, no one has pointed a finger directly at Shi yet."

"Not even Feng Mei?"

"Not even her."

I pushed off the sink. "She's afraid of him. They're *all* afraid of him. Or afraid of what he can do to their families."

"Undoubtedly."

"So, what's going to happen to Shi?"

"He returned to China last night. Not surprisingly, this has become a sensitive diplomatic matter."

"*What?* He got away unscathed?"

Slash met my gaze in the mirror. "He won't come out of this unscathed, *cara*."

"How can you be so sure?"

"I just am."

Slash returned the towel to the bar and took my hand. "Look, I don't want you to worry or think about it tonight. Tonight we are going to celebrate the start of a new life for two special friends and nothing more. Let's linger on lighter thoughts for the moment…like the party."

"What's light about *that*?" I exclaimed.

He chuckled. "It's too late to do anything but show up."

"I know. Don't remind me. I talked to Basia about half an hour ago. I'm stopping by her place in my rental car before I head over to the club."

"You're taking her to the club?"

"No." I shook my head. "I called a limo service for that. Her cousins are coming over and will go with her. I'm going to the club early to make sure everything is in place. Basia wanted me to stop by her place before I go to the club and everyone gets there."

"Why?"

"I have no idea. Probably some kind of weird girl talk."

"You're taking this all remarkably well." He tucked a strand of hair behind my ear. "But I know better. How are you really holding up?"

"Honestly, Slash? I feel like I want to throw up. This

hostess thing… I've discovered it's totally not my thing. In fact, I'm *never* going to throw a party again. Been there, done that and it's totally crossed off my bucket list. Not that it was ever there in the first place."

"You'll do fine. You've survived complicated rescue missions and saved the world. You'll survive a party, too."

"Then why am I totally panicking?"

He patted my shoulder, amused. "Basia will be among friends and so will you. Relax. I'm sure it will be memorable."

I sighed. "I sure hope so. Wish me luck."

FIFTY-ONE

BASIA FUSSED WITH her hair even though it looked perfect. "Remind me why we can't go to the bachelorette party together?"

"Because you'll be arriving in style in a limousine. Plus, I want to get there first to make sure all the decorations are in order. The limo will be here in about forty minutes to take you and your cousins, Jolka, Victoria and Katia. The others are meeting us at the club."

"Okay. I'm so looking forward to this."

"By the way, thanks for inviting Gray at the last moment. I just thought since Xavier had invited Hands…"

"Oh, please, not another word." She snapped open a lipstick and expertly applied soft pink color to her lips. "I'm beyond thrilled to finally meet Grayson. I know she played an instrumental part in saving Elvis's life, so I'm honored to have her at my party."

"You'll like her."

"I'm sure I will." She gave me a hug. "Oh, I love you so much, Lexi."

"Wait and say that *after* the bachelorette party, okay?"

"It's going to be perfect. I just know it."

"Honestly, I'd settle for satisfactory, but if you're going for perfect, I'll do my best."

"You are the best friend *ever*."

"Really?" I'd started to feel guilty I hadn't been more

involved in the party planning. "I just hope you won't—you know—grow out of our friendship."

Basia stopped fussing with her hair and turned away from the mirror. "Why would you say that?"

"I don't know." I struggled with the right words, feeling stupid. Why had I opened my mouth?

When I didn't answer, she walked over to me, putting her hands on my shoulders. Her head came up to my chin, but when she had that fire in her eyes, I felt a little afraid. "Lexi?"

"Never mind. It's nothing."

"Look, I'm getting married, not dying. I will *always* be there for you. There are many people who may walk in and out of my life, but you aren't one of them. You're here." She tapped her heart. "And here you'll stay. Got that?"

"Got it." I scuffed my foot against the floor, wishing I hadn't brought it up. But for some unknown reason, the words kept falling from my lips. "I guess I'll just miss having you around all the time, you know, telling me what to do."

She sighed. "You don't need me to tell you what to do. Just trust your heart once in a while and give that overcharged brain of yours a rest."

She threw her arms around me and we hugged. The moment seemed oddly bittersweet. I'd never fully understood or appreciated the importance of having a close female friend, but now it was starting to hit me. No matter how she insisted things would be the same, I knew I'd no longer be the first to hear her secrets or dreams or frustrations. She had Xavier for that now. Things were changing between us, much in the same way they were changing between Elvis and me.

Adapt and grow. Life kept pushing me in these directions. While it was hard to keep up, I was learning how to roll with it—at least a little.

"I'm sincerely happy for you, Basia." I stepped back from the hug and smiled. "I really am. Xavier is a great guy. He and I...well, we'll just have to figure out how to share you. I know you'll always be my best friend. But now, you'll be Xavier's, too."

FIFTY-TWO

I drove to the club, checking several times in the rearview mirror. No more FBI tail. I smiled. It felt…freeing.

I pulled into the parking lot of the After Hours Club. The sign in front of the club blinked in red, white and yellow. The parking lot was empty, so I pulled into a space in front. The lights were on in the club and Faylene had told me they would park their van in the back next to the kitchen entrance.

The club was finishing up some minor renovations that wouldn't interfere with our bachelorette party, but it meant we'd be able to have the entire club to ourselves for the evening.

The front door was unlocked. There was a coatrack near the door so I slid out of the new blue coat Slash had bought me and hung it on a hook.

"Hello?" I called out.

"Lexi?"

A woman dressed in a red flannel shirt, blue jeans and cowboy boots walked toward me. Frizzy gray hair, an unlit cigarette dangling between her lips and friendly brown eyes. She pumped my hand hard.

"Hi, I'm Faylene. Nice to finally meet you. I hope everything is to your satisfaction. It's been hard to get a hold of you these past few days."

"I know. Sorry about that."

I looked around. One large circular table had been set

up with a pretty yellow tablecloth. Ten plates, glasses, napkins and silverware had been set out. In the middle of the table was a lovely centerpiece comprised of yellow-and-red roses with some greenery surrounding a large orange candle. There were red gift bags at each place setting. One chair had a slipcover that looked like a princess throne. A gold crown with a white veil sat on the plate.

"Wow, the table looks nice."

"Glad you like it. Over here is the buffet." She led me to a long table. There were several silver-covered serving trays lined up. Underneath the trays were small burners to keep the food warm. I lifted the lid on one and sniffed.

"That smells fantastic. What is it?"

"Lasagna. It's my granny's recipe. Really yummy."

"Wow. I can't wait to try it."

I went down the table, inspecting the dishes. A few were empty, but others had garlic bread, green beans, salad, and macaroni and cheese. There were a couple of great choices for desserts, too. Chocolate cake, lemon squares and a whipped cream salad.

"Junior," Faylene shouted at a door behind which I presumed was the kitchen. "Where are my brownies?"

"Coming, Mama."

"Wow, this is really great." I spread my hands. "Thanks so much, Faylene."

"I'm happy it meets with your approval." She linked arms with me and steered me to the bar. "Now let me introduce you to your bartender for the night. Uncle Shine, you back there?"

A big man stood up from behind the bar holding a bottle of vodka in each hand and wearing a great big smile. "Right here, Faylene." He dipped his head in greeting. His cheeks were weathered and ruddy and his five o'clock shadow gave him a grizzled look.

"I want you to meet Lexi Carmichael. She's in charge of the party tonight."

"Technically, *you're* in the charge of the party, Faylene," I corrected. "But that's just semantics at this point."

"Hey there, Lexi." Uncle Shine extended a big hand and we shook. "We're going to have a great time tonight."

"I hope you're right."

"Of course, I'm right." He waved the bottle of vodka at me. "I'm the bartender, so what I say goes. Can I start you off early?"

"Oh, no thanks. I'm the designated driver."

I looked around the room. "So, what is the plan in terms of schedule?" Schedules always made me feel more in charge, more relaxed. They were linear, logical and planned. That worked for me.

"Well, as soon as the girls start arriving, have them hang up their coats and head toward the bar," Faylene explained. "Uncle Shine will get them started with a drink."

"Okay, that sounds good. Then what?"

"Then you eat. The food is ready. After that you'll play your first game. It's all set up over here."

She tugged on my arm, pulling me toward a wall next to the stage where she had hung a giant poster of a naked guy with dark hair, dark stubble and no clothes. There was a bull's-eye on his private parts. He looked oddly familiar...

Slash!

I gripped her arm in panic. "Where did you get this photo?"

She looked surprised. "Off the internet. There is a page with all these male fashion models. Between you and me, he's probably not into girls, if you know what I mean. I just blew it up and added the target."

I studied the poster closer. After a better examination, I realized it wasn't Slash. But it was a darn close representation. In the dim light, it was an easy mistake to make.

I pressed a hand to my chest, calming it. "Okay, fine. Tell me why is there a giant poster of a naked guy with a bull's-eye on his...thing...on the wall?"

"The game," Faylene said, tapping my shoulder. "Pin the Junk on the Hunk."

"What?"

She held up a red blindfold in one hand and a small bucket in the other. I glanced in the bucket and saw a variety of cartoon cutouts of a man's private part. I looked between the poster, the blindfold and the bucket and got the idea. Reaching into the bucket, I pulled out one of the cutouts and studied it.

"A hot dog cutout?" I said. "Really?"

"The bat with the two balls is my favorite," Faylene chuckled. "Although the cactus-shaped one is a close second. It's just a sexy variation of pin the tail on the donkey. Well, actually, there are sexier versions than this, but I thought this would be enough for you."

"No kidding."

"Anyway, this version involves putting the blindfold on the girl, spinning her around and pushing her toward the poster. Whoever gets the junk on the hunk closest to the target wins." She walked over to a nearby table and held up a gift bag. "Then the rest of the girls can take the cutouts home as a souvenir."

I shuddered just thinking about it. I totally didn't get the point of this game, but it wouldn't have been polite to say that, so I kept my mouth shut.

"So, you're running this game, right?" I said.

"Oh, heck no. This is your thing, honey. I'm behind the scenes in the kitchen."

"Jeez." I took breaths to calm myself. It was just a stupid game. I could handle it. "Okay. What's after the game?"

"There's more entertainment to follow, but your involvement on that will be minimal, so you can relax and enjoy."

I blew out a breath. "Thank goodness."

I started to relax a bit. Faylene did seem to have everything under control. The decorations were nice, Uncle Shine was settled in behind the bar and the entertainment was taken care of. I needed to take the anxiousness down a notch.

"Okay, Faylene, now what?"

She pointed at the door where Bonnie and Gray were just coming in. "Your guests are here. I suggest you go greet them."

FIFTY-THREE

I STRODE OVER to meet Bonnie and Grayson. They both gave me a hug and I introduced them to each other. They were already chatting so I figured they would get along just fine. I showed them where to hang their coats and sent them over to Uncle Shine at the bar to get started.

I went over to stand next to Faylene at the buffet table, knowing I was being a little clingy. Despite my fake confidence, I was terrified about being alone in managing things. She was fussing with the food arrangement.

"Junior," she yelled out. "Where are my brownies?"

A skinny guy in a red T-shirt, jeans and a backward baseball cap pushed open the swinging door to the kitchen with a tray. "No need to yell, Mama. They're right here." He passed by me and I sniffed. They smelled delicious. My stomach growled as he set them down near the other desserts.

"Lexi, this is my son, Junior. Junior, say hello to Lexi."

He pulled off his cap and smiled at me. "Hey, Lexi."

"Hey, Junior. Thanks for helping out."

Faylene put a hand on her son's shoulder. "Well, let's get going. We've got to get to the other party."

"Wait." A flicker of panic shot through me. "You're leaving? What other party?"

"The bachelor party, just down the street. He said you referred my services to him. Don't worry, Lexi. We're just going to help him get set up and we'll be right back. He said you were okay with sharing."

My eyes widened. "Wait. Are you talking about the bachelor party being run by Elvis Zimmerman?"

"Yep." She snapped her fingers. "That's the one."

"I thought you only did bachelorette parties."

"I know, but when he called, he sounded desperate. I figured a friend of yours is a friend of mine, so I decided to help. Besides, a party's a party, right? Now don't you worry about a thing. The food is all set up and ready. It's a serve yourself buffet, so no worries. Besides, Uncle Shine is here if you need something before we get back."

There wasn't much I could do and I knew Elvis needed the support as much, if not more, than I did, so I didn't protest.

Faylene and Junior disappeared through the kitchen, headed out the back entrance to their van. I peeked out the window and, sure enough, saw them driving away in a white van that said Faylene's Bachelorette Party and Supplies. Someone had written *and Bachelor* below the word Bachelorette in what looked like a black Sharpie.

I blew out a breath and turned away from the window just as more guests, including Basia and her cousins, walked through the door. Guess the limousine had arrived. Time to suck it up and be the perfect hostess, whatever the heck that meant.

I greeted everyone with a nervous smile and hug and provided instructions on what to do. It was too many women at the same time for my taste, but I smiled and tried to engage in appropriate small talk.

The bar got busy really fast. I had to give it to Uncle Shine. He had turned on a boom box with popular music, flirted and entertained the girls with the charm of an experienced bartender while deftly plying them with alcohol.

Basia oohed and aahed at the table setting and decorations. A few of the girls were pulling items out of their goody bags examining them.

"When do we get to eat?" Grayson asked, stuffing most of a brownie in her mouth. She had a drink in her other hand. "I'm starving."

"You're already pigging out," I pointed out.

"Oh, please. This is not pigging out. It's just a snack." She waved the remainder of a brownie in my face. "I'm talking about the lasagna. It smells heavenly."

I glanced at the bar and saw it was empty. Everyone who wanted a drink already had one.

"Actually, it's time to eat right now," I said. I grabbed a water goblet off the table and clinked a fork against it to get everyone's attention.

"Okay, everyone," I yelled. "Dinnertime. Please help yourself to the food. After we eat, we're going to, ah, play some games."

I was nearly stampeded as the girls rushed past me to get to the buffet line. Basia gave me a one-armed hug. She looked cute in the tiara and veil that Faylene had provided. Much more importantly, she seemed happy and satisfied with my efforts so far. "This is a great party, Lexi. Awesome. Thank you so much."

"Save the thanks for *after* the party," I said. "For now, just save me a seat next to you at the table."

"Done," she said, smiling.

FIFTY-FOUR

AS THE GIRLS piled food on their plates, I walked around making sure we weren't running out of anything. The lasagna was going fast. Jolka, one of Basia's cousins, asked if we had any Parmesan cheese, so I said I'd check in the kitchen.

I walked into the kitchen and came to a dead stop at the foot of a giant, hideous, white plastic wedding cake.

"What the heck?" I said aloud.

"Ta-da!"

The top of the wedding cake popped open and a young woman dressed in blond pigtails, super short jean cutoffs that barely covered anything and a tiny blue polka-dotted halter top fastened beneath her considerable breasts jumped out of the cake.

I yelped in surprise, staggering backward and falling over a trash can and onto my butt.

The girl who'd popped out of the cake looked at me in astonishment.

"Who are you?" she asked in a heavy Southern accent.

"Who are *you*?" I asked. "And how did you get in that cake?"

"I'm Billie Sue. Faylene is paying me to jump out of the cake for a bachelor party down the road tonight. I just got here so I thought I should practice."

There were many questions I wanted to ask, but one

seemed more significant than the others. "You have to *practice* jumping out of a plastic cake?"

"Of course. Timing is everything. Watch this." With a sweeping flourish, she yanked off her halter with one hand and her shorts with the other, leaving her naked save for a teensy-weensy red, white and blue thong.

"What the—" I said, my mouth gaping open in astonishment. "How did you do that?"

"Velcro. Cool, huh?" She put her shirt back on, fastening it beneath her breasts with the Velcro strips and then did the same with her shorts. "Looks like everything is in working order."

In spite of myself, I was impressed.

"Lexi?"

The voice came from outside the kitchen. It was Basia's voice.

Holy stripper!

I scrambled to my feet. "Billie Sue, stay in the kitchen, would you?"

"Excuse me?"

"Look, that voice you hear is the bride-to-be of the bachelor whose party you are headed to shortly. So, just wait here, okay?"

Billie Sue frowned, but stayed put. I ran out of the kitchen, nearly knocking Basia over. She was balancing a plate loaded with lasagna and garlic bread.

"What's wrong?" she asked.

"Nothing is wrong." She stared at me, so I smiled brightly.

Calm down, Lexi. A party planner is poised and in control. A calm hostess is a successful hostess.

"Look, Basia, I just want everything to go perfectly,"

I said. "But there's no Parmesan cheese. Sorry about that."

"It's okay, Lexi. Just relax. Everything is perfect, even without the cheese. Go get your food."

"Yep, I'm on it. But there is one more place the Parmesan cheese might be. Save me a seat, okay?"

I raced back into the kitchen. Billie Sue sat on a corner of the cake with her legs crossed. "That food smells good."

I pointed at her. "Why are you *here* instead of the bachelor party?"

"Faylene told me to meet her here." Billie Sue uncrossed her legs. "They didn't have room to take the cake and me on the last trip because the van was full. I don't go on until later in the party anyway, so they figured they'd just take me over shortly before I am up. Don't worry. It's not like I'm going to crash your party or anything."

"Good to know."

Still I didn't like the thought of her hanging around in the kitchen where Basia might discover her. I took out my cell and punched Faylene's number, but there was no answer. I left a message for her to call me.

I dialed Elvis's next. He answered after five rings. "Hello?" I could barely hear him over the loud music in the background.

"Elvis?" I shouted.

"Lexi?"

"Did you get Faylene to help you with your party?"

"Yes. Yes, I did."

"You *stole* my idea?"

"Shared not stole. I was desperate, okay? I figured you were on to something, so I jumped on the bandwagon. She said you ordered the deluxe package, so I did, too."

"Is she there now?"

"Yes."

"Well, tell her to get back here and get rid of the giant plastic cake in the kitchen. Basia almost saw Billie Sue."

"Who's Billie Sue?"

"The stripper that goes with the cake."

"I didn't order a stripper," Elvis yelled. I could hear the panic in his voice. "There was no mention of strippers."

"Lexi?" It was Basia's voice again outside the kitchen door.

"Oh, God, Elvis. Just tell Faylene to hurry, okay?"

I slid the phone into my pocket and came out of the kitchen with a fake smile plastered on my face. "Nope. Definitely no Parmesan. No worries, though. It will probably taste just fine without it."

She looked at me strangely. "Why are you acting so weird?"

"Me? Weird? This is normal for me in party situations. You know that."

She shrugged, probably figuring I had a point. "Okay, I saved you a seat. Come on."

"Great. Let me get some food."

I was the last guest to go through the line. There was hardly any lasagna left. We had totally decimated it. I put some food on my plate for show, but my stomach was in such anxious knots, I was pretty sure there was no way I'd be able to force anything down. At my request, Uncle Shine turned off the music so we could speak to each other at the table without screaming.

"Where's your drink?" Gray asked me as I sat and

then started laughing. She'd already plowed through half her lasagna. She looked completely toasted. What the heck was Uncle Shine serving them at the bar?

"I'm in charge of this party, Gray. I have to stay focused. Plus, I can't drink. I'm the designated driver."

"Designated driver? Are you kidding me? Basia told me we're all going to take the limo home. You included. This is a bachelorette party, Lexi. You *must* imbibe. It's the rule. I'll go get you the perfect drink."

It wasn't like I could stop her, so I watched as she staggered toward the bar. A few minutes later she came back with a drink.

"What's this?" I looked at the drink. It was green and actually smelled good.

"An apple martini. Shaken not stirred."

I took a cautious sip. "It's pretty good."

"Of course, it's good. Would I steer you wrong?" Gray tipped her glass to mine. "Good work tonight, my friend. You're sure to be voted Party Planner of the Year."

"I'm just hoping to survive the night."

On my other side, Basia nudged my arm. "OMG! Lexi, this is the best lasagna ever. Orgasmic. Who's the caterer?"

"A woman named Faylene. She's got a business doing these kinds of parties. She says it's her grandmother's recipe."

From across the table, Bonnie lifted a fork of lasagna to me. "Basia's right. It's heavenly. Great choice of menu. This is a fantastic party."

I felt some of the tension of the night unwind even if my stomach revolted at the thought of eating anything. "Thanks, Bonnie."

Everyone ate steadily while I pretended to eat and pushed the food around on my plate. I nervously kept watching the kitchen, hoping Faylene would magically appear, but so far, nothing.

Basia's cousin, Jolka, who seemed overly tipsy, suddenly stood up. "I'd like to toast the bride and wish her all the best." Her voice slurred and she burped, covering her mouth while everyone laughed. "May her days be fun and her nights filled with passion and a really, *really* big one."

Basia rolled her eyes and laughed.

"To you, my dear cousin." Jolka leaned over the table, giggling, her hand with the glass outstretched for a toast.

I saw the disaster a split second before it happened. Later I would look back and think I should have anticipated it, but I didn't. By the time I realized what was happening, it was too late.

FIFTY-FIVE

MY PHONE VIBRATED in my pocket just as Jolka leaned over tapping her glass against Basia's. Her white frilly blouse swayed and then dipped into the candle in the centerpiece. When she straightened, the blouse was on fire.

"Aaaagh!" she screamed, ripping off her blouse and throwing it to the floor.

As everyone gasped, Jolka's sister, Victoria, leaped into action. She snatched her vodka and tonic and threw it on the burning blouse. The fire surged.

"Oops!" she said. "I thought it was my water glass."

I snapped out of my trance and grabbed the first thing I could find at hand to beat out the fire. Unfortunately, the object, while big, was also light and plastic. I stared at it for a second, trying to figure out what it was.

Grayson, who was standing next to me, giggled. "It's a giant inflatable penis. It was in my goody bag. I *blew* it up. Get it?"

Holy party favor!

I tossed it over my shoulder and grabbed my water goblet instead. I dumped the contents of it on the blouse but the alcohol had made it too hot. I needed something bigger and heavier to smother it. I ran for the coat area, hoping Slash would forgive me. I yanked my new coat off the hanger and ran back to the table.

Uncle Shine already stood there. Apparently trying to be helpful, he had dumped an entire bottle of tequila on the fire. The fire surged again causing renewed shrieking.

I turned to the partygoers and shouted, "If one more person throws alcohol on the fire, I'll torch you myself."

Everyone backed off, possibly more afraid of me than the fire. I beat at the fire with my coat until it went out. There was no damage to the stone floor other than some blackening, but Jolka's blouse was a complete loss. I surveyed my coat and added that to the loss column, as well.

Sighing, I shrugged out of my sweater and handed it to Jolka.

"Sorry about the blouse," I said.

"My fault," she said, taking the sweater and slipping it on while Victoria found a safety pin to hold it together in the front.

Disaster averted. Sort of.

Where the heck was Faylene?

After a minute everyone started giggling about the incident. I was more than a bit surprised that no one seemed overly upset or worried. Instead, they just sat down and started eating again, chatting cheerfully like nothing at all had happened.

Ooookay. While I was glad everyone was taking it so well, something didn't seem right. Worried, I went to return to my seat when I noticed Basia's chair was empty.

"Basia?" I said, looking around. Where had she gone?

Basia came out of the kitchen pushing the giant plastic wedding cake on a moveable trolley in front of her. Billie Sue sat artfully on top of the cake. Thank God she still had clothes on.

"Lexi, who is this?" Basia asked me, a hand on her hip. "She just scared the crap out of me jumping out of this cake."

I sighed. "Oh, great."

"Just tell me you didn't get a female stripper for this party."

"I…ah…" I stuttered.

"Of course, she didn't get me for this party," Billie Sue said. "I'm practicing for a party down the street."

"A party down the street?" Basia blinked in surprise. "The Zimmerman party?"

Billie Sue examined her fingernails. "I can't answer that. It's confidential information."

Basia narrowed her eyes at me. "Elvis ordered a stripper for Xavier's party?"

"Well, ah, I don't think he exactly ordered—"

Before I could say anything more, the front door burst open and three firemen in full gear with duffel bags rushed in.

"Where's the fire?" the one in the front shouted.

"No, no!" I shouted, running forward and waving my arms. "Everything is fine. It was just a little accident. No one and nothing got hurt or damaged except for a blouse and my new coat."

The fireman in front nodded at me. "Oh, good. Glad you've got it under control. I was afraid we'd got here way too early. Are you girls ready to *hang* out?"

To my astonishment, the three firemen whipped off their coats. They were naked underneath except for teeny-weeny G-strings, fireman hats and boots.

One of the firemen pressed a button on his phone and music blared from a set of wireless speakers in his bag, complete with a siren accompaniment in the background.

"Let's get this party started," one of them yelled. "It's going to get hot in here!"

The girls, including Basia, apparently forgot all about the fire, the burned blouse, Billie Sue and the plastic wedding cake. Instead, they started laughing, screaming and circling around the firemen strippers.

I watched with my mouth hanging open. What in God's name was going on? Faylene had ordered fireman strippers? Really?

Worse, what had happened to the girls? They were all acting strange. It was like everyone had completely lost their minds. Or maybe this was a normal occurrence at a bachelorette party. It wasn't like I had any parameters by which to base a theory.

I glanced around the room. The life-size poster of the guy who looked like Slash stared back at me, amused. That reminded me that we hadn't even had a chance to play Pin the Junk on the Hunk yet.

If Faylene didn't get here soon, I was going to lose it.

A fireman danced over to me, presumably because I was the only one not screaming like a lunatic. He circled his hips at me. "Hey, baby, you are smoking hot. Want to check my hose?"

I winced. "Ugh. Really? That's the worst pickup line I've ever heard."

He grinned at me. "I'm burning up, babe. Be the fuel to my fire."

I was spared another *ugh* because the phone vibrated in my pocket. "Excuse me," I said, turning away from him and punching the answer button.

"Hello?" I pressed a finger to my other ear so I could hear.

"*Cara*, I've been calling you."

"Slash? I'm sorry I missed your call. There's been, ah…an incident. I'm sorry to report it involved the new coat you gave me."

"Forget the coat and listen carefully. Do *not* eat the lasagna."

"What? Why? The food is the one thing that's gone right tonight. What's wrong with it?"

"Let's just say it's not oregano in the secret sauce."

"What?"

He paused. "Do I hear a siren? Are people screaming? What's going on over there?"

I walked into the kitchen, which helped a little with the noise, but not much.

"Never mind about the siren and the screaming. What *exactly* is in the food?"

"Marijuana," he said. "A potent strain."

Holy lasagna! No wonder everyone was feeling so happy.

At that moment, Grayson ran into the kitchen, grabbing my arm. Her face was flushed and she was laughing. I tried to see if her pupils were dilated, but it was dark and she pulled me out of the kitchen where it was darker, so it was a lost cause. I tried to remember how much lasagna she'd eaten, but all I could remember was that it had been a lot.

"Lexi, they're setting up an oil pit," she screamed so I could hear over the siren and shrieking. "You've got to come see this."

Oil pit?

Oh. My. God.

Slash said something else, but I couldn't hear. "I've got to go, Slash. It's an emergency. I'll call you back later." I hung up and slipped the phone in my pocket.

By the time we ran out to the room, the firemen had already set up a small kiddie pool. It looked like two of the guys were going to wrestle each other while covered in baby oil. The third fireman had brought a chair for Basia and set it up right in front of the oil pit.

One look at Basia's face and I noticed something wasn't right. She looked…ill. Then I remembered the huge amount of lasagna she'd eaten and the fact she was so petite.

I took one a step toward her when the fireman started to grind out a dance in front of her. He wiggled, sashayed and danced to "Light My Fire." He had just started a lap dance when Basia threw up.

For a small girl, she fire-hosed that guy, thoroughly drenching him. He screamed like a girl and ran toward the kiddie pool, where the two oiled-up guys were fake wrestling and flexing their biceps. He took one step into the pool, slipped and took both of them down with him.

While I stared in horror, the three of them splashed and flailed around like fish out of water, trying to get away from each other. At that exact moment, the kitchen door swung open with a bang. I whirled around as Faylene and Junior stepped into the room.

"Oh, Faylene! Thank God you are here," I shouted, relief flooding through me. I took one step toward her, when a guy holding a gun to Junior's back followed them into the room.

I froze, my eyes widening in astonishment. "Who's that?"

Faylene didn't answer me, but she looked completely terrified. Junior wasn't looking so good himself.

"Turn the music off," the guy with the gun shouted at us. When no one heard him, he fired a shot in the air. The music abruptly stopped and the room fell silent.

The three firemen finally managed to stand in the kiddie pool.

The guy with the gun wrinkled his nose. "What the hell is going on here?"

I lifted my shoulders. "Ah…a party?"

He shook his head and then poked Junior in the back with his gun. "Okay, we're all here. Where's my stash?"

Junior jerked his head at the kitchen. "It's in my mom's oregano jar in the kitchen. It's in the large clear jar on the counter next to the stove."

The guy with the gun pointed at me. "You there. Go get it. No funny business or I start popping people. Keep your hands up where I can see them.

Keeping my hands up, I went into the kitchen. He propped open the door with his foot so he could watch me. I found the jar on the counter right where Junior said it would be.

It was a *big* jar—the size of a cookie jar. How much of the stash had been in the jar?

I handed the jar over to guy. He peered into it and frowned. "Where is the rest of it?"

Junior swallowed, his Adam's apple bobbing nervously. "I, ah, think my mom baked it into the lasagna."

The guy looked at Junior in shock. "You let your mom bake my stash into a lasagna?"

"Yeah, well, she thought it was oregano."

"Are you a complete idiot?" he screamed. "Wait.

Don't answer that." The guy waved the gun at me. "You, there. Go get me the lasagna."

I retrieved the lasagna tray and held it out for his inspection. He peered into the tray.

"This is all the lasagna that's left?" He glared at me.

I lifted my shoulders. "We were hungry."

"Exactly what kind of stash are we talking about?" Basia stalked over. She looked a lot better now, presumably because a good bit of the lasagna was out of her stomach. Somehow, she had miraculously escaped most of her own upchuck, but she was spitting mad.

"Are you saying you cooked something illegal in my lasagna?" She glared at Junior. "At *my* bachelorette party?"

"Marijuana," I supplied. "A potent strain."

"I'm *so* sorry." Junior looked at Basia pleadingly. "I panicked and dumped it in the jar. I didn't know my mom was making lasagna for the party. I didn't want to hand it over to Leo so he could sell it to the unsuspecting public, so I hid it."

"We *are* the unsuspecting public," Basia shouted at him.

"Oops." Junior swallowed hard. "Guess I bungled that good."

"How dare you!" Basia jabbed a finger in his chest. "You think it's okay to hide drugs in someone's food? Do you?"

Call it habit, instinct or just the result of a longtime friendship, but something in her voice didn't match up with her actions. On the upside, the guy with the gun didn't seem the least bit worried or intimidated by her.

His mistake.

"Well, I… I didn't think about that… I'm sorry," Junior babbled. He looked ready to cry.

"Don't give excuses," Basia said. "It isn't manly."

Her plan went down faster than I expected. Basia shoved Junior hard. He stumbled into the man with the gun who lost his hold on the oregano jar. As the jar flew through the air, I leaped forward, shoving the lasagna tray into the guy's face and twisting his arm, causing the gun to fall to the floor. Gray, giggling, kicked it across the room. I wrapped my arms around the guy trying to bring him down. But given that he and I were now covered in tomato sauce and cheese, he was slippery and hard to hold.

"A little help here," I shouted at no one in particular.

Two of the fireman leaped into action, jumping onto us, but it only caused us to crash to the ground and slide around the floor like greased pigs. No one was able to hold on to anything. As we slid across the floor, I shouted at Basia, motioning with my head toward Uncle Shine.

The bad guy managed to get to his feet and started running toward his gun. Basia, seeing where I was going with this, snatched the full bottle of whiskey Uncle Shine held in his hand. As the guy passed by, Basia clocked him in the head with it. He stumbled a couple of steps before I leaped to my feet and gave him a hard shove toward the open compartment of the plastic wedding cake. He fell inside and Basia slammed the top of the cake shut after stuffing his legs in.

"*That's* for crashing my party," she said.

At that moment, the front door flew open. To my astonishment, Xavier's entire bachelor party raced in, led by Slash.

"Cara?" he said, skidding to a halt and looking at me in horror.

I glanced down at myself. I was smeared with lasagna, baby oil and other stuff better not mentioned.

I spread my arms. "Regardless of how this looks, I'm fine, Slash."

The guys took in the scene with wide eyes—the kiddie pool, the naked and oiled firemen, Billie Sue and a giant plastic wedding cake upon which Basia now sat.

I just stood there covered in…stuff.

Junior retrieved the gun and gingerly held it out to Slash, assuming he was the police. "It's all a big mistake, Officer. I'm on probation. Leo gave me the stash to sell. I didn't want to do it, so I panicked and dumped it into my mom's oregano jar. I was just trying to hide it until I could figure out how to turn it in."

Slash took the gun from Junior and turned his gaze to mine. "Who is Leo?" he asked.

"The drug dealer in the wedding cake." I jerked my head toward the cake. "You don't happen to have cuffs on you, do you?"

Slash looked like he was trying to figure out what to say next when he saw the giant-sized poster of the naked guy that looked remarkably like him. "What's that?"

"Don't ask," I said, holding up a hand. "Please. Just don't. I'm not sure the night could get any weirder. I need a napkin stat."

I headed toward the kitchen and froze when I heard the shouting.

"Police! Everyone get your hands up and get facedown on the floor. Now!"

I turned around, meeting the determined gaze of two policemen who stood in the doorway aiming their service weapons at us. I glanced at Slash as he rolled his eyes and dropped the gun he was holding. He raised his hands above his head and knelt down.

Gray, however, swayed on her feet, giggling and waving at the policemen. "Oh, hey, Officers, come on in and join the party. Are you going to strip, too? You guys are soooo cute. You can arrest me anytime. God, I'm hungry." She winked at them and then promptly toppled over.

Hands caught her before she hit the ground.

I knelt to the floor with my hands up. "I didn't think it could happen, but things just got a lot weirder."

FIFTY-SIX

WE TOOK UP the entire waiting room at the police station. A couple of officers had to go get more chairs so we could all fit. An hour and a half later we'd all been interviewed, except for Basia, who was in the room now. They were supposedly wrapping up our paperwork so we could go home.

I sat smelling like garlic, lasagna and baby oil, drinking a horrible cup of coffee while sitting on a bench between Elvis and Slash. I'd cleaned up the best I could in the bathroom, but it didn't take the place of a full-fledged shower and a washing machine. Bonnie sat next to Elvis. It made me smile when I saw them holding hands. She shot me a grateful look and I smiled back. I saw that friendship going places and it made me happy. I leaned back against the faded blue wall of the station when Elvis got up to use the facilities.

I turned my head toward Slash. "You didn't tell me yet how you knew about the pot."

He had also leaned back against the wall, his eyes closed. He cracked open one eye when I spoke. "When they were setting up I smelled it on Junior. I'm sure he sampled a bit before or during his baking duties, but I'm reluctant to admit it didn't occur to me that he would have baked any into the food until I tasted it."

"Wait. How could you taste the pot in the lasagna?"

"I'm Italian." He spread his hands. "I know my lasagna."

He had a point.

"When I called you, I heard the siren in the background and figured the police might be headed your way. I wanted to come alone, but these guys insisted they come with me. I had no idea there was a guy with a gun who had co-opted Junior and Faylene or that you and Basia would be so successful at handling him on your own."

"There's no stopping Basia these days. Seriously. I was just along for the ride."

"I'm not so sure about that." He grinned. "Fieldwork may be your thing after all. Possibly hers, too."

"Luckily I had a tray of lasagna to use as a defensive weapon."

"A good agent uses whatever items are at hand. You acted perfectly. Look who's turning into James Bond after all."

"Ha-ha. But speaking of lasagna…" My stomach grumbled. I rummaged around in my purse, looking through the change compartment in my wallet. "Do you have any money for the vending machine? I'm starving, and only because I didn't eat much at the party, *not* because I pigged out on lasagna and have the munchies."

He had both eyes open now. "If I do have change, you have to promise me you won't eat the processed peanut butter crackers."

"I honestly can't promise that. I'll take whatever they have. I'm famished."

Sighing, he shifted on the chair and searched his pocket. He came up with a fistful of coins. He poured them all into my hand.

I sorted through them, taking a bunch of quarters and returned the rest. "Thanks, Slash. You want something? A Kit Kat bar? Coffee?"

"No. Your coffee smells awful."

I tossed my half-empty cup into the trash can as I walked to the vending machine. I looked through the glass, but it was empty. Decimated by a bunch of women with the munchies.

Jeez.

I headed back to my seat empty-handed. As I passed Hands and Gray, I heard him ask her, "Remind me again, how many servings of lasagna did you eat?"

"Shut up."

"How are you going to explain this on your next lie detector test?"

"Hands, I swear if you don't shut up—"

He burst into laughter and kissed her hard on the mouth. She wound her hands around his neck and kissed him back.

I'd just returned to my chair when the detective in charge, Jimmy Gonzales, came back into the room with Basia. She still wore the crown and the veil, although the crown was crooked and the veil torn. He looked at the sorry lot of us, shaking his head.

"So, let me run this down for everyone. I have a CIA agent, an NSA employee in possession of a firearm that isn't his and another gun and a knife that is, the CEO of a cyberintelligence corporation and a couple of his employees, four strippers—one female and three male, a robbery detective with the Baltimore PD, a Navy SEAL, a reporter for *The Washington Post*, two computer programmers, a bartender, a medical intern, a couple of students, the owner of a party supply store and her son, who happens to be on probation, and…did I forget someone?"

When we were silent, he sighed. "What the hell am I supposed to do with you people?"

I raised my hand. "Well, I—"

"That was a rhetorical question, Ms. Carmichael."

"Oh." I lowered my hand. "Sorry."

"Now, according to my notes from the interviews, Ms. Kowalski pushed Mr. Junior Markle into Mr. Leo Aultz who was brandishing a gun and threatening people. As Mr. Aultz stumbled, Ms. Carmichael used a lasagna tray as a means of divesting Mr. Aultz of his weapon while Ms. Kowalski applied a whiskey bottle to Mr. Aultz's head to knock him unconscious."

I nodded. "Yep. That's pretty much it in a nutshell."

Sergeant Gonzales glanced around the room. "For the record, I would never, *ever* recommend taking the actions that these two ladies took this evening, even though it had a positive outcome. However, that is apparently hindsight. I suppose no one in this room knew that Mr. Aultz is a notorious drug dealer in our area?"

We all shook our heads.

"Then I presume none of you knew there was a reward for information leading to the arrest of these men. Seeing as how Ms. Kowalski and Ms. Carmichael were the ones who did a lot more than just provide information—they, in fact, disarmed and secured him—we will be handing over the reward of ten thousand dollars to them. Congratulations, ladies."

I looked over at Basia in surprise. She looked delighted at the turn of events. Everyone else started clapping, cheering and hugging Basia and me.

I removed myself from Xavier's hug and shouted

over the cheering. "Wait. Does this mean we're not in trouble?"

"Well, not you." Sergeant Gonzales cupped his hands around his mouth and shouted for everyone to be quiet. When the noise in the room died down, he continued. "Mr. Markle—Junior—was on probation, so we'll be taking further action with him. I'm afraid he'll be held pending bail for the time being, but the rest of you are free to go. Just go easy on the lasagna from here on out, okay? I've had our receptionist call a bunch of cabs to get everyone home. They should be out front shortly."

The room erupted again with more sounds of laughter and talking. This time Sergeant Gonzales didn't try to quiet it down.

Basia rushed over and hugged me. "OMG! Lexi, what an utterly crazy night."

I examined her expression cautiously. "Wait. You're not mad at me?"

"Of course not, you silly goose. I'll never forget tonight. It will make a story to tell our kids for years to come. Right, Xavier?"

"Right, baby."

They seemed so happy, I felt suspicious—like the bomb would fall any minute and I would blow up without knowing what hit me. "But…you got sick, and the fireman and the lasagna…"

"I mean it, Lexi. It's all okay. It was definitely memorable."

"Really? You're not just saying that?"

Basia smiled. "Of course, not! It was a blast. Plus, we just got ten thousand dollars. Unbelievable."

Xavier slid an arm around Basia's waist. "You want the truth, Lexi? Your party just entered legendary status. What the hell could possibly top that? For a first effort, I'm totally impressed."

I glanced at Elvis, an apology in my eyes. "But, Xavier, I ruined your bachelor party by extension. Elvis worked so hard on it."

Elvis held up a hand. "Let's be perfectly clear here. I did *not* work hard on it. I turned it over completely to Faylene. Just like you did. I feel uncomfortable with any misconceptions on that part."

"No one ruined anything." Xavier laughed. "Are you two listening to us? It was a night for the books. I've always wanted to run into a party ready to save the day only to discover my badass woman has already taken care of it. I can't tell you how totally hot that is. Look, it's been a hell of a night, and I mean that as a total compliment. You two aced it. Righteous all the way." He and Elvis exchanged a high five.

Before I could respond, Billie Sue walked past and blew me a kiss. We all watched her disappear out the front door.

Xavier cleared his throat. "There is, however, the fact that I missed out on the stripper entertainment. I was not able to experience the true magic of the giant plastic wedding cake." He grinned at Basia. "I don't suppose that's a fantasy of yours, is it, babe?"

Basia elbowed him the stomach. He grunted, but a smile lit his face. Everyone seemed so happy. It was hard to tell if the party was really a success or if everyone was still feeling the effects of the marijuana. Either way, as long as people enjoyed themselves, who was I to tell them they were crazy?

As everyone filed out of the station, I lingered behind, glancing at Faylene and Uncle Shine who were sitting in a huddle, talking animatedly. Slash noticed my hesitation to leave and took my hand, a question in his eyes.

"Cara?"

"I have an idea. Come on." I pulled him over to where to Faylene and Uncle Shine were sitting.

They both looked up when I approached them.

"I'm really sorry about tonight, Lexi," Faylene said. She'd been crying. Her eyes were red and watery, the skin on her cheeks blotchy. "I'm not charging you for any of it. I didn't know about Junior. I thought he was getting back on the right track."

"It sounds to me that was what he was trying to do. He just got a little confused about the best way to do that."

She looked down at her hands. "Regardless, this isn't what I had in mind for your party."

I reached into my purse and pulled out my checkbook. "I was just told the party ranked among those of legendary status. Legendary status equals payment in my book. How much do I owe you?"

"It wouldn't be right," she insisted. "Everything was ruined."

"It really wasn't. How much do I owe you, Faylene? Seriously."

She told me. I wrote the check, signing my name with a flourish and handed it over along with a business card.

She looked at the check, her eyes widening. "You wrote the wrong amount. This is two thousand dollars more than you owe me."

"Use it to bail out Junior and use any leftover to do repairs on the club table and pay Billie Sue. Besides, I just came into a small windfall by putting Aultz away."

Her eyes filled with tears as she stood to hug me. She smelled of cigarettes and bad coffee. Her wiry hair tickled my cheeks as she squeezed me hard. When she pulled back, her smile was sincere.

"I don't know how to thank you."

"Yes, you do. Give Junior my business card and tell him to look me up when you get this sorted out. If he really wants to go down the right path, maybe I can figure out a way to give him a fresh start. I work for a pretty decent company that may have something he can do. He seems like a good kid and I believe good kids deserve second chances if he's willing to work hard."

Uncle Shine stood and vigorously pumped my hand and then Slash's. "Thank you so much. This means a lot to us."

I grinned at Uncle Shine. "You know, you're the best bartender I've ever met. Not that I've met a lot, but you have a real talent for the job. By the way, why do they call you Uncle Shine?"

He exchanged a glance with Faylene and then smiled sheepishly. "It's a nickname—you know, short for moonshine. I make my own liquor…sometimes."

I was still smiling as Slash and I left the police station hand in hand. I glanced at my watch once we were out in the cool night air. It was three forty-seven in the morning. I was mentally and physically exhausted, not to mention hungry.

"I'm really sorry about the coat, Slash. Again."

He squeezed my hand. "No worries. Next time I'll buy you ten of them."

"Two should be enough. An heir and a spare." I

rubbed my eyes sleepily. "So, where are we going tonight? My place or yours?"

He stopped and put his hands on my shoulders. "How about *our* place?"

FIFTY-SEVEN

Before I could utter a word, he pressed a finger to my lips. "Don't say anything yet. Just let me show you and then you can tell me what you think. Okay?"

I nodded and he lifted his finger from my mouth. In complete silence, we drove south on I-95 headed toward Washington, DC. My thoughts were whirling and I wasn't sure what I would say even if I could. When we got to the exit for Silver Spring, Maryland, he pulled off and wound around several roads until he pulled into an older residential area with old trees and even older houses. He pulled into the driveway of a house and took the keys out of the ignition.

"It's a house," I said in surprise. "With a yard."

"Most houses have yards," he said in amusement.

The house was the Colonial style architecture that was popular in this area. I had never imagined Slash in a house, but suddenly I could see him in one, enjoying the space and yard, perhaps upgrading from the minimalist design of his current apartment.

"I thought it was time to graduate from a condo," he said. "I'm still renovating. The location is halfway between the NSA where I work and Crystal City where you work."

That didn't seem like a random coincidence, but I didn't say anything. I climbed out of the car and we walked to the front door together. I observed the small cameras mounted to the windowsill from the upper floors. The lights were blinking red.

"Just give me your assurance that no one will be able to hack into those security cameras," I said.

He held his hand against his heart. "I swear."

He unlocked the door, tapped in a password on a security pad and flicked on the light. The house seemed ordinary on the outside, but on the inside it was sleek, modern and updated. To the left of the entrance was a living room and to the right were new, modular stairs. Directly in front of us, I got a glimpse of a brand-new kitchen.

He shut the door behind me and locked it. "It's nearly done, but I'm still working on the bathrooms and the safe room."

He tugged on my arm, directing me to the living room first. It had a big bay window, a fireplace and a lot of room for…whatever you put in a living room this size.

"The piano could fit here," Slash said, spreading his arms, as if he had read my mind.

He played the piano beautifully, something I hadn't known about him until recently. "So, you're not keeping it behind locked doors and soundproof walls anymore?" I asked.

"No. Not anymore."

He pointed at the bay window. "By the way, every window in the house is bulletproof."

"Well, that's good to know."

He smiled as I wandered into an empty dining room, which had a side door to the kitchen and large French doors that opened to a backyard. It was too dark to see the backyard clearly, but it looked private with lots of trees and a wooden fence surrounding the lot.

"Who is going to mow that?" I asked.

"The LawnBott 43621." Slash grinned. "I understand it will practically mow the lawn by itself. If not, it's never too late to learn how to operate a regular lawn mower or develop a more intelligent one, I suppose."

I chuckled and walked into the finished kitchen. It was big with modern stainless steel appliances, dark wood cabinets, steel handles and a gray, white and black backsplash. A center island had a lot of counter space and another sink. Some sleek silver lighting dropped down from the ceilings over the counter area, breakfast bar and center island. I liked the clean lines and the logic of the design, even if I knew squat about how to arrange a kitchen.

"This is amazing, Slash."

"Do you think it's big enough to invite Nonna to visit and do some cooking?"

His grandmother in Italy was the best cook in the world…the universe…probably the entire galaxy.

"It's more than big enough, although it's not like I would know." Cooking was not my thing, but with Nonna's help, there was hope I might someday be satisfactory.

He laughed and took me downstairs to the basement next. It was completely finished with a large open entertainment area and a full dark mahogany bar. I followed him down a small corridor to a complete suite with an adjoining bathroom and small kitchenette.

"Wow, it's another complete apartment."

"Technically it's referred to as a nanny suite. I thought to use it for our guests and my family. The basement was fully finished when I bought it. It's one of the reasons I purchased the house. It provides everyone with a high level of privacy."

I stopped, looked at him. "Has any of your family ever visited you in the States?"

"Not yet. But I'm going to change that. I'm going to change a lot of things."

I stared at him for a moment and then followed him back upstairs. There were three more finished bedrooms, one of which he'd clearly intended to be his workout room, and a bathroom. Another room Slash identified as the future location of the safe room was located next to the master bedroom. It was nothing more than wooden beams and a lot of dust at this point.

"There's still a lot of work to be done in here, including special wiring to get this room just the way I want it."

After that he led me to the master bedroom suite. It was a large room with a small sitting area beneath a smaller bay window. The sitting area had a built-in bench and two small bookshelves beneath it. It looked like the perfect spot to curl up with a laptop and a hot cup of coffee. The bedroom also had a small stone-and-glass fireplace. At the moment, the room was devoid of furniture except for a blow-up mattress and a couple of blankets.

"You've already spent the night here."

"A few times when I needed to meet a contractor."

I walked around in a circle. "This is a lot of house. It doesn't look that big from the driveway."

"Good. As long as it blends in and isn't pretentious, I'm happy."

I walked into the master bathroom. It still needed some tile behind the double sink, but it was mostly finished. There were towels hanging on the rack and toilet paper in the holder.

I examined the shower. "You did the three showerhead thing again?" I opened the glass door, observing them.

"Absolutely."

"That massage one is the best. You do know you've ruined me for all other showers."

"I'm not sorry about that." A smile touched his lips.

I leaned back against the sink, crossed my arms against my chest. "Slash, when did you buy this house?"

"About five months ago."

"Five months?" I studied him. "You kept it a secret all this time? Why?"

He blew out a breath and walked over to me. "Because I wasn't sure if I would keep it or sell it."

"And now?"

He cupped my cheeks. "Now I'm sure. I know it's a big step for you...for me. Move in with me, *cara*. You can keep your apartment for a while, so if you don't think it's working out, you can leave at any time. We can take one day at a time, one week at a time, whatever you want. No strings attached. I want you to be comfortable. I want you to be as happy as I am."

I tilted my head. "Basia would tell me that moving in would be taking our relationship to a whole new level."

"She'd be right." He took my hand. "I know this past week hasn't been easy for either one of us. You've seen more sides of me than anyone ever has—including the sides I don't normally show anyone."

"Why were you afraid to show me that part of you?"

The expression on his face was pained. "Because I wasn't sure you could accept that part of me. I also worried about corrupting…tainting you. In the end, it didn't turn out like that. You were far too strong. I didn't corrupt you at all. Instead, you saved me."

"Not true." I covered his hand, which was still cupping my cheek. "You didn't need saving. You were pursuing peace, or at least détente, the entire time. But you had to be prepared in case that didn't happen. I understand that now."

"Thank you," he murmured. He closed his eyes, leaned his forehead against mine.

I let out a breath and spoke from my heart. "The truth is, Slash, I want to be with you. But it has to be *all* of you. The good, the bad, the dark and the complicated. It goes both ways. I've got my issues, too. I'm not an expert on relationships, but I'm pretty sure that's what love is all about. We have to trust each other enough to share those kinds of things with each other. Deal?"

He paused and then nodded. "Deal."

We stood there in silence. My emotions were running the gamut of terrified to exhilarated. I wasn't sure how to sort them out, and I could no longer ask Basia what to do next. Actually, I no longer *had* to ask her. Trust my heart, she'd said. That's what had convinced me to get into the relationship with Slash in the first place. So far, the relationship had worked out far better than I'd ever expected, so trust my heart is what I'd do now.

Still, my hands trembled as I spoke. "Here's the bottom line, Slash. I understand living together will not be easy. It's going to be a lot of work. If I'm honest, it already is. So, if we decide to do this, we have to agree to work at it every day."

"Agreed."

"Then, my answer is yes. I'll move in with you. Let's consider it a new level, a new beginning for us."

He pulled me tight against his chest. He rested his chin on the top of my head, his arms tight around me. His embrace was warm and safe, the thud of his heartbeat reassuring. I didn't know where this next step would lead us, but for now it was enough to know I felt confident enough to take it.

"I love you, *cara*," he murmured. "I can't wait to see where it takes us."

"Me neither. And just so you know, Slash, I'll be leaving my apartment in Jessup when I move in with you. I'm going into this on faith. I can't believe I'm saying that, but I am. Let's make it all or nothing."

His arms tightened around me as he pressed a kiss against my hair. "Perfect. I like my odds on that."

FIFTY-EIGHT

IT FELT GOOD to be back in China. As much as Jiang Shi enjoyed traveling, he preferred to be home among his networks and computers. From China he could go wherever he wanted, *whenever* he wanted, anyway. Like right now, for example. He was having a special little tour of New Jersey.

Shi tapped a few keys on his favorite keyboard and slipped into the outer ring of security of the Public Service Electric and Gas—the major electrical grid for New Jersey. A couple of more layers and the power would be his to command. On or off. He could do whatever he damn well wanted with a single keystroke.

He had just started a complicated coding string when his door opened. Who had dared to enter without knocking?

Furious, he swiveled around in his chair ready to provide a suitable tongue-lashing when two men dressed in dark suits and ties strode into his office. One of them closed the door behind him.

Jiang Shi stood up in surprise. The man in front was Liu Chunlin, Deputy Director of the Ministry of State Security. Shi didn't know the second man.

Shi masked his concern by bowing low to the men. "Gentlemen, welcome. I wasn't expecting you. To what do I owe this honor?" He waved to two chairs on the other side of his desk. "Please have a seat." He hated himself for it, but his hand trembled, so he put it in his pocket to keep it out of sight.

Chunlin and the other man didn't answer and both remained standing. The serious looks on their faces began to concern Shi. He fidgeted on his feet, afraid to be quiet but too nervous to speak.

Finally Chunlin stepped forward. "Jiang Shi, you have been accused of theft, money laundering, bribery and defrauding the citizens of the People's Republic of China."

"What?" Shi took a step back in shock, his mind reeling. Whatever his concern, this level of accusation had not crossed his mind. "That's outrageous. Who brings these charges against me?"

"Three hidden offshore accounts in your name containing money directly siphoned from the ministry have been brought to our attention."

"By whom? I don't own any such accounts. This a ridiculous charge."

"The accounts in your name have been confirmed, as has the cyber trail, which leads directly back to you. What do you have to say for yourself?"

"What do I have to say for myself?" Fear turned to anger. Shi slammed his hand on his desk. "I'm being framed. That's what I have to say. It's most certainly the Americans who are behind this. They are trying to get back at me. It's revenge. A plot to dishonor me."

To his surprise, Chunlin smiled and sat down. The other man remained standing and expressionless.

"Things haven't been going well for you lately, have they, Jiang Shi?"

Shi blinked, confused by the change in his demeanor and the question. He took a wary step forward, choosing his words carefully. "I have encountered a few setbacks, but that's to be expected in a profession such as mine."

"Setbacks. That's a mild word. You've made a lot of promises to the ministry. Promises you haven't fulfilled. Despite your best efforts in Papua New Guinea, we have no quantum microchip and no useful intelligence on the inner workings of the NSA cybersecurity department. Instead your brother, Jiang Quon, also a member of your cyber team, was captured and is apparently assisting the Americans in their study of our own cyberstrategies. A Chinese citizen, and the nephew of one of Sinam Tech's executives, has been arrested for his part in a hacking plot that was undertaken without the Ministry's knowledge or approval. Three other Chinese citizens, including Feng Mei, have also been arrested in the US and charged with kidnapping a reporter for *The Washington Post*. Feng Mei also faces the far more serious charge of the murders of two NSA employees, including the director and deputy director of IAD. Finally, you intended to launch a cyberattack against the United States without express permission from the general secretary or the state council. We had to stop said attack with only minutes to spare before the Americans launched their own attack against us. I would say that all equals to a lot more than a few *minor* setbacks."

Sweat trickled down his left temple. It was becoming hard to breathe. "I promise I can fix everything. The cyberattack was a misunderstanding. I've already explained in great detail what happened. Right now I'm this close to a hack into—"

"Jiang Shi—" the deputy minister interrupted and

leaned forward. His eyes were cold. "We don't tolerate broken promises."

"They're not broken. I can take care of everything. I have a plan. A good one." Shi's words had started to slur together. Panic gripped his throat.

"What about the matter of the fraud?" Chunlin continued. "You are in possession of millions of yuan siphoned from the ministry. What do you intend to do about that?"

"You can have all the money back. I never took it in the first place."

"I see. And the six million yuan still missing?"

"What? I...don't have it. I swear." Shi's eyes widened, he reached up to touch his throat. "I've been framed. You know that. The Americans are trying to get back at me."

Chunlin crossed his legs, inspected his fingernails as if he had nothing more important to do. "How incompetent you must be to have allowed yourself to be framed so easily. I'm afraid, Jiang Shi, you are a weak spot for us."

Shi staggered backward. "No. I am not weak. I am strong. I will handle this or resign. You have my word."

Chunlin lifted his gaze. "Resign? You think we would allow a man of your knowledge and experience to resign? You're far too dangerous to us to be set loose. You should know that."

Shi couldn't breathe. His knees were weak. He braced his hand against the corner of his desk. "Please." The plea came out as a whisper.

"I'm afraid you've outlived your usefulness." Chunlin stood up, brushing his hands together. "Jiang Shi, you are hereby charged with crimes against the Chinese people. Please come with us."

The big man, who had stood so silently near the door, pulled a pair of handcuffs out of his pocket and approached Shi.

Shi's fear burst from within. *"No!"* he shouted and collapsed to the floor.

SLASH WALKED INTO the NSA, flashing his badge and submitting his palm print for identification before checking his weapon with the guard and walking through the metal detector. He headed straight for the elevator, taking it to the third floor and past two more security checks before being ushered in to see the director of the NSA, General Maxwell Norton.

Slash had expected the summons, but now he was here, he wondered how Norton would play it. Norton was a straightforward guy, honest and had a good grasp of the threats presented on the cyber front. But he was also politically savvy and was required to answer personally to Washington. That was another complicated layer added to an already complex situation. It was hard to predict how the meeting would go.

As Slash was ushered into his office, Norton rose from behind his desk and shook his hand.

"Slash, good to see you, son. Thank you for coming. Sit down."

Slash sat. Instead of returning to the chair behind his desk, Norton came around and sat in the chair beside him, looking at him with kind and experienced eyes.

After a short pause he spoke. "So, I understand you finished the code."

Good. Norton wasn't going to waste time with meaningless chatter. "Yes, sir, it's finished."

"Excellent." He leaned forward. "May I ask where it is? Our experts have been all over that laptop you had at the hotel and we can't find it."

"The code in a safe place." Slash kept his gaze even on Norton's. He didn't have to say more. Norton knew exactly what that meant.

The general studied him for a moment. "I see. That's how it's going to be."

"That's how it's going to be," Slash confirmed. "That's how it *has* to be. It's safer that way for everyone."

To his surprise, Norton didn't try to argue or persuade him to turn it over. Instead he looked relieved.

"Agreed. So, your team, Slash—the ones who worked on the code with you—I'm well aware they're the best and brightest America has to offer. We owe you and them a debt we can't ever repay. The Zimmermans…did they prove to be helpful as expected?"

"Exceptionally. But they didn't touch the code itself. They created the security sheath and protocols, that's all. The black code—that's on me alone."

Norton sat back in his chair and steepled his fingers. "Alone? Really? According to the FBI report I read, you were hit with a dart and were out for a significant amount of time during the operation. Perhaps you had a little extra help somewhere else, then?"

Slash remained silent. No way would he confirm Lexi's participation or drag her into this, even if it seemed obvious to Norton.

Norton smiled. "It's okay, son, your secret is safe with me. I'm well aware of Ms. Carmichael's abilities.

I also know she was the one who sent the code into hiding. She was the last one with her hands on the laptop. I'm damn sorry we lost her here at the agency. The lure and freedom of the private sector is killing us. Despite that, she's proven to be quite an asset to the US government. She's a special woman."

He tensed and Norton patted him on the knee. "Stand down, Slash. I don't intend to use her as leverage. You have my word."

Slash relaxed slightly, leaning forward, his hands on his knees. "How's Charlie?"

"He's fine. Recovering nicely. There's a certain young FBI agent who is now facing charges of attempted murder for injecting him with an unauthorized medication."

"The agent was on Jiang Shi's payroll?"

"We're still working on tracing the connection, but it looks that way. Charlie will be fully reinstated, of course."

"Who created the offshore accounts in Charlie's name?"

Norton raised a silver eyebrow. "Who do you think?"

"Sam." Sick betrayal swept through him. "What's happening to him?"

"He's in FBI custody. He will face prosecution on a number of serious charges. We're exploring the charge of treason, as well. How do you feel about that?"

His jaw clenched. "I feel good about it." His voice was cold, his conscience clear. "Do it. Are the agents who were at the FBI safe house recovering?"

"Two of the three agents who were inside with you have been released from the hospital and are expected to have a full recovery. The third, Agent Knott, remains hospitalized, but apparently he's going to make it. He's a tough old bird."

Slash closed his eyes for a moment, relief easing a bit of the tension coiled in his gut. "That's good to hear."

"Yes, it is." Norton crossed his legs, studying Slash for a moment. "I need to ask you something, son. Are you intending to leave the NSA?"

Slash examined Norton, wondering why he'd asked the question. "Not today, sir."

Visible relief crossed Norton's face. "Good, because you're the most important talent this agency has right now. It's a personal priority for me to see you are well taken care of and protected. You are hereby promoted from acting director to Director of IAD."

Slash blinked. "You want me to permanently step into the directorship?"

"I do. You've earned it. You'll be the youngest Director of IAD in NSA history, but we want to keep you. We *need* to keep you. The world is changing and we must keep up."

Slash considered for a moment. "I'd be honored to receive the promotion. I will accept…if my conditions are met."

Norton raised an eyebrow. "Conditions? Such as?"

"Such as, no agents in my house. I've built myself a place with sophisticated security equipment. I will permit you to examine it to assure you that it meets the NSA's rigorous safety standards. I can live with the detail outside and in the car, but they stay outside. I can drive myself, too."

Norton stared at him for a long moment and then nodded. "Granted."

"I'm also scaling back my hours. That means no

more regular sixteen—and eighteen-hour days. I can be flexible and accommodating depending on the mission, but only to a point."

Norton leaned forward, his expression curious. "I see. I presume things are getting serious with a certain young lady?"

Slash didn't answer, but a broad smile crossed Norton's face.

"Look, I don't have the foggiest idea why you put up with our crap, but I'm damn grateful you do. Your adopted country thanks you and so do I. I know—perhaps better than most—what you sacrifice for us. That last condition is granted, as well. Welcome aboard. We're fortunate to have you." He held out a hand and Slash shook it.

Slash started to rise, but the general waved him back to his seat. "Wait. There's something I want to show you."

Norton stood and walked over to his desk, retrieving a small package from atop some files and handing it to Slash.

"I received something today. Open it."

Not surprisingly, the small box had already been opened. Any packages coming in and out of the NSA were opened at an off-site location. Norton already knew what the box contained, but he watched Slash examine the package.

Slash studied the brown packaging paper that had been folded around the box. It was addressed to Norton.

Slash lifted the lid and pulled out an object, unwrapping the tissue paper. A large silver coin fell into his palm.

"Do you know what that is?" Norton asked.

"I do."

Slash examined the silver coin owned by Jiang Quon, Shi's brother, still in CIA custody. Slash had mailed it to Shi after he'd captured Quon and now it was being returned. Things were coming full circle. There was only one person who could have gotten his hands on the coin and known where to return it.

Liu Chunlin.

A small piece of paper had been folded at the bottom of the box. Slash pulled it out and unfolded it.

TELL SLASH WE'RE DOING OUR PART FOR CYBER DéTENTE. YOU'RE WELCOME.

Slash handed the paper to Norton. "It's confirmation of the stalemate. Mission accomplished."

"Well-done, son." Norton laughed and slapped him on the back. "Well-done, indeed."

As Slash walked out of the NSA, he put his sunglasses on. The sun warmed his shoulders and neck, releasing some of the tension he'd stored there for the past few days.

Lexi would be waiting.

She'd be home from work, probably playing Magic Shorn, sitting on the couch with her computer on her lap, hair wound up in a ponytail. Her bare feet would be on the coffee table, a bowl of dry Cheerios, or perhaps an apple, within reaching distance. When he walked in, she'd look up and smile at him.

"Hey, Slash. How was your day?" she'd ask.

He'd set down his briefcase and kiss her on the check, suggesting they cook dinner together. Maybe he'd even try to teach her to make gnocchi…again. While they were cooking, he'd tell her about his promotion. She'd remind him that even though she was new at offering emotional support and understood he couldn't share classified information she'd be happy to listen when he worried about the latest injection vulnerabilities or insufficient encryption techniques. They'd discuss which was the more important of the two and then make a mental list of actions they'd take if faced with such a crisis.

Later, while lying in bed, they might talk about the upcoming move and their new house. He'd pretend to argue with her about who would get the sink on the left in the master bathroom, then let her win once he figured out which side she really wanted.

Eventually he'd close his eyes, her body warm next to his, strands of her hair soft against his cheek. He'd sleep, really sleep, because somehow life had become more than just a series of problems to fix for someone else. It had become about him. About her.

She centered him…somehow she *always* centered him.

And he loved her for it.

* * * * *

*Stay tuned for the next
Lexi Carmichael Mystery series,
No Living Soul.*

ACKNOWLEDGMENTS

A novel is rarely a solitary effort and this book is no exception. Thanks to all of my true-blue tech head family: my nephew, Kyle, who works at Google; his wife, Julia, who works at Yahoo; my brother, Brad, who is brilliant at all things tech and storytelling; my sister, Sandy, who is a great writer and always knows everything about everything (really!); my mom and dad, fantastic editors and Lexi's first fans; my niece, Katy, who also beta reads for me; my sister-in-law, Beth, who watched Lucas more times than I can count so I could do the writer thing; and Carina Press editor extraordinaire, Alissa Davis, for knowing Lexi and the gang inside and out and always making the BEST freaking suggestions. Love you all! oxoxo

ABOUT THE AUTHOR

Julie Moffett is a bestselling author and writes in the genres of mystery, historical romance and paranormal romance. She has won numerous awards, including the 2014 Mystery & Mayhem Award for Best YA/ New Adult Mystery, the prestigious 2014 HOLT Award for Best Novel with Romantic Elements, a HOLT Merit Award for Best Novel by a Virginia Author, a PRISM Award for Best Romantic Time-Travel and Best of the Best Paranormal Books of 2002 and the 2011 EPIC Award for Best Action/Adventure Novel. She has also garnered additional nominations for the Daphne du Maurier Award, the Colorado Romance Writers' Award of Excellence and the Gayle Wilson Award of Excellence. Her book *A Double-Edged Blade* was an Amazon #1 bestselling novel.

Julie is a military brat (air force) and has traveled extensively. Her more exciting exploits include attending high school in Okinawa, Japan; backpacking around Europe and Scandinavia for several months; a year-long college graduate study in Warsaw, Poland; and a wonderful trip to Scotland and Ireland, where she fell in love with castles, kilts and brogues.

Julie has a BA in political science and Russian language from Colorado College, an MA in international affairs from The George Washington University in Washington, DC, and an MEd from Liberty University. She has worked as a proposal writer, journalist, teacher, librarian and researcher. Julie speaks Russian and Polish and has two sons.

Visit Julie's website at www.juliemoffett.com or follow Julie on social media.

Facebook: Facebook.com/JulieMoffettAuthor

Twitter: @JMoffettAuthor

Instagram: Instagram.com/julie_moffett/

Get 2 Free Books,
Plus 2 Free Gifts—
just for trying the Reader Service!

HARLEQUIN
INTRIGUE

YES! Please send me 2 FREE Harlequin® Intrigue novels and my 2 FREE gifts (gifts are worth about $10 retail). After receiving them, if I don't wish to receive any more books, I can return the shipping statement marked "cancel." If I don't cancel, I will receive 6 brand-new novels every month and be billed just $4.99 each for the regular-print edition or $5.74 each for the larger-print edition in the U.S., or $5.74 each for the regular-print edition or $6.49 each for the larger-print edition in Canada. That's a savings of at least 12% off the cover price! It's quite a bargain! Shipping and handling is just 50¢ per book in the U.S. and 75¢ per book in Canada.* I understand that accepting the 2 free books and gifts places me under no obligation to buy anything. I can always return a shipment and cancel at any time. The free books and gifts are mine to keep no matter what I decide.

Please check one: ☐ Harlequin® Intrigue Regular-Print ☐ Harlequin® Intrigue Larger-Print
(182/382 HDN GLWJ) (199/399 HDN GLWJ)

Name _____ (PLEASE PRINT)

Address _____ Apt. #

City _____ State/Prov. _____ Zip/Postal Code

Signature (if under 18, a parent or guardian must sign)

Mail to the **Reader Service:**
IN U.S.A.: P.O. Box 1341, Buffalo, NY 14240-8531
IN CANADA: P.O. Box 603, Fort Erie, Ontario L2A 5X3

Want to try two free books from another line?
Call 1-800-873-8635 or visit www.ReaderService.com.

*Terms and prices subject to change without notice. Prices do not include applicable taxes. Sales tax applicable in N.Y. Canadian residents will be charged applicable taxes. Offer not valid in Quebec. This offer is limited to one order per household. Books received may not be as shown. Not valid for current subscribers to Harlequin Intrigue books. All orders subject to approval. Credit or debit balances in a customer's account(s) may be offset by any other outstanding balance owed by or to the customer. Please allow 4 to 6 weeks for delivery. Offer available while quantities last.

Your Privacy—The Reader Service is committed to protecting your privacy. Our Privacy Policy is available online at www.ReaderService.com or upon request from the Reader Service.

We make a portion of our mailing list available to reputable third parties that offer products we believe may interest you. If you prefer that we not exchange your name with third parties, or if you wish to clarify or modify your communication preferences, please visit us at www.ReaderService.com/consumerschoice or write to us at Reader Service Preference Service, P.O. Box 9062, Buffalo, NY 14240-9062. Include your complete name and address.

HI17R

Get 2 Free Books,
Plus 2 Free Gifts—
just for trying the Reader Service!

Get 2 Free Books,
Plus 2 Free Gifts –

just for
trying the
*Reader
Service!*

YES! Please send me 2 FREE novels from the Essential Romance or Essential Suspense Collection and my 2 FREE gifts (gifts are worth about $10 retail). After receiving them, if I don't wish to receive any more books, I can return the shipping statement marked "cancel." If I don't cancel, I will receive 4 brand-new novels every month and be billed just $6.74 each in the U.S. or $7.24 each in Canada. That's a savings of at least 16% off the cover price. It's quite a bargain! Shipping and handling is just 50¢ per book in the U.S. and 75¢ per book in Canada.* I understand that accepting the 2 free books and gifts places me under no obligation to buy anything. I can always return a shipment and cancel at any time. The free books and gifts are mine to keep no matter what I decide.

Please check one: ☐ Essential Romance   ☐ Essential Suspense
                                    194/394 MDN GLW5   191/391 MDN GLW5

Name _____ (PLEASE PRINT) _____

Address _____ Apt. # _____

City _____ State/Prov. _____ Zip/Postal Code _____

Signature (if under 18, a parent or guardian must sign)

Mail to the **Reader Service:**
IN U.S.A.: P.O. Box 1341, Buffalo, NY 14240-8531
IN CANADA: P.O. Box 603, Fort Erie, Ontario L2A 5X3

Want to try two free books from another line?
Call 1-800-873-8635 or visit www.ReaderService.com.

*Terms and prices subject to change without notice. Prices do not include applicable taxes. Sales tax applicable in NY. Canadian residents will be charged applicable taxes. Offer not valid in Quebec. This offer is limited to one order per household. Books received may not be as shown. Not valid for current subscribers to the Essential Romance or Essential Suspense Collection. All orders subject to approval. Credit or debit balances in a customer's account(s) may be offset by any other outstanding balance owed by or to the customer. Please allow 4 to 6 weeks for delivery. Offer available while quantities last.

Your Privacy—The Reader Service is committed to protecting your privacy. Our Privacy Policy is available online at www.ReaderService.com or upon request from the Reader Service.

We make a portion of our mailing list available to reputable third parties that offer products we believe may interest you. If you prefer that we not exchange your name with third parties, or if you wish to clarify or modify your communication preferences, please visit us at www.ReaderService.com/consumerschoice or write to us at Reader Service Preference Service, P.O. Box 9062, Buffalo, NY 14240-9062. Include your complete name and address.

READERSERVICE.COM

Manage your account online!
- Review your order history
- Manage your payments
- Update your address

> ### We've designed the Reader Service website just for you.

Enjoy all the features!
- Discover new series available to you, and read excerpts from any series.
- Respond to mailings and special monthly offers.
- Browse the Bonus Bucks catalog and online-only exculsives.
- Share your feedback.

Visit us at:

ReaderService.com

Get 2 Free Books,
Plus 2 Free Gifts—
just for trying the Reader Service!

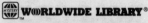

WWLI7R

Get 2 Free Books,

Plus 2 Free Gifts—

just for trying the Reader Service!